PERSONAL
DEMONS

JAMES BUCHANAN

mlrpress

MLR PRESS AUTHORS

Featuring a roll call of some of the best writers of gay erotica and mysteries today!

M. Jules Aedin
Maura Anderson
Victor J. Banis
Jeanne Barrack
Laura Baumbach
Alex Beecroft
Sarah Black
Ally Blue
J.P. Bowie
Michael Breyette
P.A. Brown
Brenda Bryce
Jade Buchanan
James Buchanan
Charlie Cochrane
Gary Cramer
Kirby Crow
Dick D.
Ethan Day
Jason Edding
Angela Fiddler
Dakota Flint
S.J. Frost
Kimberly Gardner
Storm Grant
Amber Green
LB Gregg

Wayne Gunn
Samantha Kane
Kiernan Kelly
J.L. Langley
Josh Lanyon
Clare London
William Maltese
Gary Martine
Z.A. Maxfield
Patric Michael
Jet Mykles
Willa Okati
L. Picaro
Neil Plakcy
Jordan Castillo Price
Luisa Prieto
Rick R. Reed
A.M. Riley
George Seaton
Jardonn Smith
Caro Soles
JoAnne Soper-Cook
Richard Stevenson
Clare Thompson
Stevie Woods
Kit Zheng

Check out titles, both available and forthcoming, at
www.mlrpress.com

PERSONAL DEMONS

JAMES BUCHANAN

mlrpress

Copyright 2009 by James Buchanan

Published by
MLR Press, LLC
3052 Gaines Waterport Rd.
Albion, NY 14411

Visit ManLoveRomance Press, LLC on the Internet:
www.mlrpress.com

Cover Art by Deana C. Jamroz
Editing by Maura Anderson
Printed in the United States of America.

ISBN# 978-1-60820-062-7

First Edition 2009

Desert heat sucked the sweat from Special Agent Chase Nozick's pores. "Give it up, Garcia!" he yelled. Somehow, he'd managed to shrug into the soft body armor as he slid out the car. Sweat pooled under the vest, plastering his suit jacket, dress shirt and tie to his skin. *Damn, it was hot.* Chase snorted as he leaned over the hood of his Bureau-issued car. The last thing he really needed to care about was how hot it was.

He aimed his 9mm at the driver's side window of a pinned Escalade and yelled again, "I mean now!"

Chase never felt calmer. The situation flew by in sharp focus. He smelled oil burning off his Buick's engine. The pop and hiss of the SUV's radiator puking over the trunk of the Buick stung his ears. In his peripheral vision, Chase watched Jason crab-walk around the back of the SUV. Sand shifted under the feet of Chase's partner, Jason Olhms, each grating grain distinguishable from another. Overlaid across it was Garcia's cursing as he fought with his seatbelt. The impact from Chase's car must have jammed it when he reversed the Buick directly into Garcia's fleeing vehicle. One of Garcia's ever-present goons lay slumped against the dash, his mirrored sunglasses hanging off his face at a bizarre angle. The spider web fracture on the windshield and open doll eyes told Chase the guy wasn't going anywhere in the near future.

"Come on, Garcia!" he barked.

Garcia looked up. An evil, murderous smile ripped across his mouth. Flat brown eyes, soulless eyes, stared out from under a heavy brow. Chase heard the snap-click of a hammer going back. A hole burst through the SUV's door. One, two, three rapid blasts shattered the air. A pair of bullets whizzed by Chase's head. Then the vuv-pop of a ricochet sounded. Pain bloomed in the back of Chase's neck.

He blinked. Garcia twisted. The gun hidden in his lap came up and pointed out the passenger side of the SUV. Jason stood.

Chase's voice froze as he tried to croak out a warning. Red mist exploded where Jason's face had been. Chase pulled his trigger. Once, just once. Garcia slumped in his seat.

The world shifted, spun as Chase tried to stand. Hot and sticky, blood pumped down under his vest. Chase sucked in a breath and pain rampaged through his body. There wasn't time to check Garcia's status. Jason...Chase figured him for dead already. Even if he wasn't, every second counted for his own survival. Knees weak and stomach rolling, he reached up and pressed his free hand to the torn flesh of his neck. Chase shook so bad he could barely keep the gun trained on where Garcia had been.

He had to get help. He had to get help fast.

Chase staggered back to driver's side of the Buick. It took all his will to wrench the door open and slide into the driver's seat. He fumbled the mike, trying to key it. Slick with blood and sweat, it slid to the floor. Chase almost cried. Bending down sent waves of agony screaming through his neck. He took a deep breath and reached for it.

The world went black.

CHAPTER TWO

Five years later

Chase flipped through the photos in his file and chewed a piece of Juicy Fruit gum as though it aided his ability to recall important facts. In a way it did. Jason had always had a pack stuck in his pocket and a piece stuck in his mouth. A small, tenuous connection to one of the few people Chase ever really cared about.

In the grainy snapshot, Almandeto Famosa-Garcia, drug smuggler, extortionist, arsonist and general bad-ass boy glared over his shoulder like he hated the world. Three of his goons, his *Muertos*, with their mirrored shades, shaved heads and all black clothing, surrounded him. Why a hit man surrounded himself with hired muscle always confused Chase. The best he could figure was for show. God knew Garcia was lethal enough on his own.

Ages ago, Chase committed Garcia's mug to memory. The man lived in Chase's memory, haunted his sleep, seeped into his mouth with each chew—both Garcia and Jason. Garcia poisoned his soul with vengeance. Jason, Jason tainted every moment with regret.

Regret that Jason died.

Regret that Jason's badge had been lost at the scene. Chase, as his partner, presented his widow with nothing but a standard flag, issued from inventory and never touched by Jason's hand. A cold and impersonal reminder of death in government service.

Regret that Chase, with no one special to mourn him, had lived, and Jason, with a bereft wife and two fatherless children, hadn't.

Chase glared at the photos, willing them to tell him where Garcia was. Shaved head, squared-off jaw always sporting a five o'clock shadow, Garcia's eyes brooded dark under heavy brows. Various images of Almandeto Garcia at dinner in some restaurant, jaywalking through traffic, arguing with some guy on a street corner—some guy who'd wound up dead not a week later—captivated him. Chase knew them, every pixel capturing the brutal Cuban-American hit man for the Colombians, carved into his memory.

Two other photos stood out from the rest. One a mug shot of a penny-ante criminal, unremarkable except for a star-shaped scar on his cheek. Renaldo Fuertes. The other the graduation headshot of Renaldo's sister, Carmen.

Chase spit the gum into the cocktail napkin on the flight tray before fishing a roll of antacids from his pocket. Popping two to quell the low-level throb in his gut, he studied Carmen's photo. Pretty enough with almost curly red-brown hair, her full lips set off pale brown skin and dark eyes. Carmen made the unfortunate choice of shacking up with Almandeto for a time. The fast-life siren-call sucked her in. Watching two guys get popped for welshing on a meth deal sent her running for cover. Chase would find her, bring her in. The cooperation noises were there. Chase just had to sift out the good girl hiding under all that fear.

Then he'd put Garcia away for good.

He owed Jason at least that.

The whine of the engines combined with the subtle sinking feeling in his gut told him the plane had started its descent. The familiar bone-weary grind, from reading with his head down, settled into his neck. Chase stretched as much as possible in the cramped seat. His row mate shot him a nasty look. Chase chose to ignore it, turning instead to stare out the window as he worked his fingers over the scars. Miles and miles of endless human habitation baked under a reddish-brownish haze and stretched from mountain to seashore. Wildfires tinged the ever-present smog. South, north and east, the plumes billowed into the sky. Chase snorted, closed his eyes and tried not to think as the plane touched down and taxied to the gate.

The cabin attendant flashed him a seductive smile as he passed her on the way out. He smiled back at her. It wasn't interest, just habit. Attention was one of those things he was used to. Being a Special Agent of the Federal Bureau of Investigation often garnered it. Beyond that, Chase wore forty like an expensive old suit. Good fabric, strong classic lines, but starting to go shiny at the seams. To the right person, he guessed he came off as sexy.

The moment he hit the gangway, the scent of charred wood seeped into his nose. Shit, the recent round of fires had to be bad to overcome the reek of diesel and exhaust that normally choked the lungs in Los Angeles. Then he passed through into the twice-processed and re-circulated air of LAX. Spider webs, ghoulish caricatures and baskets of candy decorated the various counters, kiosks and terminal storefronts. Every TV monitor not devoted to plane schedules carried news of the nine fires across several counties that'd been burning for at least a day already. Another one had started way before dawn.

Chase threaded his way slowly through the crowd. Chase rarely rushed, it paid to take his time and observe. Some woman and her guy, fighting but not fighting, passed him. A mom struggled with a demanding child wanting some pre-Halloween treat, both danced on the precipice of breakdown. Chase edged around a pair of businessmen conducting a negotiation best left to private boardrooms, not airport terminal walkways. About thirty different cell conversations, or at least one half of them, granted Chase a tiny and likely unwanted insight into the speaker's lives.

Discretion, as the Bureau taught, was the better part of valor and the antithesis of espionage. The more secure a target believed his own private box to be, the easier it was to tap into. Garcia, paranoid son-of-a-bitch that he was, didn't think anything was secure. It made him damned hard to pin down. That and he had more lives than a freaking cat. Somehow he and Chase both managed to survive that afternoon. Chase bore the shrapnel wedged in his spine; he always wondered if Garcia'd been as lucky.

Chase shifted his briefcase and huffed. Tomorrow he had a meeting at Bureau headquarters. They'd decided to saddle him with some LAPD specialist. Just what Chase needed, a gung-ho cop dogging his tail. Jason was the only partner who ever managed to stay in step with him, met Chase move for move. And now the Bureau set him up to get his toes stepped on by a boy in blue.

Well, until then he was pretty much on his own. Anything and everything was open in the City of the Angels. If it was to be had, you could find it in Metro-hell. A smirk twisted up the corner of his mouth. Okay, not quite on his own. A clean-cut kid in a suit scanned the faces of arriving passengers and fussed with his tie at the bottom of the escalator.

Bureau fresh meat.

Male or female, black, white or purple polka dot, once an agent graduated from the academy, they all assimilated that uniform FBI appearance. The kid's blue eyes passed over Chase and then quickly jumped back; like recognizing like. As Chase stepped off into the chaos of baggage claim, the kid sidled up and stuck out his hand. "Agent Nozick?" Chase nodded and took the proffered shake. "I'm Agent Britt, stationed here at LAX. Did you check luggage?" That fast-paced patter had Chase out of breath.

Chase ran his hand through his own close-cropped brown hair and drawled out, "Yep."

"Great." Britt's smile didn't hide the fact that this was a crap assignment. Anybody who'd been in the Bureau longer than a week would know it. Forcing a gung-ho attitude, Britt snapped, "Let's grab 'em. I've got your hotel information." His words rattled off in a clip only outmatched by his pace towards the baggage carousel. Chase strolled and counted off how long it took Britt to realize he wasn't trying to keep up. Britt turned and irritation flashed over his features. Not like running would make the bags come any faster. Chase sauntered up and Britt huffed. "I'm to give you a ride to your BuCar. The Special Agent in Charge wanted me to remind you that the meeting starts at nine tomorrow. Over in Westwood." He paused and, apparently not receiving whatever clue from Chase he sought, added, "You know, So Cal headquarters."

Spelling the title out like that, instead of using SAC, the kid had to be greener than grass. The less time Chase spent in Britt's company, the happier he'd be. Newbies grated on his nerves; too rough around the edges and anal about policy, procedure and principal. "I know." Chase tried to defray his distaste with a smile. If you acted like you meant it…well, once you learned how to fake sincere, the rest of life was a cake walk. "I've got two bags. As soon as I can, I'll head out to the hotel…get out of your hair." Chase flashed another insincere smile, which Britt echoed. "I just want to hit the shower and crash."

"Fine." Britt seemed pleased enough with Chase's stated intentions. Handing over a manila folder he added, "I printed out the route for you. You're early enough. The 405 shouldn't be a parking lot yet." Chase flipped through the loose printouts of routes and confirmation numbers. A cough from Britt caused him to glance up. Britt shrugged. "The hotel's not too far from HQ and pretty nice…within budget."

Inwardly, Chase groaned. Within budget hopefully meant the beds didn't vibrate. The images of some rat-infested flea bag ticked at Chase's mind while he grabbed his luggage and Britt ferried him to his BuCar. Chase always wondered why they didn't call them BICs. It seemed a better acronym for Bureau Issued Car than BuCar. Of course, the term "boat" might work just as well. Big, old and navy colored, Chase'd been assigned the typical American four-door. Maneuvering out past the light pylons signaling the exit of the airport, Chase knew he stood out as government issue.

If he was going to do what he wanted to do for the evening, he'd have to ditch the car.

Mid-day traffic crawled up the Sepulveda Pass. No amount of time or asphalt could ever relieve the chronic congestion. Luckily, he didn't have to go far and his faded memories served well enough to keep him off the freeway. A few jumps up through El Segundo, Century City and finally into Hollywood found him at a decent enough Residence Inn. Someone in the

Bureau had some foresight. Special Assignments were hard enough. Living in a standard hotel room for more than a week made them torture. Chase walked into the lobby and reveled in the spartan, shabby, but clean surroundings.

Credit card imprint exchanged for keys and Chase was home; at least his home for however long this Special lasted. He dragged his bags down a hall of peeling wallpaper and stained rust carpet. For one-twenty-nine a night it wasn't bad and at least he had two exits. His room had a sliding patio door opening out onto the parking lot. Once his bags were stowed, Chase'd move the BuCar so he could keep an eye on it.

He knew his choices were either the central Los Angeles areas, which could be pretty dodgy on the best day, or near the airport. Chase never slept well near the airport. With the Bureau's budget, the location could have been a lot worse. And, allegedly, it was only about five miles from FBI HQ. Chase made sure to give himself a good hour tomorrow to go those five miles. Los Angeles measured distance in traffic time, not asphalt under the tires.

The door swung open into a cramped but survivable one-bedroom mini-apartment. Surveying his temporary home, Chase bypassed the first opening on his left and headed for the door at the end of the short hall. Then he threw his bags through the doorway where the hall ended and jogged left—the bedroom. A few more steps brought him to a living room barely big enough to merit the title. A loveseat-sized sofa backed up against a half wall. A few inches of space between the couch, an oversized chair and the TV cabinet would probably mean bumped shins in the morning. The view through the open blinds was all parking lot. At least the efficiency kitchen, Chase noted as he leaned over the bar, boasted a real refrigerator and a two burner range. It was more than he expected.

Chase stripped as he headed back toward the shower. Always the first order of business, wash the road out of your skin. Water needled out the kinks of a big man trapped in a small airline seat for too many hours. Then he staggered out of the bath, towel around his middle, and collapsed on the bed.

As he stretched, the familiar snaps sounded from his spine. Chase tugged the towel open and let himself air-dry. It felt so good to just laze around in the buff. Chase reached down to give his dick a good hard rub. Hell, maybe he was a closet nudist…or maybe Chase just needed to be out of his agent persona for a while. To manage that, Chase stripped to the raw. Heavy, wood-smoke tinged air blanketed Chase's bare body. He couldn't believe it was October. The temperature hovered at a good eighty plus degrees.

Lazily, Chase fumbled the remote off the nightstand. Mindless blather occupied most every channel. Suited Chase just fine. It stripped more of the Bureau off his bones. One evening to not be who he was on the outside, so he could be who he was on the inside; God, it was eventually going to drive him crazy. It was, however, the life he'd chosen, the life of a chameleon—gay in the FBI.

Chase rolled over to hang off the bed. He dug into his bag, under the suits, the ties and the dress shirts, searching until his hand slid over the hard surface encased in plastic. Rolling back, Chase pulled the bottle along with him. Took him a moment to drag the cool glass out of the zip-lock, then he cracked the top, lifted the bottle to his lips and drank straight from it. Warm and comfortable, the burn slid through his body.

Chase took a little time to reminisce with his good friends, Jack Daniels and his hand. He couldn't be bothered enough to hunt down ice or a glass. A hand-over-hand slow stroke-off got his hips jerking and he dropped his knees wide. Chase cupped his balls, squeezing for the delicious pressure. Once the whiskey haze settled into his joints, Chase stretched again. The pops and grinds out of his back weren't half as noticeable. The heat of his palm moving over his prick melded with the glow of the booze.

Tonight, come hell or high water, he was going to taste dick. He promised himself he would. The vow shot sparks through his balls. God knew he couldn't go looking while wrapped up in a Special. If he didn't get laid tonight…well, best not to go down that road.

He hissed and fucked his own fist in earnest. The muscles in his chest twitched. Chase bit his lip and thought about some nameless hot guy. It really didn't matter much what he looked like, so long as he could fuck. Chase spread his legs wider and slid his other hand down to tickle his ass. He brought his hand up and, imagining a mouthful of hot cock, spit-slicked his finger. Then he reached back down and shoved inside. A good, heady burn as his finger breached his ass.

Fucked or sucked, Chase really didn't give a shit which. He just needed to get off. Chase's tongue stroked the roof of his mouth. And get off on something other than a one-handed date. Chase gave in to his fantasies. A dick up his ass, another in his mouth and some mouth on him...an invisible orgy. His hand flew over his prick, sending shocks through his gut. Body tense, Chase jerked. His balls sucked up into his body and then shivers blew through his frame. Chase shuddered as he milked spunk from his prick. Then he groaned and collapsed, spread-eagle, on the bed.

Intense, but not, the stroke-off got it out of his system for a bit. Chase didn't need an orgy, one real person would do.

He slid out of bed and went to clean up. Relaxed jeans came out and on, fuck wearing shorts or undershirt. Then Chase shouldered into a burgundy button-up shirt, which he didn't button up all the way. A pair of loafers on his feet and Chase headed out the door looking like anything but an FBI agent.

He rolled the cuffs back while waiting for a cab. The unremarkable monstrosity, courtesy of the Bureau's auto pool, would sleep in the hotel parking lot. Cars like that marked you as a Fed. Plus Chase knew better than to drive on a night he planned on drinking hard. Explaining off a DUI earned in West Hollywood to his SAC, not good. Chase ducked into the cab and gave the guy an address on Santa Monica. When the cabbie flashed a knowing smirk into the rearview, Chase debated on whether to tip. Fuck it, he finally figured, it was nobody's business but his own if Chase wanted to head into boys' town.

Hours later, Chase stared at the drink in his hand. Maybe this was just a bad idea. He'd been in the City of Angels for four hours, tops, and he hadn't even talked to anyone yet. Well, during dinner, he'd chatted it up with a waiter who looked way too young to be serving drinks. The kid recommended the joint housing the bar Chase leaned on now. Relaxed, trendy—but not—and way crowded; Silverlake's low-key answer to West Hollywood's forced urban hip.

Nude women stared vacantly off red and gold walls. Chase figured he should have specified somewhere more overtly gay and less just gay-friendly when asking for recommends. People, of all orientations and ages, lounged on Moroccan-styled couches along the wall. Maybe he would have had better odds on a weekend, Chase mused into the amber liquid swirling in his glass.

"Wow." A voice at his shoulder jerked Chase's attention from his self-pity.

He looked up into a bright smile and warm skin. "What?" Damn, the guy was good looking. Not in that stunning movie star kinda way, but with a pleasant face, easy body language and dark eyes. A choker of red and white beads flashed at the open collar of his white shirt. Both colors set off the man's caramel skin.

Another smile flashed as the guy tapped Chase's tumbler. "You managed to get a drink." He laughed and the sound traveled straight down Chase's spine to his hips. "Takes an act of Congress to get service here."

"Oh," Chase's face felt strange. Then he realized it was from an ear-splitting grin. Shit, if that didn't come off as desperate, Chase would eat his badge. He coughed and raised his glass to his lips in a badly concealed effort to mask the smile. "I laid the money down before I ordered."

The guy slid onto the stool next to Chase. "Explains it then." He leaned in and drummed his fingers on the bar. "My name's Enrique, I don't think I've seen you here before."

Enrique's hip pressed against Chase's thigh. When Enrique shifted, a hard bulge rubbed Chase through his jeans. Okay, Chase mused, so maybe the waiter had been on the money about the place. "I would be surprised if you had," Chase nudged back a little, letting Enrique know he felt it. "Just in town for business."

"What kind of business?" The question came loaded. Chase wasn't sure with exactly what. A strange wariness seemed to lurk under the words. For a moment, Chase toyed with a few implausible explanations and then figured he just didn't care. Because the hand that dropped down onto his thigh wasn't wary in the least. Easy, light, Enrique traced the inseam of Chase's jeans with his fingers.

Refusing to elaborate, Chase muttered, "Just business," as he knocked back his drink. Chase shrugged and spread his legs a little wider.

"Really," Enrique moved in closer. "I thought it might be scoping twenty-somethings out looking for their sugar daddies." The faded edge of cologne threaded under the scent of guy in a hot, crowded bar.

Chase snorted. A sense of humor, he liked that. Not that it was a requirement, but it made it nice, friendly. "The problem with twenty-somethings is they're twenty-something." He slid his arm around Enrique to cup a nicely toned ass through expensive slacks.

Damn, if Enrique moved any closer, he'd end up on Chase's lap. "How 'bout a thirty-something then?"

"You're, ah, pretty direct there." Chase teased. Actually, for a bar pickup, Enrique was beating about the bush a lot. Half the time a nod, a smile and a jerk of the chin arranged everything.

Enrique leaned in and laughed in his ear. "No, pretty direct is 'do you wanna fuck?'"

He squeezed Enrique's butt. "Is that an offer?" Felt good.

No laughter this time. Enrique hissed, "Want it to be?"

"Yeah." Chase stood.

"Then it's an offer." Pressing against a warm, solid body, one that was about to be all Chase's, sent anticipation thrumming into Chase's hips. Enrique's fingers hadn't stopped drumming Chase's skin, he just moved the touch more front and center. "Your place?"

A long, frantic fuck in bed, God it sounded great. Chase wasn't about to go down that road. "My place's no good. What about your place?"

Enrique glanced over at the bartender. The guy raised an eyebrow full of piercings. Enrique smirked and the guy jerked his head toward a door. "How about you just come with me?"

"Shit." Enrique must have been a regular, 'cause Chase sure didn't merit that kinda trust out of the staff. He was certainly glad Enrique did. "Okay." Chase dropped his glass on the bar as he turned. Enrique moved first, shoving his way through a throng of patrons.

Into the back, heading towards the can, Enrique paused once to chat up one of the bouncers. The burly guy seemed to laugh, but by the time Chase caught up, Enrique was on the move again. Enrique slipped into a dim hall, Chase close on his heels. Past the bathrooms, Enrique turned and bumped a door with his butt. He smiled, watching Chase approach, and turned the handle. Pushing the door open with his weight, Enrique's smile dissolved into something a little more feral. He balled his hand into Chase's shirt and pulled him inside.

It wasn't more than a broom closet, hardly enough room for two men to move, let alone get on all fours or anything. The tiny space smelled like ammonia and gym socks. Likely the owners would deny it until judgment day, but they damn well knew what went on in their empty little closet. Before Enrique let the door swing shut, Chase grabbed a condom out of a plastic bucket perched on a hamstrung bar stool. A trash can finished the limited furnishings.

The door snicked shut and the room went dark. A few blinks adjusted Chase's eyes to the almost nonexistent blue lighting. Chase took a deep breath and found Enrique with his fingers. Desperately, he pulled the other man to him. They met in a hard, open-mouth kiss and grinding hips. All he had to do was press the packet into Enrique's palm and it settled who did what to whom. Nobody talked in places like this, you just fucked.

Sliding his hand down, Chase cupped Enrique's dick. It was hard as hell, hard as Chase's own. For a while they let it build. Chase felt up Enrique, sliding his hand over a thick, trapped dick. Each stroke earned him a groan and a grind. He licked the salt on the other man's throat. Enrique's hands roamed over his denim-enclosed butt and prick. If they were somewhere else, Chase would have stripped Enrique and licked every inch of skin.

Enrique found his mouth in the dark. Chase bit at Enrique's lip. When he opened his mouth, Chase forced his tongue in. Enrique tasted of rum. Their tongues wrestled, never in one mouth too long. Without stopping the kiss, Enrique worked the button and fly on Chase's jeans. When they popped open, he yanked the material down enough to free Chase's raging hard-on.

No ceremony, no messy conversations, Enrique dropped to his knees and sucked Chase down. Chase hissed. His hips bucked. Enrique's mouth was hot and wet. The guy could definitely suck dick. He licked the crown and then down the length, sending chills running down the back of Chase's knees. After a bit of that tease, Enrique added a grip around Chase's cock. One hand pumped Chase's shaft. The other massaged his balls. Each time Enrique wrapped his lips over Chase's throbbing head, Chase lost a little more control.

The touch left his sac, moving back. A finger circled his hole. Chase swallowed and dropped his head back against the concrete wall. Enrique pushed and the exploring digit slipped inside. A bit of pain made Chase hiss again. Too long without that kinda contact and his body forgot what it was supposed to do. Slow, easy, Enrique pumped him, finger-fucked him, opened him up. The raw burn became sweet, swelling heat in Chase's balls.

As fire built in his gut, Chase slid his fingers through Enrique's sweat-damp hair. Cupping the back of Enrique's head, Chase shoved his dick down that hot throat. Face-fucking the other man, he made Enrique take it all the way down again and again. With each thrust, a rolling mass of pent-up desire fractured every cell.

"Gonna happen." Chase mumbled through tight lips. Enrique pulled off. He wrapped his hand around Chase's prick and jerked. Two strokes and Chase shot, cum spattering the floor.

Enrique stood. Chase reached out and found a hard dick already wrapped in a condom. Fuck yeah, no time wasted. Rough and demanding, Enrique grabbed his shoulders and spun Chase to the wall. Chase hooked one foot on a low rung of the stool, leaned over what was left of the back and pulled the tail of his shirt up a bit. His hand pressed against the far wall for support. Not the best position, but it would do. Enrique's dick pressed against his hole.

Chase savored that demanding and so male contact.

With a grunt, Enrique thrust. Chase's body balked and he jerked against the broken stool. It'd been a hell of a long time. Insistent but slower, like he sensed Chase needed to adjust, Enrique keep pushing. When resistance gave, both groaned. Damn, Chase needed that feeling. Needed that prick up his ass. Enrique spread him wide. As his body remembered, opened up, Chase bit his lip. That thick cock reached deeper inside him and touched things impossible to touch. Chase rocked back to get more.

Enrique ran his hands over Chase's ass and exposed thigh. The touch shredded Chase's already frayed nerves, made him shiver. Slowly, Enrique seated himself. When his dick was buried down to the balls, he shuddered. His fingers latched onto Chase's hips. Two short, sharp thrusts and Enrique started to pound. Enrique's grunts mixed with the slap of his balls against Chase's own. Sweat ran along the line of Chase's jaw. It mixed with the spicy tang of his own spunk drying on the floor and the heady scent of Enrique. He moaned and bucked against Enrique's movements. Fucking back as much as he was fucked. Too short, too quick, Chase felt Enrique jerk as heat welled in Chase's hole. Panting heavily, Enrique pulled away.

Behind him, Chase heard the thunk of the condom hitting the trash and then the grate of Enrique's zipper. He stood on wobbly legs to yank up his jeans. Enrique stepped in and licked

Chase's ear. "Thanks, man," he muttered over the rattle of the doorknob.

"No problem." Chase managed to respond, but Enrique was already out the door. Chase righted his clothes. Then he slipped out and headed first to the can, and then back to the bar for another drink. Enrique had vanished. Didn't matter much. Most guys didn't even say thanks, much less goodbye.

CHAPTER THREE

Running his hands over the top of his skull, Chase debated whether to get out of the BuCar and head inside. Chase's capacity for self-abuse amazed even himself. What was the use of really tying one on the night before if you didn't even suffer a full-blown hangover in the morning? All that seemed to manifest for Chase was a slight sense of heavy unease, like he wore someone else's soul, and the taste of cotton wool in his mouth. He'd skipped breakfast in favor of a roll of antacids.

Chase popped the sedan's door and eased out of the car. Whiskey didn't seem to do it much anymore. Wine came off too fem and just made him sick. Gin gave him a headache before the alcohol even swam warm through his veins. He needed to find something harder, with more bite. Hands shoved in his jacket pockets, Chase started the long walk toward the Los Angeles HQ. There had to be something out there that would create the demons-building-houses effect inside his skull. Drunk or hungover, both kept him from thinking too hard.

Wedged in his pocket, next to a pack of Juicy Fruit gum and the remainder of the roll of antacids, the FBI's wanted sheet on Almandeto Famosa-Garcia weighed heavy. He'd memorized it years ago. Chase kept the crumpled paper as a token reminder of all the years of hunting and tracking, only to have Garcia slip through his fingers. Now they were closing in. Not just on Garcia—he'd go down for Jason—but the real nuts and bolts to put a kink in his whole organization.

Chase was nervous about this new Special. He was known as the go-to-it guy, the one who could fit in anywhere and work with anyone. He was a chameleon; his life suited him for undercover work.

Single meant no encumbrances, irate spouses or missed softball games to worry about while he was on assignment. He was forty and looked all of thirty. Added to that, an indiscriminate heritage that let him slide anywhere from white middle class to low-rung, but light-skinned Hispanic, meant Chase could move from boardroom to boardwalk with little effort. Training kept him in shape. A military background, Rangers, gave Chase the survival skills most agents wouldn't even begin to know where to pick up.

The dark glass and white concrete of the sixties' era headquarters loomed; the ashen countenance a stark counter to the muted brown sky. At least it didn't look half as bad as the monstrosity of the Hoover building. Antiquated, dated, and stuffed beyond capacity; over a thousand staff members and agents were farmed out to the Resident Agencies, like LAX. There just wasn't any room for them all. The grinding oppression of it meshed with Chase's already miserable mood and clicked perfectly.

Mostly, he mused, his ability to blend and disappear was because he was gay, which meant every day of his life in the FBI was spent pretending he was something he wasn't. Chase headed across the massive parking lot, loosening his tie slightly as he walked. Gay and FBI were not words that went together. Even after Buttino's suit shredded the Bureau for its stance on the issue, it hadn't changed. Now the discrimination was just more subversive.

The degraded lump of last night's stupidity wormed through Chase's chest, sliding down to curl up, warm and comfortable, in the pit of his stomach. Chase swam in a perpetual stew of self-loathing. Miserable after tying one on, wound tighter than a spring detonator most other times…getting drunk seemed the only way to relax. Problem was, he relaxed too far. There was no mental stop sign. His internal monitor, conscience, whatever you called it, got bombed right along with him. Instead of *hey, we need to back this down*, it went to sleep under the table.

Drawing in a deep breath, Chase shoved the thoughts aside and stepped through the maw of the beast. Procedures, check-ins, sign-outs and general bureaucratic nonsense distracted him for a while. Still, Chase realized he'd risked his career last night for a quick fuck in a back room. Chase filled his career with riskier and riskier moves. He was his own worst enemy. Every so often he managed to kick his own ass, although so far he was lucky enough no one else had. Only a matter of time, if he kept up like he was.

A plastic smile slid onto his face when he rounded the corner and ran into a grim older man. "Special Agent Donaldson?" Chase spat out with an overabundance of enthusiasm. Chase recognized him from the briefings and portfolio he'd read on the plane. Donaldson, the Special Agent in Charge of this Special Assignment, turned and glared. The wizened gnome, if Chase remembered correctly, made his name in paper chases. Unlike some agents, Chase didn't sneer at the more academic in the Bureau. It took a certain type of genius to not only work out the trail of receipts, payola and lifestyle, but to put it in a coherent form for lesser minds. "Just who I was told to find on this Special." Everything in the FBI was just so freaking special: agents, assignments. At least Donaldson wasn't one of the three Big SACs, just an SAC. Chase wasn't sure he could stomach a Big SAC on top of last night.

"Agent Nozick?" Donaldson growled.

Chase let the critical once-over of Donaldson's eyes pass without either ire or overt notice. "Yes, sir." If anything his smile stretched, just a little more confident.

"You're too goddamn upbeat before my third cup of coffee."

"Ah," Chase snorted, finding he liked Donaldson without really wanting to, "that's 'cause I'm on about my sixth." None of them had managed to wash the taste of tin off his tongue.

"That explains it. You up to date?" When Chase nodded, Donaldson grunted. "Alright then. We got everyone ready. The local boys showed up about an hour early." Donaldson's gnarled hand shot out to grab the lever on one of a myriad of doors. "You'd think they'd never worked a task force or something." He grumbled and shoved. Donaldson rolled through, holding the door for Chase with the tips of his fingers. As soon as he sensed Chase was far enough through, he let it go. Chase caught the door with his shoulder. With what he'd learned about Donaldson in the past few moments, Chase chalked it up to a guy so wrapped up in the next assignment that he just didn't pay attention to anything, or anyone, else.

Dun walls and green linoleum, the room definitely felt like government issue. File boxes stacked around the perimeter made it seem cramped. God, Chase hated these windowless holes. Sure, they were secure, but you had to breathe re-circulated air and paint fumes. Lighting never seemed adequate. Fluorescents, reflected off an eight-foot gray amalgamate conference table, gave off a sickly vibe. Between the boxes and the beat-up executive chairs, there was hardly room to move.

That and the six other bodies crammed into the room didn't ease Chase's sense of claustrophobia.

Donaldson shoved through the narrow space to the end of the room. Waving at an assembly of men and women, all in suits, he started introductions. "Agents Tyler and Craig," Donaldson jabbed at the only two women in the room. "Craig's your first point of contact for anything you need. They both work organized crime." The meaty finger swung to point at a thin black man in a subdued suit. "Jamison here is our gang expert on this one."

All the agents caved to the bland uniformity of the Bureau. Even their unique features of sex or race wouldn't make them stand out in a crowd of other agents. Of course the only thing about Chase's clothes that stood out was his wine-colored tie. Otherwise, his charcoal suit and white shirt disappeared into the sea of government-issue clones.

One of the unidentified men stepped up and offered a nail-bitten hand. Rumpled, with a bright blue shirt, no jacket and a blue tie emblazoned with handcuffs and revolvers marked him as not FBI. "Detective Sergeant Grant Hill, LAPD." Hill's grip was dry and strong, a power handshake. "Heard all about you, Agent Nozick." Like Donaldson, Hill made a slow, calculating once-over of Chase.

The remaining two feigned disinterest. A wannabe military clone, sporting bulging muscles, shorn brown hair and a glare, leaned against the wall and tried to stare Chase down. Chinos and a polo shirt separated him from the agents as well. Chase refused to even rise to the bait. If you acted like it didn't matter, then it didn't matter. The other guy sat in one of the broken-down chairs, his back to Chase. Long legs in expensive slacks stretched across to bump the back wall. The most Chase could make out of the guy was a mop of black hair, one brown arm and the edge of a cinnamon short-sleeved shirt. Hill jerked his chin towards big and burly.

"This is Rod Hungwell." Chase tried not to choke when he heard the guy's porn star name. "Rod's a D outta Central and works organized for us." Rod barely grunted and didn't move.

Hill's hand landed on the other man's shoulder. The guy rolled his head back to smile at Hill. The partial profile churned Chase's memory, but he couldn't put a bead on it. "Enrique Rios-Ochoa." Hill beamed. "We're lending him to y'all on this one. He'll get you in, out and sideways into the Cuban community." Enrique spun the chair round and stood. Holy shit, the dark eyes, those hit Chase first. The first name, the face, finally clicked.

Chase blinked. Before Enrique could do a double-take, Chase grabbed his hand and squeezed...hard. "Damn," he smiled to take the bite out of the grip, "You look just like a guy I served with." Pleading with his eyes for Enrique to take the cue, Chase tried not to puke.

For a moment, Chase thought Enrique might blow it. Then Enrique squeezed back. He popped Chase's shoulder with his other fist. "Never been in the military, man."

The rising tide of panic faded. "Good," that was mostly for Enrique. He feigned a comment for the group to cover, "to meet you all," and dropped the shake. Turning to Hill and Donaldson, he managed to act casual, maybe even relaxed. "So, I understand I'm gonna be partnered up with one of your men for this Special." Chase hoped he'd misheard Enrique's introduction.

"Enrique's your man. Nobody better." Hill beamed. "He's got a lot of experience with organized crime and is one of our resident experts on Voodoo and crap."

Shit, he hadn't. "Well, good then." Chase managed to stutter out without coming off overly strained. The fake smiles were getting harder and harder to maintain. "Shall we get the briefing started then?" Chase edged around the table and chose a seat where he wouldn't have to look directly at Enrique. Before dropping heavy into the chair, he reminded himself he'd pulled off more dangerous charades. Nobody had a gun pointed at his head—yet. And Enrique seemed willing to play along. Thank God.

Everyone settled into a space and the routine of an interagency briefing. Information and objectives flew across the table. They discussed Garcia and the whys of him not popping up on the radar recently. Questions about his *Muertos* came up and remained largely unanswered. Mostly, they all tried to figure out how to find Carmen or whether they would find her in one reasonably whole piece. Chase voiced the opinion, and no one knew enough or had enough balls to blow him down, that Garcia liked to possess things: cars, people, money. He'd get every last bit of sadistic fun from his former girlfriend before dumping her. Nobody walked away from Garcia, but he liked to keep them around long enough for them to understand that, fear it.

The briefing hardly helped Chase forget who sat two chairs down. Not that he honestly cared all that much. It was nothing more than a fuck and suck, he reminded himself, but shit, he just hadn't geared up to run into one of his casual lays at HQ. The situation tugged all his senses the wrong way. Intensely aware of Enrique, his smile, his voice...his smell, Chase found himself risking a glance again and again. Luckily, this go round didn't require much input from Chase. All he had to do was sit down and soak up info.

Halfway through, or what Chase assumed was about the halfway point, Hill's cell phone rang. The man jerked it off his hip, flipped the clamshell open and glared at the screen. Whoever called must have been important because the Detective Sergeant rolled his chair back and answered the call. Everyone tried to ignore the short conversation punctuated with, "uh-hus," "un-uhs" and "yeahs." With a final grunt, Hill snapped the phone closed. All attention turned to him.

"Okay, Enrique." Hill's grin was feral. "You get to show FBI guy here how the LAPD does business. Northwest's got a 187 with a possible hit on the Person of Interest the Bureau sent over. That Fuertes guy. LA River, Griffith Park area. Call Northwest dispatch and get the details as you roll."

"Yes, sir." Enrique pushed back from the table. "How will you get back to the station if I take the car?" he asked as he stood.

Before he could stop himself, Chase offered, "I have an assigned vehicle. We can take mine." Shit. He mentally kicked himself for the slip. Of course, the lack of an offer would have stood out. His own reputation grabbed him by the short hairs again. "I can drop you off wherever when we're done."

Donaldson smiled. "Sounds like a plan then. Get! Go! We can wrap the rest up another day."

Spared from much interaction by a group walk to the lobby, Chase tried to not think. The agents stayed, the cops followed them to the BuCar, keeping up a steady tide of patter as they walked. Chase slid into the driver's seat. Enrique clambered into the passenger side. Two doors slammed, locking them in a Detroit-built cell. All the conversation gambits Chase knew, those for bumping into a casual fuck, didn't seem appropriate to the moment. Instead he said nothing and started the car.

Enrique broke the ice first, with business. "Got something I can write on?"

"Yeah, in the back seat, there's a portfolio." Chase pulled out of the space, heading through the lot towards Wilshire.

"Okay, FBI." Leaning between the seats, Enrique added, "Jump up to Santa Monica, head east to Vermont and then north up to Los Feliez. That'll keep us from having to go 'round the mountain or through downtown." He slid back into the seat and fumbled with his shoulder belt. Then he dug out his cell phone, saving Chase the need to try and figure anything out. A one-sided conversation where Enrique jotted notes saved Chase from dealing with the situation.

Upscale Beverly Hills mansions gave way to the trendy West Hollywood strip as Enrique talked. When he hung up, Enrique spoke into his notes. "Looks like we've got a male Hispanic, mid-twenties with a scar on his left cheek. His details pinged with the APB on Fuertes." Flipping through the few pages, he reviewed the information before adding, "There's pretty obvious gunshot trauma. Coroner will have to give a definite yea or nay on the cause of death. They're holding the scene for us where it's at, they don't have to clear for use. Middle of the fucking LA River."

"Middle?" Chase gave half his attention to Enrique's running commentary, the rest he reserved for driving. WeHo slowly dissolved into rundown warehouses and low-rent production studios before Chase turned onto Vermont.

"Yeah. The river's pretty low. Even when it's not, there's a lot of, I'd guess you'd call them islands?" Enrique flipped the pad shut and stared out into the LA barrio. "Derelicts, druggies sometimes use them for camps. Apparently someone scrounging found the body this morning."

As they crossed Sunset and finally made Los Feliz, the city's character again changed to upscale residential. High-priced condos and apartments lined either side of the wide boulevard. Thirty minutes and four different economic zones, Chase shook his head and snorted.

"What?"

"Nothing." So far, they hadn't talked about anything that happened. Most situations and Chase wouldn't have needed to. Something needed to be said. "Look, last night." He held up a hand to forestall a comment from Enrique. "Don't care. Doesn't matter. It was fun, but look, I'm not out at work. The Bureau doesn't deal with the issue well. So the subject's dead, right?"

Enrique stared at him for a moment. "LAPD ain't exactly a gay-friendly environment, FBI. I hear you. This is work." Chase nodded, glad that Enrique understood. A few moments passed before Enrique spoke up. "Go past the park, hit the freeway for a bit. We'll go over to the soccer field and walk from there."

Following the signs onto I-5 and then off onto Zoo Drive, they found a set of uniforms directing traffic. The road was open, but they'd closed off the parking areas on either side. After checking IDs, they directed Chase to park at an already searched spot near the off-leash dog runs. He and Enrique jogged along the asphalt, their way guided by a line of police tape to an opening in the chain-link fence that bordered the concrete wash of the river. A rope had been tied to the opposite railing at the edge of a narrow bike path. Chase silently thanked whoever had foresight to string it. The concrete sloped down sharply before leveling out into a silted-up concrete basin.

Gnawing on another handful of antacids, Chase splashed across a muddy rivulet following the line of police tape. Every inch of the river could hold clues. LAPD didn't want investigative personnel mucking up the scene, in this case a scene that could stretch a good mile or more in any direction. The yellow plastic ribbon meandered toward the gargantuan supports of the intersection of the 5 and 134 freeways.

Ahead and slightly to the left brooded an island of broken concrete, river-rock and silt. In the dry season the Los Angeles River hardly rated as a creek. Visitors wondered what all the fuss was about. Half a mile wide, the steep-sloped concrete seemed a pretty large prison for such a little stream. Come winter, when the rains hit hard, it wouldn't be half big enough to contain the hell. Chocolate-silted flow would boil from rim to rim, everything between concrete lips swept to the ocean.

Chase clambered up onto the drier ground and pushed through thick stands of non-native bamboo. As he picked his way across the rubble, things scurried away from his feet. Behind him Enrique muttered, "Fuck, every time I get a pair of new slacks, I fucking land a murder scene. Shit, FBI, you're supposed to keep me outta this shit. You guys never get down and dirty in the trenches."

"Shows a lot you don't know." Chase paused, waiting for Enrique to catch up. After fishing the pack of gum from his pocket, he pulled a piece for himself and then offered it out to Enrique. "Gum?" He needed something to break the chalky film left by the antacid tablets.

Enrique raised an eyebrow at the bright yellow package. "Juicy Fruit?" Then he snagged a piece.

Chase shrugged as he unwrapped his piece. "Yeah, my last partner got me stuck on it when he quit smoking." Before folding the gum into his mouth he pocketed the wrapper. Enrique did the same. Good crime scene etiquette; don't pollute the scene.

As they started walking again, Enrique jumped back to the previous thread of conversation. "Really, FBI." He snorted, going back to Chase's first comment. "What's the worst scene you ever processed?"

"Oklahoma." Chase paused again and stared up at the sepia-toned sky. There were some memories he'd just rather forget. Jason Olhms' murder ranked second only to that.

Enrique stopped beside him. "What, some farm bureau hick get nabbed?"

"No, years ago." Chase resumed picking his way across the rubble, underbrush and broken bottles. "My first real posting. First day on the job and my crappy car's fucking battery died. I'm thinking 'Man I'm fucking dead. The SAC is going to chew my ass.' I got there just in time to see the front of the building go." Blowing out the rest in a huff, "Green as fucking grass and I'm working a home-grown terrorist bombing for my home office."

"Fuck." Enrique hissed. That was about the most appropriate comment that Chase could come up with most times. One word that summed it all up.

A plastic yellow ribbon with "Police Line, Do Not Cross" emblazoned in black blocked the path. Chase took another deep breath, as though that might free his thoughts, and stared at a sky mirroring the sepia tones of the river.

Up the banks, to the left, warehouses succumbed to the ravages of acrid smog and dayglow graffiti. An endless sea of lurid gang code swept up the concrete banks and into Glendale. Traffic screamed by on the right, heading up and down I-5. Just beyond that the scarred hillsides of Griffith Park sheltered the zoo, pony rides and museums from the ravages of Los Angeles' rampant sprawl.

Enrique nodded to a uniformed officer and held the tape up so they could enter the scene. "You okay there?" His dark eyes looked tired, as tired as Chase felt.

"Yeah." He ducked under. "Let's get this dog and pony show started." A bit more ducking through weeds and fast-growing reeds brought them to the heavy, sweet scent of death. Chase and Enrique followed another winding line of police tape toward the scene. It took them out of their way, but kept them off any place where the detectives thought evidence might be found.

Without much warning, Chase came face-to-face with the scene. Rodrigo, Chase recognized his mug from the pictures, lay on his stomach, head turned to the side, and one arm flopped across his back. The other flung out to the side and rested across the ring of marigold blossoms that circled his body. Flies crawled across glassy eyes, and crosses in white and red painted Renaldo's face and down his arms. Each line ended in a dot, an arrow or a fork.

Well-rehearsed, the LAPD team of specialists did their dance around the body. At the periphery, a coroner's crew waited with their bright blue body bag to take custody of the corpse.

A woman, her hair pulled tight back and wearing a better suit than her male counterparts, caught sight of them. In fact, she and Chase were the only two wearing actual suits, everyone else barely qualified as business casual. She said something to a trio of techs before picking her way toward Chase and Enrique. After introducing herself as Detective Wyatt, exchanging the brief necessities of rank and protocol, she filled them in. "We figure he was shot first over there," Wyatt waved one manicured hand back the way Chase'd come. "About fifteen feet and crawled back this way. They shot him twice more as he crawled. The last bullet, the one to his head, likely killed him where he ended up."

"Why do you figure a *they*?" Enrique spoke the question Chase'd been thinking.

Wyatt glared, like she thought Enrique yanked her instead of just asking the first obvious question. Her response was clipped with the efficiency of a woman used to being treated as slightly inferior to the men she outranked. "Rodrigo's a big guy, a bad ass, ballsy guy. One man wouldn't have been enough to intimidate him into coming down here. Drag him down, neither."

This time Chase, keeping his tone as neutral as possible, asked the question. "What if he walked down on his own?" Or they had enough guys to make it impossible to fight.

"Hard to see someone who doesn't want to be down here," Enrique folded his arms over his chest, "being dragged down here."

"Think he was meeting someone?" Chase asked the question of both detectives.

"I'd bet on that..." Wyatt's mouth went tight. "Not a hundred percent thing, but damn good odds."

Enrique paced a few steps, looking at the body from various angles. "I think someone he trusted lured him down, maybe." Looking to Wyatt, his tone said he was asking her opinion, not overriding her. Careful not to disturb the ring of flowers, he squatted near Fuertes. "Or maybe someone he didn't trust, but that he had to meet even if he didn't want to." Enrique turned his attention back to the corpse.

"So, Ochoa," Wyatt studied Enrique as he studied Fuertes. The cool, calculated once up and once down echoed a woman used to sizing up co-workers as potential opponents. "What's with the flowers? And the X's all over him? You know about this shit right?"

"Some of it. The marigolds are a Mexican thing. Americans leave roses on graves, Mexicans leave marigolds. Why they're with Fuertes, I don't know." Enrique's gaze flicked up. "Those," he traced the air indicating one of the marks on the dead man's skin, "are the symbols of Eshu."

Without thinking, Chase responded with a, "Bless you."

That rated Chase a glare from Enrique and a snort from Wyatt. "I didn't sneeze." Enrique coughed. "Eshu, also Exu, Echu or a bunch of other variants, is a deity in a lot of Afro-Caribbean religions."

"Eshu?"

"Eshu is the devil…sort of." Standing, Enrique crossed his arms over his chest and thought for a moment. Slowly, like he felt a little embarrassed at knowing what he knew. "Okay, the quick and dirty version. Religions of the Caribbean come from slave religions that got all mixed up with Catholicism. The master said pray to his god, and he was likely Spanish or Portuguese. So, his god had saints who all meant something and you prayed to them. It wasn't so hard to say this saint of water is this god of water, at least if you didn't want to get beaten for praying to your old traditional gods. Stick their statues in with your symbols and everyone thinks it's cute that the dumb slaves like the statues."

"And Eshu is the devil?" Wyatt didn't sound like she was buying.

Without seeming to take offense, Enrique shrugged. "Eshu is like Lucifer because he's always in conflict with Ologun the creator. But in many Caribbean religions Eshu is also the only one who speaks directly to Ologun. If you want something done, you ask Eshu…" he smirked. "Just be careful of what he asks for in return."

"Well, okay," Chase looked back over the scene. "Heavy possibility of ritual murder then. Although the marigolds don't fit. Our guy's Cuban."

"Well," running his hand over his jaw, Enrique seemed unsure. "The marigolds came to mind as Mexican because Halloween is coming up and they're part of the Day of the Dead celebrations. But, it could be someone pretending at the religion, so they mixed shit up…all Latinos are alike after all." Enrique rolled his eyes at the absurdity of his own statement. "Or some priest told whoever did it that Eshu wanted marigolds."

"Okay, so square one." Exasperated, Chase shook his head. Time to focus on more concrete investigations. He turned to Wyatt. "When do you plan on doing the autopsy?"

"If it's a quiet night, they'll do it tonight if we push a rush. Otherwise, tomorrow. You guys'll attend?"

"I'd like to." Chase shoved his hands into his pockets. "See if you can pull strings. We need what we can get fast. This guy's sister has dirt on a hit man we want big time. Hopefully he didn't rat her out."

"Could be why they popped him, he wouldn't rat."

"Naw," Chase's tight smile held no amusement. "Garcia is a cold-hearted son of a bitch. He'd have done it just to make a statement." Swinging his arm back, indicating the scene, "And that is one hell of a statement."

CHAPTER FOUR

Wyatt managed to pull a massive favor out of someone and got Renaldo squeezed into the daily round-up of forty plus bodies the Coroner's office handled. They grabbed convenience store coffee and danishes on the way to Mission Road and the County Coroner's building. A whitewashed concrete homage to seventies box architecture greeted them with a blue-painted sign: Department of Coroner. Administrative offices and forensic labs were separated by a concrete patio.

"So," Chase jogged up the steps after Enrique, "I'm still stumped about the flowers and the symbols, why they were there."

Pausing, Enrique waited for Chase. "Well, like I said, it could be someone trying to make it look like a Voodoo or Santeria killing. Usually, though, those aren't violent religions so that's why I'm thinking somebody is trying to make it look ritual. Of course, could be Palo Mayumbe, but I didn't see any sticks. A lot of times in a Palo-associated killing you find sticks stuck into the ground near the body."

Chase thought for a moment. The char in the air filtered onto his tongue and made the world taste like hell. "He was in a stand of bamboo. Lot of sticks."

"True." With a nod, Enrique started toward glass double-doors on the left. "I should have said I didn't see any that seemed overly ritual. Although with Palo it's sometimes hard to tell." When he got to the door, Enrique held it open for Chase. "I told the techs what to keep an eye out for."

The moment he walked into the lobby, Chase regretted eating before they came down. He'd been to many an autopsy. They all held a particular disturbing feel. But few of the morgues and funeral homes he'd seen matched the creep show factor of LA County. Enrique and Chase followed Wyatt through the dingy labyrinth. They passed big meat locker doors stenciled with numbers and framed by rusty pipes as they headed to the lab. Corpses, wrapped in white plastic and resting on rolling metal tables, lined the left side of the hallway. Above the swathed forms hung posters of body parts.

"Goddamn," Enrique held his hand over his mouth and nose. "I hate coming down here. It's like some freaking horror show."

While not overpowering, the whole building seemed saturated with the stench of formaldehyde and less identifiable scents. The tang crawled up Chase's nose. He could almost taste the decomposing flesh in his mouth. To mask it, he snagged a piece of gum. Jason's habit had a plus side. Cinnamon, nutmeg and the slight fruity tang squashed some of the worst of the scents. Chase offered the pack around. Everyone seemed thankful for the offer.

Wyatt shrugged as she stuck the gum in her mouth. "Well, the main locker is stuffed with like four hundred bodies. They still haven't really fixed the six hundred series lockers although they claim the rats don't get into the long-term storage anymore."

"If you believe that," Enrique snorted, "I've got a good piece of beachfront property in Nevada to sell you."

Another metal door ahead of them opened and a bespectacled technician in blue scrubs trundled out. She looked up from under short-cut bangs. "Detective Wyatt. I was waiting for you. Gloves and masks by the door, I'll be back in a sec. Make yourselves comfortable."

Enrique rolled his eyes for Chase's benefit as they filed through the doorway the woman just left. Baby blue tiled walls and steel sinks, scales and trays harbored no comfort for the living and the dead didn't seem to care about the amenities. Wyatt passed out the medical gloves and masks. "Rosa is good. She bent the rules a little to fit our case in." As Chase was tying his mask on, Rosa rolled back through, pushing a metal gurney. Renaldo's milky eyes stared at the ceiling.

Angling the table over a floor drain, she chuckled. "Welcome to my world." Rosa grinned and pulled a set of gloves over her stubby fingers. "Who am I entertaining besides the elegant Detective Wyatt and the late Renaldo Fuertes?"

Nodding instead of offering his hand, Enrique introduced himself. "Enrique Rios-Ochoa, outta Central." A jerk of his head indicated Chase. "This is Special Agent Chase Nozick, FBI."

"Well, well, well." Rosa moved around the table, her attention focused on the dead man. "Not many FBI agents find their way here." She grabbed a clipboard off the lip of a battered steel sink. "Detective Wyatt, if you'll do the honors of recording weights and stuff, we can move quicker. Either of you gentlemen," another round-faced grin popped up before Rosa settled a face shield over her head, "good with a camera?" Rosa waggled her fingers toward a shelf holding various saws, pries and pruning shears. Among the junk sat a digital camera.

Chase sidled around the table and grabbed it. "I can manage that." He hated autopsies. Having something official to do would help the low-grade nausea that crept into his stomach whenever someone started cutting. Rosa began the physical exam of Renaldo, detailing the type of shirt, shoes and jeans he wore and examining the possible entrance and exit wounds still concealed by clothing. Every so often she'd have Chase snap a picture of something interesting: powder burns on the shirt, grass stains on Renaldo's knees or the dirt under his fingernails. Each of the painted symbols was digitally captured for the investigation's files. With that done, Rosa began the removal of personal items and clothing. Wallet and keys came out of his jeans pockets.

"We didn't find any abandoned cars at the scene." Wyatt frowned. "We'll have to do a wider check, maybe he came onto the scene from the opposite side of the river."

"Or maybe someone drove his car off the scene. Hotwired it and dumped it somewhere if there was evidence they didn't want found."

Rosa's "Aha!" interrupted their speculation.

"What did you find?" Wyatt stepped closer to the gurney. Chase and Enrique quickly followed her.

"A card." Rosa held it up for their inspection. "Located in the front pocket of his T-shirt." All three crowded around her to try and decipher the black ink against red paper as Rosa held it up to the florescent light.

Chase read off the title as a question. "Santario de Luz: Botanica?"

"Spiritualist." Enrique nodded as though it made complete sense. "They import Mambe, Santaria and Voodoo supplies. Candles, incense, that kinda crap."

This time the question was Wyatt's. "Why would Rodrigo have it?

"Oshun." Enrique whispered the word.

"Oh-what?" Wyatt glared at him.

With a heavy sigh, Enrique plastered on a thin smile and explained. "He's a child of the goddess Oshun."

Now Chase was perplexed. "How do you know that?"

"The beads around his neck." Enrique pointed to the corpse and, more importantly, to a string of beads made from gold and yellow glass. Now that Renaldo lay on his back, the choker was visible just above his collar. "The colors are those of Oshun."

It clicked for Chase. The red and white string about Enrique's throat, a different pattern but the same style of bead made up the choker. "And the ones around yours?"

A slightly embarrassed smile blew across Enrique's face. "Shango," he muttered.

"What?" Wyatt brayed. "I know you're supposed to be some kinda guru on that shit, but you don't really believe in that crap, do you?"

Rosa shook her head and dropped the card in an evidence bag. Chase noted her jotting the date and collection time in permanent ink on the clear plastic. Ignoring them, she plucked a pair of heavy-duty scissors off a tray and started the business of cutting Renaldo out of his clothes.

Enrique's defensive, "Yeah, actually I do," caused Wyatt to take a step back.

"That's like scary shit there, Ochoa." She tried to turn it into a tease with her tone. "People biting heads off chickens and shit."

"Not quite." Both words received heavy emphasis.

"Whoa, okay," Chase literally stepped between them. "We're here to work a murder right? Not get into a philosophical discussion about religion. So, Enrique," Chase hated the law enforcement habit of calling everyone by their last names and refused to use it. "You know the place?"

Not really mollified, Enrique growled, "No." He shook his head and ran his teeth over his bottom lip. "I know *of* the place. I got some numbers at home I could call, arrange to talk to the owner and see what he knows. If we do it that way, more likely to get cooperation."

"How soon can you get on that?"

"As soon as we're done here and you drive me back to my place."

"Okay then," Chase palmed his face. The smell of the surgical gloves almost masked the pervasive low-level reek of the room. "Let's get back to work."

Rosa added a, "Great then." They turned to find her holding a scalpel raised in one hand, the fingers of the other resting on Renaldo's clammy breast bone. "I'm ready to cut."

CHAPTER FIVE

A grayish box of a house, its windows shaded by metal awnings, sporting security bars over every entrance and a concrete front yard hulked behind a wall of cinderblock and wrought iron. Blood orange and smoky, the sunset threw lurid shadows over the cement. Every direction Chase looked, smoke plumes billowed across the sky.

Enrique jumped out and unlocked the gate. Chase pulled the sedan in behind a reasonably new Nissan 350Z. As Enrique closed the gate, Chase unbuckled himself, popped the door and looked back. "Heck of a freaking car for a detective to own." The damn thing was nicer than anything Chase could afford. Sleek lines swept the car in a bullet shape and the shiny black paint job made it look like a stealth plane.

Enrique didn't look over from shutting the gate behind Chase's car. "I guess."

"Where'd you get it?"

"A friend." Enrique's tone said Chase wasn't about to get a better answer.

He pried anyway. "What kind of friend?"

"A good friend." A glare was thrown on top of Enrique's attitude. "The kind of friend who buys you nice cars."

Friends who bought really nice cars tended to be rich daddies keeping young studs entertained, enthralled and wrapped about their dicks. "Still with that friend?"

"No." Turning, Enrique leaned on the gate and added, "Not for a while."

"Why?"

"We broke up." Blank, showing almost no emotion, Enrique mumbled. "It was amicable." By the way Enrique said it, Chase figured it may have been amicable, but it wasn't pleasant.

Chase didn't know a whole lot about Enrique, but he was a few years past party boy twink. Daddy Big-Bucks, whoever he was, probably traded up for a newer model. *Thanks, it's been fun, here's the keys to your parting gift and have you met my new boy toy?* "Well, I would hope so if he let you keep the car." Chase shrugged out of his suit jacket and tossed it into the back seat. Changing the topic because he really didn't want the whole story any more than Enrique seemed to want to tell him, he asked, "So this is your place huh?" Next thing to go would be his shoulder rig, but he couldn't really leave that in the car.

"Yep." Hands tucked into his pockets, Enrique sauntered over to stand by the open car door. "Not much, but mine." The butt of his own service pistol peeked out from under his shirt.

Up on the hill where they were, Chase could just glimpse the lights of downtown. Muted sparkles barely cut through the haze. Enrique referred to the place as Silverlake. They'd driven around the edge of a reservoir and past some funky shops before meandering farther up into the hills. "Nice neighborhood."

"It can be." Enrique stared hard at him. "Look, FBI, we can beat around it all you want while you sit here in the car in my drive." With a shrug, he headed to the concrete stoop. "Or you can come in."

For the space of five heartbeats Chase just sat; he could say 'no thanks,' ask Enrique to open the gate, pull out and go back to his hotel. Temptation wouldn't have a chance to rear its head. Drumming the steering wheel with one hand and his knee with the other, Chase weighed all the good reasons not to go inside. None of them made all that much sense. He got out of the car, slamming the door behind him before he walked up to Enrique. "You know, this is an assignment." The comment was more for his own soul than Enrique's benefit. "We shouldn't get all involved or anything."

Key in the door, Enrique paused. "FBI, it was fun." He smirked. "I'm not seeing anyone right now. You got someone who's got you on a leash?"

"No."

"Then why, FBI, is it such a problem?" With a clank, the security door unlocked. Enrique opened it out, unlocked the front door and stepped inside.

Chase stood on the stoop and chewed his lip. The reasons not to bit at the back of his brain. His sex drive shot them all down. "One condition."

"Conditions, FBI?" Enrique's voice drifted out from the front room of the house. Lights flickered on and Chase caught a glimpse of wood floors and red walls.

Sucking in his breath, Chase stepped through the door into a tiny living room with ten-foot ceilings. "Yeah, my name is Chase." Off to his left a low sectional couch took up the entirety of the front and sidewalls. A huge wood coffee table squatted over an area rug of bright red geometrics and a small entertainment unit sat caddy corner from that. "Hell, you can do that cop thing and call me Nozick if you have to, but stop calling me FBI."

A large basket of laundry, clothes folded neatly and smelling of fabric softener, sat on the coffee table. Enrique pushed it off to the side. "Okay, Chase."

Masks carved from palm fronds and painted with bright colors hung on the walls. "Your maid do windows, too?" Chase fingered one and glowered at Enrique.

On the top shelf of the TV cabinet sat a small box painted white with red and gold trim. Three wood dolls, one wearing a gold crown, knelt around a rough wood bowl. Chase couldn't see what was in the bowl except for the strings of red and white beads spilling over the lip. The red hues almost matched the color creeping into Enrique's ears. "My mom."

"Your mom does your fucking laundry?" Chase laughed out loud. "Your fucking mom does your fucking laundry." Enrique frowned as he moved off to his right and Chase followed through an arch into an even smaller dining room. "I'm so out of here if she comes over and tucks you in at night."

Various tourism posters for 1940's Cuba livened up the spare space. "No, I'm an adult." A pass-through breakfast bar set up sported three stools and looked onto a bright white-tiled kitchen. Otherwise, the room had been converted to more of a bar. "She lives down the street. She just does mine when she does hers. Not a big thing. Makes her happy that she can still do things for me." Enrique quipped and, like he realized it really was a little weird, darted through a door leading to the back of the house.

"So she does your laundry." Chase stepped up and leaned on the frame. "And rich friends buy you cars." Holy shit, it was like following Alice down the rabbit hole. Each room got dinkier and dinkier. This room was maybe half the width of the one at Chase's back. "Who cleans your place?"

A heavy sigh sounded as Enrique dropped into a worn office chair and started to thumb through an old Rolodex on his battered desk. "My sister comes over every other week." He glared, daring Chase to say more.

Through the sliding glass doors, maybe six feet in front of him, Chase glimpsed a porch railing and open sky. The window to Chase's right looked out onto a cinderblock wall. "Hey, if I could get someone to clean my place, I guess I'd take it." Of course, he wouldn't let his sister do it, or let his mom do his laundry, either. Enrique needed to cut the apron strings.

Enrique apparently found the number he wanted. He pulled the card from the Rolodex and dropped it on the desk's surface. Above the desk's short edge hung a print of a balloonish man, shirt open, belt half-buckled and bare feet wiggling at the viewer.

"Wanna drink?" Painted in vivid, primary colors, one of his hands held a cigar, the other a bottle of rum. It added a very Caribbean ambiance to an otherwise functional room. "I've got a full bar."

"Sure." Chase never turned down a drink. "Got anything to eat though?"

"Probably can find something worth eating in the fridge. Should be stuff for some sandwiches." Enrique grinned. "Make me one while you're at it? Haven't had anything on my stomach since before we cut open Renaldo. Give me time to make a couple of calls."

"Sounds good." Wandering back through the dining area and into the narrow, galley-style kitchen, Chase rummaged through the few cabinets. First, he found a decent bottle of scotch and poured himself a belt. Then a bit of digging garnered him a couple of hoagie rolls, some shaved ham and Swiss slices, pre-sliced pickles and mustard. Everything needed for a decent ham and cheese.

Enrique strolled in, phone jammed between his ear and shoulder. The part of the conversation Chase heard was all in the warm, lispy Spanish of Cuba. Somewhere Enrique'd ditched his weapon. Another one of Chase's law enforcement survival skills: instantly racking up a tally of who in a room was or was not armed.

For some reason his hoagie expertise rated a glare out of Enrique. He pushed past Chase and opened the fridge. "*Ahoritica*, Nina." Next to Chase's fixings, Enrique dropped a small tub of margarine and a packet of sliced roast pork. "*Momento.*" Cupping his palm over the receiver, Enrique hissed out instructions for Chase. "There's an electric pancake griddle over there," he gestured with his elbow toward the appliance. "Butter the rolls and grill them up. Use the pancake thing to flatten 'em. Melts the cheese and all. That's how my mom made 'em."

Chase glared right back. "Do I look like your mom?" Their relationship hardly even rated a fuck-buddy status and Enrique was telling him how to cook his food.

Enrique grinned, "No, you're uglier," and pulled a beer out of the fridge. "Trust me though, you'll like it." Then he twisted the cap and resumed the conversation with whoever was on the phone. As Chase fixed the sandwiches, Enrique ended one phone call and started another. He leaned against the counter, watching Chase move about the kitchen. Each time Chase looked over his shoulder Enrique offered up a sly smile. Finally, Enrique hung up the phone. "Okay, that's all done." He dropped the handset on the counter and pulled a couple of plates out of a cupboard.

Chase took them out of Enrique's hands. "So you're in." A sandwich on each was about as fancy as Chase got. He poured another drink and followed Enrique into the living room. As he walked, Chase tugged his tie off and then tossed it on the coffee table.

"Not yet." Enrique flopped onto the couch. "They're going to call some people for me." He took a large bite out of his sandwich, chewing and speaking at the same time. "Hopefully we'll know tomorrow."

Tearing into his own sandwich, Chase admitted to himself it was damn good. Warm, crispy bread, good meat and all the flavors smashed together by the grill. "So I guess it was your place after all." No way in hell would he give Enrique the satisfaction by saying anything remotely complimentary.

"What?" Enrique mumbled around another mouthful.

"Your place or mine? We ended up at yours."

"Yeah, we did." Not talking much beyond that, they wolfed down their food. Enrique drained his beer and dropped his plate onto Chase's. Grabbing both, he stood. "Want another drink?"

"Sure." Chase stretched out, handed over his tumbler and watched Enrique move off into the kitchen. That man's butt was fine. The fabric of his slacks clung in all the right places. Of course his dick rated pretty high as well. And his mouth. The only thing left up to Chase's imagination was how it would feel to fuck that fine ass. He planned to remedy that soon. Food, booze and sex, it was turning into a pretty good evening.

The phone rang. Chase saw Enrique pick up, check the caller ID on the handset and drop it back on the counter. Chase eased himself out of his Jackass Rig shoulder holster. "Didn't really want to talk to them?" He liked the model since it didn't have to be tethered to his belt yet sat flush under a jacket.

"No." Enrique grinned through the arch as he poured more drinks. "My mom. Calling to check up on me, probably."

Folding the holster over the ammo case, Chase set the harness on the table. "Why?" He'd rather have stowed it secure, but he wouldn't know where in this house.

Enrique wandered back. "Because your car is in my drive and the gate's shut." He handed over another belt of scotch and settled down next to Chase. "Means I've got company and she wants to pry." A little too comfortably, his body melded itself to Chase's form. "Should I call her back?" Enrique teased. Without letting Chase have a drink or answer, Enrique kissed him. Hard, passionate and warm, Enrique's mouth devoured Chase's senses. He hadn't been kissed like that in ages. Hell, he hadn't made out in ages. Backroom fucks didn't usually get that intimate.

Chase tried to breathe. The moment his lips parted, Enrique's tongue slipped inside. The warm caress stroked sparks along his nerves. Chase groaned and wrapped his free hand around the back of Enrique's skull, pulling him in closer. Enrique's crotch rode his thigh as his hand wandered over Chase's chest and stomach. God, he was so fucking in deep shit, but Chase couldn't really muster the reason to care.

Finally, Chase pulled back. "You know, I'm forty."

Fingers wandering over the inseam of Chase's slacks, Enrique answered, "Yeah, so," as he took a swig of his beer.

"Just want to make sure you're not expecting an all night sex marathon or anything."

That made Enrique snort foam. "Hey, *Compa*, I ain't no twenty-year-old who can get it up at the drop of a hat either." He cupped Chase's dick and squeezed. The contact felt damn good, even through slacks and briefs. "Not that far behind you on the age thing."

"Mmhh," Chase lifted his hips into the touch. "And just how far behind is that?"

"'Bout five years."

Knocking back the scotch in one go, Chase savored the burn. He leaned over and slid the tumbler onto the table. "You're just a baby. Wait 'till you hit the big four-oh." He watched Enrique tongue the mouth of the bottle before downing another swig. Those dark eyes in that sharp, cinnamon face grabbed him. He wanted to see Enrique naked. Lick his body. Explore every inch. The want throbbed through his cock.

Those things were luxuries Chase usually didn't have time for. "I wanna screw you good."

Enrique smiled. "Yeah?" He reached out, using the beer bottle to trace the line of Chase's arm.

"Yeah. Show me your bedroom." He balled his fist into Enrique's shirt. Tugging on the material, Chase stood. "Couch is too uncomfortable for this old man."

"That 'old man,'" Enrique let himself be pulled to the edge of his seat. He buried his face in Chase's crotch. Mouthing around the hard outline of Chase's prick, he finished the thought, "Looks damn fine to me." He ran his hand up Chase's thighs, cupped his butt for a moment. Then Enrique tugged the shirttails out of Chase's trousers as he leaned over and dropped the bottle next to Chase's abandoned glass.

Chase pulled Enrique up next to him. "Come on."

Enrique kissed him again. God, did Chase miss kissing. At least kissing like this. Warm lips that held a connection, even if it was brief, tenuous and whisper-thin. They stood chest-to-chest, hard cocks pressed together, hands exploring the outlines of each other's bodies, moving from fabric to skin and back again, and just kissed.

Finally, Enrique pushed Chase back and jerked his chin toward a door behind them. "Bedroom's that way." He took a deep breath and smiled. "And if we don't move soon, we're just going to end up fucking on the couch."

"My back," Chase hooked his fingers through the belt loops on Enrique's slacks, "would never forgive me." He used the grip as a leash to lead Enrique to the door and through into a room barely big enough for the queen-sized bed and dresser. More reds and browns on the walls and heavy curtains gave the room a sensual feel. For the little time he'd known Enrique, that hit it about right—warm and sensual. Enjoy life. Revel in it.

Releasing his hold on Enrique, Chase flopped back onto the mattress. Like everything else the bed was thick and comfortable. Chase looked up, watching Enrique slide the short-sleeve shirt off his shoulders and then pull his undershirt over his head. "You're a hedonist, you know that?" Chase teased as he worked at getting out of his own clothes.

"Hedonist?" Enrique tossed the T-shirt at the bathroom door. Chase guessed it connected through to the office. "You have a problem with that?" He dropped his slacks and Chase licked his lips. Enrique rolled his shoulders and then removed the red and white choker. His hands up and back like that made everything flex and Chase hissed. Brown skin, just enough muscle to be firm, dark hair fanning out over his pecs, and a tight ass in white shorts; Chase could look at that body for ages. Enrique gently set the choker on the dresser. Again the slight twist and turn set off his body just right.

When Enrique shucked his briefs as well, it just got better. A thick, dark prick stuck out half-mast from a black nest of curls. There hadn't been enough light at the club to see the whole package.

Chase wiggled out of his dress shirt and undershirt. Then he shoved his slacks and briefs down in one motion, kicking off his shoes in the process. Business clothes did not make for easy access. He stripped off his socks. Lying back, Chase rolled his neck a few times to work out the kinks.

Enrique stood over him, watching, his hand roaming over his prick. Each stroke got it a little harder. "Nice, Chase." He clambered onto the bed. "What horse you steal that dick off of?"

There was no way he was even half that impressive. "If you're gonna stroke me," Chase teased back, "Use your hands, not words."

"That I can do." Electric kisses burned down Chase's neck as Enrique's hand wrapped over his prick. Chase's hips bucked into the touch. Drifting under the contact, Chase savored the feelings. So different from the casual fucks. Not that it wasn't a casual fuck, but this had more of the *take your time and get to know each other* feel. The kisses and the touches melded into a warm buzz running through Chase's frame.

Chase hissed when Enrique leaned over and licked the throbbing head of his prick. The warm, wet caress bubbled across his skin. With a shudder, Chase reached down and grabbed Enrique's face. "Uhn, ah, we've been around the block there already."

"So?" Enrique chuckled. "Not good enough for a repeat?"

"No, it was spectacular. But this old body of mine, well, I'd hate to run out of steam before I got to the main course."

"You keep talking like you're seventy or something."

"It ain't the years, it's the mileage." Chase's fingers danced down Enrique's chest.

Rolling onto his back, Enrique mumbled, "Definitely wouldn't want you to run outta steam." He stretched and smiled. "I was hoping to get a taste of what you got."

Chase savored the sight. Not fat, not too thin, but enough meat covering his bones to make everything comfortable. A good-sized prick throbbed against his flat belly. Heavy balls rested in a thick patch of black fur. All of it wrapped up in light brown skin and a sexy, sensual smile.

Chase bent over and licked from Enrique's navel up toward his sternum. Enrique arched into the caress. Salt and smoke flavored his body. Every inch Chase could reach got tasted. So much of what he'd wanted. The warm, brown nubs of Enrique's nipples rose to the light flicks of his tongue. Chase sucked on each for a while, enjoying the feel of Enrique shivering under the attention.

Tracing Enrique's ribs earned him moans. When he nuzzled into the heady warmth under his arm, Enrique mumbled, "Damn, Chase." Spicy, male, Enrique's skin hinted at long afternoons spent lazing in the sun.

Rocking onto his knees, Chase pulled away. His prick throbbed so hard, it burned. "God, I wanna fuck you."

"Good, *Compa*, 'cause I wanna be fucked by you." Enrique grinned.

He stretched and reached across the bed to dig what they needed out of the side table. Then Enrique's fingers wrapped around the back of his skull, and pulled Chase down. Kisses and Enrique, that sensuous mouth seemed made for it. A bit of fumbling and messing while they kissed got Chase ready. Once accomplished, Chase forgot about it for a bit and just kept kissing, exploring Enrique's mouth with his tongue. The touch of Enrique's lips, where his hand teased down Chase's spine, how his fingers kneaded the back of his skull, all churned into one rolling mass of desire eating Chase inside out.

Walking his fingers down Enrique's flat belly, Chase marveled at how responsive Enrique was to his touch. Every movement earned a half-drawn breath or shudder. When Chase found that hard, eager cock, he groaned into their kiss. He twisted the prick through his fist. A fucking gun covered in satin; hard and soft all at once.

As Chase stroked, he eased down against Enrique. He wanted slow, long and hard. With his neck and back, that meant lying down. Using his weight and movement, Chase tried to convey what he was up to. Saying something might have been easier, but then he would have had to stop exploring Enrique's hot mouth. He really didn't want to give that up just yet. Enrique seemed to catch on, rolling slightly so that Chase could snuggle in behind him. Reluctantly, Chase let go of that thick prick, sliding his hand down the inside of Enrique's thigh. The ghost of his cock tingled on Chase's palm. He tugged on Enrique's leg. A few pulls, pushes and wriggles angled him into place.

Enrique lay on his side, legs spread over Chase's hip. Another, smaller round of shuffles and Chase's cock bumped up against Enrique's ass. That tight, puckered hole was all for him. He broke off the kiss and moved his hand to his own slicked up, sheathed down cock. A firm grip helped him adjust. He licked the line of Enrique's shoulder and both of them trembled.

"Come on, Chase," Enrique mumbled, his voice all thick with lust, "give it to me."

At first, Enrique's body resisted. They both groaned in frustration and want. Chase rolled his hips slightly. Enrique arched his back a little. Everything lined up to perfection and Enrique's ass just opened up. Chase drove into the tight heat. God, it felt so good. Enrique stroked himself as Chase reached around his frame to toy with Enrique's heavy balls. Nothing but perfect in the way they moved together.

So slow and easy at first, feeling that ass spread for his cock. Enrique rolled his head, brushing Chase's chin and cheek with his lips. More kisses, Chase could do more kisses. He shifted until their mouths found each other. The heat of Enrique's body surrounded his cock and boiled Chase's blood. He rocked them, thrusting deep.

Enrique's fist flew over his own prick. The shush of rapid strokes on skin, their panting and the slap of their thighs resonated in the pit of Chase's stomach. He slammed into Enrique's tight hole, picking up speed even as he wanted to linger. It touched him too deep. The waves already rolled in his hips. Chase broke off the kiss and buried his forehead in the crook of Enrique's brown neck. He tried to hold off, give Enrique a better ride, but three more thrusts and it overwhelmed him. A roiling mass of pleasure swept him away with shudders.

Chuckling, Enrique kept stroking. He must have realized Chase was trying to hold off. With focused abandon, Enrique rammed himself on Chase's still stiff prick. "Fuck, Chase!" he hissed out as spunk shot between his fingers. For a while, they lay panting together. Chase lost himself in the sensations of having someone wrapped up in his arms. Finally, Enrique shifted. The slick shine of cum still coated his skin. "For an old man," he teased, "you sure fuck like gangbusters."

Chase snorted. "Give me the right motivation and I guess I can work with it."

"Good." Enrique's hand ran through Chase's sweat damp hair. "I'll motivate you some more in a bit."

CHAPTER SIX

"Man, that manager is a bitch." Enrique snorted from across the BuCar. Glass and concrete towers rose to either side of Wilshire, keeping the wide boulevard cloaked in shadow. Traffic eased along at a speed just above that of molasses flowing downhill. Drumming on the steering wheel, Chase tried not to keep looking over at the passenger side, Enrique's side.

A single day without Enrique and Chase missed him. They'd already fallen into a partners' groove. It was scary how fast it happened. Of course, some of the closeness might be due to a level of intimacy that most partners never even wanted to achieve.

Chase smirked and offered a non-comment as a response. "Really?" It certainly felt better out in the field with Enrique jibing him from the front seat of the BuCar. Then again, yesterday had been eaten up with all the paperwork a Special required. Coffee, Tums by the fistful, and sheer determination kept him working through a muddled cloud over his mind. Chase'd almost done a quarterback dance when Enrique called him and told him that their meeting was set up for the next day. Fieldwork kept his mind in high gear. Stuck in the office, the fantasies of his first drink after work dogged his thoughts.

"Yeah. Damn near had to threaten to arrest her before she'd let me park in the lot."

Around them, the neighborhood began to slide. "Sorry. If I knew it would be that kind of problem I would have just met you at Parker Center." Sagging facades, veins of graffiti shooting up supports, softened corners; the avenue was losing the battle of age.

"S'okay, but why do we got to take your car?"

"I drive." Chase tried not to sound churlish—or anal. Neither attitude fit the image of a gung-ho FBI agent. "There's plenty of lunatics on the road. I don't want to be stuck in the car with one. No offense man, but I don't know how you drive, but I assume like everyone else in LA. I mean, Jesus, I'm coming back from this deli yesterday and some moron almost ran me over as I'm crossing the street to get back to my car. Never even fucking stopped." Chase growled. "All I wanted was a decent cup of coffee and a ham sandwich and I ended up wearing both for the rest of the day." Not that he would have tasted it much, just something to put a temporary damper on the constant gnawing his belly.

"You get the license?" Enrique stared out the window. "I could have the guys over at traffic run it."

"Partial. Arizona plate. I wrote it down. I'll give it to you later."

"So how'd it go yesterday?"

"Well, other than almost becoming a hood ornament for a Cadillac, I netted a whole lotta nothing. There's no trace of Carmen Fuertes. She's a smart girl. I'm sure she knows if we can trace her, so can her ex-boyfriend. I'd want to keep Garcia off my tail too." MacArthur Park, with its man-made lake and sparse lawns rolled past. Piñata and discount stores, bright awnings dulled by the hazy sun, took the place of the more office-oriented structures. "Other than the sightings of Garcia a month ago, a call to Carmen's mom from out here that we suspect was Carmen checking in, we've netted one dead guy. You?"

"Worked on reconstructing Fuertes' day. We know he was at Porto's Bakery in the morning, the one in Burbank. Not surprising."

"Why not?"

"It's the only place to get *decent* Cuban pastries in LA." With the inflection, Enrique made Los Angeles sound like some backward hick burg instead of a major metropolis. "There's one in Burbank. The original's in Glendale, and there's always a line out the door in the morning there."

"Did he go anywhere else?"

"He bought some shirts at a discount place. Ran a few post office, toothpaste kinda errands; we tracked those through receipts the coroner found in his pocket. Then, from that, I tracked him to this little Cuban place in Van Nuys for lunch. Which is a good thing, 'cause it's a mom and pop storefront with, like, seven tables."

"How'd you get from receipts to a greasy-spoon?"

"Cunning and intense police work."

"You got lucky?" Chase shook his head. Investigations often took a meandering and sometimes haphazard path.

"No, that was with you." Enrique grinned across the car. Chase managed to dredge up a laugh for the jibe. "Sort of. All those chain drugstores stamp the store number and time on the receipts. The store he was at around eleven-fifteen in the morning. I'm there at around one in the afternoon, and I ain't eaten yet. Sol Cubano is only about two blocks away."

"So you went for lunch…" Chase prompted.

"And thought I might as well ask." Enrique snorted. "Our stomachs apparently think a lot alike."

"I'll keep that in mind." They rolled across the 110 overpass. Like a switch had been thrown, high-rises sprang back up and dropped the street into midday twilight. Businessmen and bums held conversations with invisible participants. Secretaries spruced up business clothes with track shoes. Bustling crowds from every level of working and nonworking society choked the sidewalks. Braver souls chanced fate and darted between through traffic. Cars weren't the most dangerous hazard, messengers whipped between vehicles on ten-speeds as though legalities like 'right of way' didn't apply to them.

"So, the owner's daughter is working it and says she remembered seeing Fuertes and that he took a call on his cell. He got real hot, arguing with whoever was on the other end. Stormed out without getting his food." A few blocks and the bustling downtown office scene stopped dead. Garment factories, discount jewelry stores and warehouses sprang up in its place. "Right now, that's where Fuertes falls off the face of the earth, at least until some trash picker finds him the next morning. We're going through the process of getting his cell records so we can see who called him."

"Okay, well, that's good."

"Also my cousin Nina, she came through. It turns out her son's godfather's sister, Elizabeth, the owner of the Santorio De Luz, the Botanica, is her cousin."

"Everyone's just all kinda interrelated there?"

"Cuba. Small island." Thumbs and index fingers making a square in the air, Enrique teased. "Everyone is either related to you or knows someone who's related to you. You may have to go back a few generations, but they'll find it. The owner's going to be there today, which is why I called you. Figured we might as well go over together and let you get a taste of it. We can double-team him on questions about Fuertes, see if he knows anything." Jerking his chin towards the sidewalk, Enrique added, "If you see a spot just take it. We'll have to hoof it a block or so, but you'll never find any parking, legal or illegal, near Santee."

Narrow, hot and crowded, Santee Alley exuded the aura of an old world bazaar. Knock off Prada on the left, buckets of turtles stacked on top of cages holding tiny bunnies on the right. Rows of T-shirts and gauzy shawls hung from awnings. Everywhere people swarmed. Santee Alley wasn't actually a single alley. A warren of shops and carts spider webbed off from one corner of the garment district. Chase shouldered through throngs of shoppers. Men reached out to tug his sleeve hawking Viagra, Green Cards, and watches; all of it counterfeit.

Dodging around a man loaded with blow-up toys, Chase dogged Enrique's steps. Two seconds of distraction and he'd lose the cop for sure. About a block in, Enrique stopped before a black-painted storefront. Little distinguished it, at least at first glance, from a dozen other shops on either side of the narrow street.

Scrawled across the red awing in yellow, the signage announced *Botanica. Productos Naturales. Articulos Religiosos.* A narrow window displayed a dozen plaster saints, Christ figures, Indians and Buddhas backed by white plastic shelving. Row upon row of brightly labeled products filled the shelves with names like High John the Conqueror spray, Money House Blessing air freshener and Compelling perfume. Four large, glazed ceramic urns sat at the very top. To the left of the window, a yellow sign proclaimed with red script *Tenemos Santos! Productos Cubanos, Mexicanos y Domincanos* and was matched by one below the window that reiterated *Botanica* in letters a foot high. The neon in the window spelled out *Santario de Luz.*

Enrique pushed open the door to the sound of chimes. Framed in the glass of the door Chase noted one more sign next to the placards for Visa, MasterCard and Discover: *Se Hacen Consultas* with a translation in small print below, *spiritual consultations here.* He shook his head and followed Enrique inside.

Directly in front of them a six-foot-high plaster statue of Jesus greeted patrons with a classic pose of benediction. To his right a wooden cabinet held a smaller version of the same statue within. A huge crystal pitcher flanked by brass candelabras sat on top of that. Behind the display, a row of more white plastic shelves stretched down the middle of the store. The far left wall held more shelves and bins of herbs, trinkets and loose beads.

Through the gaps in the merchandise, Chase spotted two young women seated on the floor sorting baubles into the bins. Dressed in T-shirts and jeans, with warm skin and dark hair, the teenagers looked oddly out of place in the strange setting. One looked up and caught his glance. She flashed a wintry smile, whispered something to her companion and then returned her attention to the beads. Chase dogged Enrique's steps down the right-hand side. Racks of beaded necklaces in rainbow mixtures brushed his shoulder. He had to dodge around drums piled on the floor.

A short, wide man looked up from behind the counter as they made their way back. Huge brown eyes stared at them, through them almost. "You need help?" What sounded like coins rattled in his palm. A corkboard behind him was barely visible under tacked memos, receipts and family photos. The candid shots outnumbered the other papers three to one. Most of them captured the image of the man they spoke to and a varying set of children in backyards, amusement parks and playgrounds. The same faces repeated time and again. If Chase had to guess, he'd either started late, but been prolific, or he had a shitload of grandkids.

"*Hola*," Enrique smiled. "I'm looking for Miguel Finale."

The man propped his elbows on the glass case in front of him. A wide brass cuff cut into the fleshy mass of his wrist. "That is me."

"Enrique Rios-Ochoa, LAPD." Enrique flipped open his badge case with a smile. "This is Chase Nozick from the FBI. Elizabeth Gutierez called, told you we'd be coming."

"Ah yes." When Miguel nodded, his jowls shook. He looked like a very pleased bulldog. "She said you were looking for someone."

Chase took the opportunity to jump in. Slipping the photo of Fuertes across the counter, Chase explained. "This man is dead. And we need to find someone he was protecting. Do you know him?"

Without even glancing at the photo, Miguel growled. "No, I do not think I know him."

"Then," Chase hated this dance—the I-don't-want-to-be-involved two-step, "do you know why he might have a card from your store?"

"Lots of people have cards." His eyes went narrow. "I sell many things they need."

"Look again." Enrique tapped the photo as he leaned in. His red shirt gaped open, showing a flash of the beaded choker about his neck. "It is very important. There's a woman in trouble." Staring into Miguel's eyes, he added, "This man, he knew where she was. He was a Santero. We owe it to him, to his Orisha, to help."

Miguel jerked his chin at Chase. The wattle of his neck was about a second behind the rest of the movement. "Why does that man want to help? He is not a Santero." With that, he rocked back on his stool and crossed his arms, defensively, over his chest.

"He is FBI. A man who is also looking for this woman has done many bad things."

"The *policia* say many people have done bad things that maybe are not so bad." Miguel still hadn't looked at the picture.

Chase expected this kind of reluctance. The nature of investigative work and who you had to deal with often cultivated it. Not because the people you were dealing with were bad or had something to hide. Rather, human nature said don't get involved. Gossiping about gory details was not the same as having cops show up and ask you questions.

Rubbing the back of his neck, where the scars pocked his skin, he thought for a moment. "A woman was home with her children. Her husband had gone out. He owed some money to Garcia, the man I want to find." Chase let himself remember the scene, the aftermath. "Garcia came to this woman's house to get the money. She didn't have it and she didn't know where her husband had gone. Her little boy, who was six, told us what happened." With each word a little more anger crept into Chase's voice. "Garcia tied them all up and when his mother couldn't tell them where his father was, shot the little boy first. Then he shot the two little girls and finally the mother, because she didn't know. Only the little boy lived. That was," Chase tapped the picture, drawing Miguel's attention down to the glossy photo, "under anyone's definition, a bad thing. But then, my partner and I, we found him. We almost had him. I still have the bullets in my neck. I was barely out of the hospital when they buried my partner. So, yeah, I think he's a bad guy, that's why I'm here. And it's personal."

Staring at the photo, Miguel seemed to mull things over. His lips moved as though he were talking to himself. Then, Miguel shook his fist, coins jangling within. He rolled his eyes up toward the ceiling and tightened his mouth into a thin line. Without further ceremony, he threw them onto the counter. Four pennies spun on the glass, wobbling until they fell: two heads, two tails. An even split. Muttering, Miguel ran his fingers over the coins.

Miguel looked into, almost beyond, Chase's eyes. "I think I might know him." His stare bored in hard and pulled God knew what information. "Well, not so much this man, but who may know where to look." As he spoke, he kept nodding, like someone was whispering in his ear.

Enrique's relieved sigh echoed Chase's own. "Great. Whatever you can do for us, whatever you might have is great."

"I will call someone. First, there are things we must do. If you do this, you must do this right." Miguel reached under the counter and pulled out a small, lidded bowl. Cradling the white porcelain tureen in his arms he stood. "You need to be protected."

It took a moment before Chase realized the man spoke to him. "Protected?"

"Yes, I see that there will be some very dangerous situations in your future. You should be protected from them." Miguel stepped behind a beaded curtain.

"What the hell?" Chase turned to Enrique. "What is he talking about being protected?"

"I think that he means protection from or by the Orishas."

"The what?"

Enrique pointed to several statutes of saints. "The Orishas."

"Saints?" Chase just stared. He had no clue what Enrique was talking about.

"No, Orishas. Each Orisha has a saint it is in sympathy with. No, not sympathy. Shango," Enrique lifted the bead choker from his skin with one finger, "is Saint Barbara." With his other hand, he pointed to a statue of a woman wearing a red cape and standing on a castle, brandishing a sword. "Saint Barbara is Shango." Dropping the necklace, he shrugged. "I think he believes you need an Orisha to watch over you."

Going above and beyond for an investigation was one thing, participating in some weird-ass rite another. "He wants to initiate me?"

"Oh, no. It takes much to be a Santero, an initiate. Many years. I am only *aborisha*, a devotee, but not initiated beyond that." As if he read Chase's confusion in his face, Enrique foundered a bit. "Think like someone who has been baptized, but has never gone through first communion." Chase wasn't certain that clarified things. Still, he didn't interrupt. "But he can find your Orisha, the one who protects you, like a guardian angel." Enrique looked up as Miguel leaned back through the curtain and motioned to follow him. "It will help."

"It will?" Chase dropped his voice to a whisper.

"Yes." Keeping his voice low as well, Enrique agreed. He caught Chase by the elbow and led him around the counter. It kept them close so they wouldn't be overheard. "If you walk into a building and you see another man with a badge, you know you can ask him for help. We're all part of the same club." As he swept aside the drape of brown and white beads, Enrique added, "He will determine your Orisha and give you a *collare* in that Orisha's colors. Well, not really." Miguel disappeared into another opening to their left. Maneuvering through a narrow space, around boxes and cleaning supplies, Enrique and Chase headed after him. "To really find your Orisha is a long ceremony and takes three *santeros*. I think that Miguel will find who is helping you with our search. Who is looking out for you right now, not over your whole life."

Through the door was a small room. Lemon yellow walls were decorated with pictures of mountain streams pulled from calendars or nature magazines. In the center of the room, Miguel sat cross-legged on a straw mat, the bowl resting between his legs. The lid had been removed and three large, oval stones bearing arcane markings rested within. "And people will think I'm part of the club?" With a smile and broad gestures, Miguel beckoned them farther into the small room, indicating they should sit on the mat.

"In a small way, yes."

"Okay." Chase grunted as he knelt in front of Miguel. A cabinet, like one of the ones out front, sat behind Miguel. Inside rested a tiny statue of a queen standing upon a brass throne. Gold veils flowed from the top of her head to her feet. Both she and the babe she cradled in one arm were crowned in gold. Peacock tail feathers fanned out behind her like rays from an iridescent sun. As they settled in front of him, Miguel tied a yellow bandana about his head. Then he draped a small shawl, embroidered with the "eyes" of peacock feathers and trimmed in gold fringe, over his shoulders. At his side sat a small basket full of peanut-sized shells the color of butterscotch.

With his balled fist, Miguel rapped three times on the cement floor. "What day were you born?" He asked as he reached into the basket and began counting out shells.

Again it took Chase a minute to realize Miguel questioned him. "January 18—"

"No." Miguel interrupted him. "What day of the week were you born on?"

"Oh." Chase rolled his eyes and offered a sheepish grin to Enrique. "A Friday, I think."

"Do you know what time?"

"My mom said the middle of the night, but I don't think she was being literal."

Miguel nodded and began to whisper just low enough that Chase couldn't make out the words. The only things he caught were what sounded like names, "Eleggua," "Oshun," "Xhango." Three times Miguel kissed the cowry shells in his hand. Then he held them out in his cupped palms. "Tell them your name."

Feeling just a little stupid, Chase answered, "Chase Nozick."

"Your mother?"

"Why the fuck does that matter?" Enrique's hand on his leg stopped him from just getting up and leaving. FBI didn't give up information on their relatives. It was a good way to lose your family.

Gently, Enrique explained, "Santeria is not just about the Orishas, but also who your ancestors were." Squeezing his eyes shut like he was thinking hard, Enrique added, "Your family who have died, the Orishas can use them to help you. But they need to know who these people are." Miguel nodded and smiled. "So you must tell him their names. Trust me, Chase."

It felt awkward and wrong, but Chase answered. "Alina Nozick."

"Father?"

"Paul Nozick." They played name all your relatives for a time, at least until Chase started getting stumped.

"Good." Miguel smiled. He held out the shells in his palm. "Kiss them."

"The shells?"

"Yes." As Chase bent over and quickly kissed the shells, Miguel spoke. "Everyone is ruled by an Orisha. You have one for your head," he tapped his temple, then his chest, "and one for your heart, because they are your parents. They guide you, like your mother and father."

"So men always follow men and women always follow their moms?"

"Not so much. A man may be ruled by a female Orisha. My Orisha is Ochun, the Virgin of Charity." He smiled before putting his finger to his lips, forestalling more questions from Chase. "Let me pray and consult the shells, then we will talk."

Chase studied Miguel. The man closed his eyes and began to chant in Spanish. Most of it was too soft for him to understand. He glanced over toward Enrique. A soft smile played about those sensuous lips when Enrique caught Chase's attention. Chase could drown in those chocolate eyes and never regret it. Already, he was getting used to Enrique's presence, starting to trust him. It'd taken him months to find that comfort zone with Jason. Of course, he hadn't fucked and been fucked by Jason. A whole level of interaction he'd never had with his former partner.

Miguel's shout yanked Chase's attention back. The cowry shells rattled onto the mat. Rocking on his heels, Miguel studied the pattern. Then he swept them back up into his hands. Cupping both palms around the shells, Miguel whispered more prayers. Again, he yelled and tossed the shells onto the mat. Three more times he repeated the ritual.

The cowry shells went back into the basket. Replacing the lid on the tureen, Miguel bent and kissed it. Then he smiled at Chase. "I see Ochossi watches over you." Miguel seemed pleased. "The warrior, the hunter, the one who provides justice. St. Norbert." With a grunt, he stood and offered his hand down to assist Chase.

Ignoring the proffered assistance, Chase gained his feet. Needles shot down his legs as the blood flow returned. "So, what do I have to do?" He couldn't believe that was it, that they were done. A lot of build up for not much at all.

"Go out front and your friend will help you find a *collare.*" Miguel waved toward the curtain and the front of the store. "Equal strings of blue and gold for you. Something you like that speaks to you is best. I will make a call. The man you look for, Ochun says I should help you." Miguel thought for a moment before adding. "He came here. He wanted someone to do a spiritualist reading for him. I will see if she will talk to you."

"Thanks, I'll give you my card." Enrique offered Chase a knowing smile as he fished his wallet out of his pocket. "Call me and let me know. We all know it's the right thing to do."

Miguel took the card as he ushered them from the room. "Maria-Elisa," he called out and a muffled thump and bang answered him. "My goddaughter, she will help you. She is learning, but knows this." When the girl appeared, sweeping aside the curtain of beads and peering through, Miguel instructed her. "A *collare* for Ochossi for this man." He patted Chase's shoulder and gave him a gentle push to the front of the store.

Maria-Elisa barely spoke, just nodded and smiled as she presented Chase with a series of beaded necklaces. He finally selected the most subdued, plain piece he could find. Small turquoise stones and brass beads; it looked simple and earthy although the sticker price hit as a small shock.

"Forty freaking bucks," he grumbled to Enrique when they got back to the BuCar. "What a rip." Fingering the choker, the sales gal insisted he wear it out, Chase slid behind the wheel. "So where are we off to now?"

Enrique slammed his door and buckled in before answering. "I got some follow-up to do, but it's not urgent. Run me back to my car or tag along and see how real police do work?"

With a snort for Enrique's stab at humor, Chase spared a quick glance over his shoulder for traffic and pulled into the street. "Real police, huh?" he teased. "Like reality TV police? Or guys who actually get down and dirty?" He risked a quick glance at Enrique who rolled his eyes.

Chase looked back to the road. Stepping off the curb was a young mom and maybe two kids, or a stroller and a kid—

"Shit!" Chase slammed the brakes. The BuCar's front went down and ass went up. The belt jerked hard against Chase's chest. Like a slow-motion soundtrack, he heard it. Another set of tire squeals overlaid across his. A second slam into the seatbelt was accompanied by a brittle plastic and glass crunch. Before Chase really even registered they'd been hit, a big, black blur of a car whipped around the BuCar.

"Are you okay, Enrique?"

"Yeah, that *cabron* just ran off, didn't he?" Enrique certainly sounded more pissed than injured.

"Fucking LA drivers!" Chase spat. A quick scan showed Enrique rubbing his neck and the woman with kids shaking on the curb. Well, at least everyone walked away. "Fuck, let's call this crap in and see what the damage is. You didn't happen to catch the plate, did you?" When Enrique shook his head, Chase blew out an exasperated breath. "Well, shit then." Not quite three in the afternoon. Two more hours to go and Chase could have that good, hard drink to file the edge off the day.

And this day needed filing with a belt sander.

CHAPTER SEVEN

Chase woke, shaky and disoriented. The dim shadows in the room seemed to ripple when Chase opened his eyes. A thin sheen of booze-sour sweat coated his body. His skin felt alternatively too tight and too loose to belong to him. He coughed, trying to force the raw, sandpaper feeling out of his throat. The taste of tin swam in his mouth.

A warm touch ran up Chase's arm and Chase froze. "You okay there, *Compa*?" Enrique mumbled, his voice still heavy with sleep.

"Yeah, man." Holy crap, Enrique. In bed, at—Chase rolled his head and tried to focus on the LED clock—four-thirty in the morning. "I think I'm getting a touch of something." Chase couldn't remember the last time he'd actually *slept* with someone he slept with. It scared the hell out of him.

"Yeah," Enrique's snort blew the hairs on the nape of Chase's neck. "It's called a hangover."

"I don't get hangovers." Chase growled. He didn't, not really anymore. Hangovers were a special breed of hell. Feeling like he did this morning was a constant. He also couldn't remember the last time he *hadn't* woken feeling completely like crap. That no longer held terror. It was merely a state of existence pounded into functionality by strong coffee, aspirin and antacids. Only one thing that made it bearable; another drink.

Warm kisses replaced the breath on Chase's skin. "Do you always hit it that hard?"

"Why do you care?"

"Just want to know." Enrique's strong arms wandered across Chase's torso. He pulled Chase in tight against his own body. "*Mofuco* will fuck you up man. You're a good cop, I mean agent. Hate to see anybody slide their career down a bottle. You know, 'cause for some fucked up reason, I like you."

"Well, it's how I mellow out, deal with things, the stress and all." Shifting, Chase cocked his head to stare into Enrique's deep brown eyes. Worry, understanding and a lot of something Chase didn't want to think about lurked there.

"There's other ways," fingers playing in the fur on Chase's chest as Enrique chided, "to deal with stress."

It was Chase's turn to snort. "Pills?"

"Exercise." He gave a double jerk of his eyebrows and reached down under the cover's to tug at Chase's prick. "Sex."

"Okay," Chase swatted Enrique's exploring hand. "The sex thing all rolls up into why I'm stressed. If it ever came out, they'd find some way to get rid of me. The Bureau is a lot more subtle about it now. No three-day interviews about how many dicks I've sucked. I'd just get shuffled into some crap assignment and my performance ratings would go down. Harass me until I quit."

"*Mofuco*, the booze, it ain't gonna solve that." With a grunt, Enrique rolled away. "Look, I'll make some coffee. We'll get an early start on the day." He stretched and swung his feet off the edge of the bed. "I'll get you something to put in your stomach, that'll help.'

"Nothing major." Easing up on his elbows, Chase stared as Enrique walked around the bed and headed to the door. "Although, you know, breakfast in bed. I might get spoiled." He could definitely get spoiled with that lean, brown body wandering around his hotel room naked.

"Nope." Enrique grinned from the doorway. "Simple." At that, he disappeared down the hall. Chase could follow his progress from the john to the tiny kitchen by the clunks and bangs. Chase eased out of the sheets and headed to the can for a bit. When he finished, he slipped back under the covers. Hell, he could have joined Enrique in the kitchen, but he secretly liked the idea of being taken care of. The last time someone had brought him breakfast in bed, he'd been at his parents' place and come down with the flu. That had to be, what, more than ten years ago. And Mom forcing chicken soup down his throat didn't quite have the sensual quality of a guy bringing him caffeine in the nude. Chase drifted in low-key fantasy until he heard Enrique cursing in the hall.

Balancing a plate of toast on top of one mug and with a tight grip on the other mug, Enrique reappeared. Gingerly, he walked back into the room. Damn right he needed to be careful. Hot coffee and bare dicks didn't mix well. With a sly grin, Enrique slid the mug and toast onto the dresser serving as a bedside table. "Hope you take it black." He set the plate on the scarred surface and then passed the coffee to Chase, "And strong."

"Black's fine." Chase breathed the heat and smell in deep. "The rougher the better."

"What, brown and smooth's not good enough for you?" He teased as he settled onto the bed.

Chase took a deep swig. Three times as strong as he would have made it, the sharp flavor hit Chase with a jolt. Exactly what he needed. After savoring the taste for a bit, he shook his head. "That's just fucking corny."

Enrique reached over, broke off a bit of toast and dipped it in his coffee. "But true." He grinned and popped the sopping piece into his mouth.

Somewhere between amused and confused, Chase asked, "What are you doing?"

"Eating breakfast," Enrique mumbled around his food, "What does it look like I'm doing?"

"Dunking your bread in your coffee."

Enrique snapped off another bite of toast. "It's good." After dunking it in his coffee, he held it out toward Chase. "Here, try it."

Cautious, Chase let Enrique feed him the morsel. Mushy toast flavored by coffee; Chase could have done without it. He swallowed. "I can think of other things I'd rather have you stick in my mouth."

With a leer, Enrique purred out. "I can, too." Then he leaned over and set his mug on the table.

"You know," Chase slid his coffee next to Enrique's. "I'm not twenty any more. Three times in five days may be more than I can manage." The protest was half-hearted at best. He slid one arm across Enrique's lap and let his hand drape over his hip.

"Chase, you're not dead either." Still bent forward, Enrique shifted until he straddled Chase with one arm on either side of his chest. "Quit acting like you're over the hill and washed up."

Chase jabbed Enrique in the ribs with his thumb. "See, now, you invited yourself over last night." Enrique swatted his hand away. "Here you are in my bed. You're mooching my coffee, eating my toast, getting crumbs all in my sheets. And now you want me to give you head. What do you think I am?"

"Fucking sexy." Dropping even closer, Enrique growled. "You're the one who insisted on driving and then kept inventing reasons why I needed to hang out with you and have dinner." He eased his body down onto Chase. "Why should I go home after that?"

The weight was comfortable. The sensation of skin-on-skin incredible. It worked its way through Chase's senses. Things Chase didn't think could be up and running that early in the morning woke. "Yeah, and then you stay all night." He shifted, trying to get a little more contact without being obvious.

"I was too relaxed to take off...not like someone in this room." Enrique's tone was lighter than Chase would have expected.

Still, the dig hit Chase in a lot of places he liked to keep buried. "Hey," he hedged, "I'm just not used to actually sleeping with the guys I sleep with." So much so, he'd bailed on Enrique the other night, bolting out the door without his tie. Excuses didn't really cover the fight-or-flight reflex that welled up inside when the sex ended. Chase couldn't face Enrique snuggled next to him. He'd caved. He'd fled. And now he had to face it.

"You did alright last night." Lust, approval and need echoed in Enrique's voice, all of it wrapped up with a good deal of understanding.

"Yeah, I did." Usually, Chase tossed and turned with someone else in his bed. He never felt really at ease with any of his prior hookups. With Enrique, they'd kissed and touched for a bit before drifting off. Chase'd slept straight through the night. A terrorist attack couldn't have woken him. It was a little unnerving. "I slept pretty good."

Wicked, Enrique smiled. "That's 'cause I fucked your brains out last night."

Chase reached up and grabbed a hank of Enrique's hair. "How 'bout I blow yours out now?" He used the grip to tug Enrique closer.

"So long," Enrique let himself be pulled down, "as you're not talking about doing it with your service weapon."

"Definitely not that weapon." Chase ran his tongue along the line of Enrique's jaw. Morning stubble roughed up the flavor of salt. Enrique certainly tasted better than the bitter ghost of Jack Daniels.

Enrique groaned and shifted his hips. "Then how 'bout," the movement rubbed their half-hard pricks together, "we make it a little mutual weapons maintenance."

Working down a warm brown throat, Chase murmured, "You know we're just getting silly now."

"Hey." Enrique rolled onto his back. One brown arm went behind his head, his left knee splayed out, he grinned. "*Compa*, at our age, sex starts to get pretty silly anyway." Enrique's prick rested heavy against his hip.

Already, Chase anticipated the taste. He bent over and kissed Enrique's dick, moving along the thick vein toward the head. Every time his lips touched skin, that prick got a little harder, a little hotter. Buttery satin skin slipped under his kisses. Musky and spicy and male. Chase blew a breath across the already red crown. Enrique shuddered.

Then Enrique tugged at Chase's thigh and shimmied over. Pulling, twisting, rearranging, Chase snorted a laugh when his knee bumped Enrique's nose. That doubled as Enrique almost racked his nuts with an ill-timed elbow. "Shit, man." He looked back down the line of Enrique's body. "I'm getting too old for these kinda acrobatics."

Enrique's tongue reached out to flick Chase's prick. "You're just about as coordinated as a three-legged dog on crack."

"You," Chase choked back a laugh, "should never insult a man with his teeth near your family jewels." He punctuated the thought by nipping the skin at the base of Enrique's balls.

"*Singao!*" Spat Enrique as he smacked Chase's butt.

Chuckling, Chase nuzzled Enrique's balls. Fur tickled his cheek. That soft, warm weight against his face, the heady smell of last night still clung to Enrique's skin. Slowly he worked up the length of Enrique's prick. There was magic in feeling Enrique come fully alive under his lips that couldn't be matched by anything else. When he wrapped his lips over Enrique's cock and sucked him down, Chase hit heaven.

Chase hissed as Enrique's tongue flicked out to tease his prick. Enrique grabbed the base and squeezed, causing Chase to hiss again. Pumping, licking, sucking, he brought Chase to full attention. The man's tongue was incredible, roaming Chase's shaft with abandon.

Chase moved lower, back behind Enrique's balls. Spreading Enrique's cheeks with his hands, he licked until he found that tight hole. Soft, but resistant to his explorations, Enrique's puckered flesh fought his tongue. Chase probed until his ass opened up. Thick, warm and a little bitter, the taste of a guy first thing in the morning rewarded him.

Chamois-smooth skin slid under his palm as Chase wrapped his fist around Enrique's prick. Under him, Enrique bucked into the combined forces of his mouth and his hand. Damn, it was almost better feeling Enrique respond than getting his own prick sucked—almost. His hips jerked, fucking the mouth circling his cock. As much as he wanted to, Chase couldn't manage to stay bent over in that awkward position. The mileage he'd put on his body just couldn't handle it. With a parting lick, Chase came back up. He swallowed Enrique's dick in one motion. Lips bumped fingers as he jerked and sucked.

Giving and getting all at once, few things could equal it. Two mouths working hard flesh had them both moaning. Enrique's hands wandered over Chase's butt and thighs. The touch wove fire under his skin. The prick in his mouth stretched his jaws with a low, needful ache. It all seeped through his frame until Chase was nothing but a mass of sensation.

He felt it, the flying rush as orgasm hit. He shook. Heat blew through his body, massing in his core until the final explosion of feeling. When his heart rate dropped and his breathing stilled, Chase looked back between their bodies. Enrique's neck and chest were splattered with ropes of cum.

His half-lidded, lust-filled eyes stared right back at Chase. With a sly grin, Chase pumped the cock in his fist. Enrique bucked into the grip. Three, four strokes and Enrique hissed out, "*Singao!*" Spunk shot from his dick in a thick white fountain.

Chase chucked and flopped over onto the mattress. "I could get used to that every morning."

Lazily, Enrique reached out. He flicked Chase's softening prick with his thumb and forefinger. "You couldn't take that every morning," he paused before adding, "old man."

"Fuck you!" Chase rested his cheek on Enrique's knee. Hand stretched out, he made intentionally futile motions toward the nightstand. "Give this old man his coffee. Then we should get a move on." When Enrique passed his mug over, Chase sat up. It'd cooled slightly, making the taste bitter. Oh well, Chase figured he could live with it. "I'm hitting the shower…you?"

Enrique took a swig from his own cup. The grimace that flashed across his face told Chase his coffee was just as nasty. "You go first. I'll make a fresh pot and trade you out."

"Fair enough." With a groan and various pops from his joints, Chase rolled off the bed. It didn't take him long to hose off. He literally traded the soap for another cup of coffee as he stepped out of the shower. Enrique jumped under the spray right behind him and showered while he shaved.

Reasonably clean and presentable, Chase ambled back to the bedroom to dig out some clothes. Enrique'd be stuck with last night's kit and slacks, but Chase dropped one of his dress shirts on the bed. No sense being incredibly obvious that Enrique hadn't changed. As he buttoned up his pants, Enrique wandered in, drying off his hair. Everything else gaped open for Chase's view. Damn that man was hot.

Dropping the towel on the bed, Enrique retrieved his shorts from the floor. "Since you're mostly dressed, why don't you get us some more coffee?" He grinned and tucked himself into his briefs.

"Sure." Chase shoved his arms into his shirt. "I can do that." He snagged the cups off the dresser and headed down the hall. Cutting round the sofa without banging his knee, Chase slid the mugs onto the counter. Time to wake up and face the day. He stepped over the coffee table and yanked the drapes back.

"Enrique!" Chase stood before the sliding door, staring out at the parking lot, fists still balled in the drapes. His brain processed but couldn't quite comprehend what he saw. A scrawny black rooster, wearing ropes of beads, lay on the hood of the BuCar. Its wings spread out to either side and its feet curled against a feathered belly. A coarse black powder dusted the dead bird and clotted up the blood running over the hood. Red and black, green and black, Chase started to wonder if someone had a thing for black. Pins dotted the bird's breast. Each one pierced a blood soaked scrap of paper. Finally, he managed to sputter out, "There's a chicken on my BuCar."

From down the hall, Enrique questioned, "*¿Qué?*"

"There's a dead chicken," Chase paused, trying to make sense the scene, "wearing a necklace, on the hood of my car."

Enrique's next question threw Chase. "What color is the chicken?"

He spun, pointed out the window and sputtered, "It's dead…with jewelry…on my fucking car. What the fuck does it matter, 'what color is it?'"

"Because," Enrique shrugged, as he headed toward Chase, his voice muffled by the undershirt he struggled to pull over his head, "different colors mean different things."

Still not comprehending what Enrique meant, Chase rubbed his temples and tried to forestall the impending headache. "It's black." He wanted, no, he needed a drink. A good stiff belt might just make it all go away, or make Chase not give a fuck. Either outcome was acceptable.

Pushing past, Enrique moved to the window. He stared, silent, for a while. Finally he turned back to Chase. "Not just black. Everything about it is black." Arms crossed over his chest, Enrique chewed on his bottom lip. He looked worried. "This is not a good thing."

Understatement of the year there. Not good equaled a flat tire. This crept into the realm of creepy horror flicks. He had to think and it was hard with the fuzziness that went with rocky sleep. "Enrique, make some more coffee, really strong." The craving for alcohol hadn't vanished, Chase just shoved it down and promised to pacify it, temporarily, with caffeine. He knew the booze need would come back later and stronger. "Shit," Chase squeezed his temples between the heels of his palms. "I got to call this in."

CHAPTER EIGHT

"Damn it." God, the day started off so promising—a blow job, a hot guy—and then degenerated into police tape and dead poultry. Life in the Bureau—insanity at all hours.

Looking up from pouring himself another round of coffee, Enrique asked, "What?" It barely carried over the coffee shop bustle.

Chase picked up his coffee and waved it toward the window. Somewhere, behind the shrubbery, in the parking lot, police worked over the Ford. "My BuCar has become a crime scene. I'm going to get such shit for this." The dead chicken jokes would spread like wildfire. Chase knew, just knew, that any Special he showed his face on, there'd be some little joke as a reminder of this day. It'd be years before it wound its way out of the collective conscious of the FBI. Elephants and law enforcement possessed long-term memories.

"We have a larger issue." Enrique plunked the carafe down with a thump. "Somebody wants to curse us."

"Right." Without drinking from his own mug of lukewarm coffee, Chase set it back down on the table. Then he laced his fingers together and settled his chin on the back of his hands.

Enrique glowered. "Believe or don't believe, but someone went through a lot of trouble to find us, find your car, kill a chicken in a motel parking lot, and set that scene up so that we would find it in the morning and *know* that we had been cursed." His tone chided Chase as though Enrique's thought process should be plainly obvious.

Chase slouched back into the booth and rubbed his eyes with one hand. He so did not need this insanity thrown onto his investigation. Enough legitimate crap came flying at him from normal investigative pot-stirring. Chase didn't want the abnormal thrown in for good measure. And so far, no one had asked *why* Enrique happened to be in Chase's motel room at five-forty in the morning. Luckily, Enrique's car was parked at the opposite end of the lot from Chase's, up near the lobby. Otherwise they'd be trying to explain how a seasoned cop missed a scene you'd have to be blind not to see from fifteen feet away.

Peeling the foil off a roll of cherry-flavored Rolaids, Chase grumbled. "How do you know the chicken was killed here?" Chase's long-suffering huff punctuated the end of the question. He tossed three of the tablets in his mouth, ground them to paste and swallowed them down with a mouthful of crummy coffee.

Mouth tight and eyes narrowed, Enrique studied his finger as it circled the rim of his cup. "I don't know for certain." With a shake of his head, like he was clearing his thoughts, Enrique glanced at Chase. "I'm taking an educated guess by the amount of blood on the car. That size carcass, it would have bled out in a matter of minutes." Tapping his middle finger on the mug's handle, Enrique explained his thoughts. "So they either killed the thing on the car or brought a bucket of blood with them. Honestly, I don't know why, but I prefer a guy slitting a rooster's throat here and now to some *cabrone* hauling around baggies of blood. Possible, but not probable. Crime scene techs will tell us for sure."

"Great, so someone is trying to spook us." Chase lifted his mug and downed another swig of coffee. Enrique made better by far, strong enough to peel paint, but not bitter. This crap made Chase grimace. "I don't spook easy." Still, he drank it to distract himself.

"I think," Enrique shrugged before gulping his own coffee. The scowl that hit Enrique's face told Chase it was just as nasty as what occupied his mug. "We should go find someone to remove the curse."

"We're not cursed."

"Look, yesterday we got clipped by that hit-and-run. You damn near got run over crossing the street the other day." He took another swig and shuddered. "Coincidence, maybe." Once he set down the coffee, Enrique spread his hands and smiled, one of those ingratiating but slightly intimidating smiles that law enforcement cultivated. It said *'believe me because I can arrest your ass.'* "But, curse or no curse, why chance it? Besides, you're missing the big point."

Chase favored Enrique with his own version of police attitude—narrowing his eyes and letting the rest of his face go slack. "Which is?" His expression said *'you're feeding me a line of bullshit and I ain't biting.'*

"Someone wanted us to *know* they cursed you." Ultimately reasonable, Enrique had a point there. "That they found you and know where you're staying." Ice water chills slid down Chase's back. He'd tried to avoid dwelling on that issue. Damn Enrique for bringing it up. "If we go to have the curse removed, whoever did this will see that they cannot intimidate us...at least that way. We just turn around and neutralized them." Another shrug, then he added, "It's a psychological thing."

"Okay," Chase conceded. "I'm not biting one hundred percent, but I'll run with you here."

Enrique smiled. That smile hit deep inside Chase, a place he didn't even remember existed. Chase swallowed and then realized Enrique was speaking. "And the person we go to, we go as supplicants, not as big shot cops." Shit, he'd missed the first part. Chase hoped it wasn't too important. "Please help us, we respect you and your faith at least enough to say if it comes through your gods, it should be removed by your gods. I can guarantee you that the person who removes this curse will want all the details of Miss Fuertes' disappearance...at least what we can give them. Then we've gotten the word out to someone who can say 'while I was removing their curse, the Orishas spoke to me and we must help.' Then it's not just police work, it is the Orishas' will. It may make the visit with the psychic we're trying to set up go down easier. We appeal to her professionally first and then roll the concerned citizen crap in on top, after."

You had to admire someone who thought like that. "You are a sneaky, cagey bastard." Chase punctuated the praise by using his coffee mug to salute. Hell, he already admired Enrique for a ton of reasons, that one just added more icing to the cake.

Another smile flashed. Chase determined to find more ways to earn those. "From you, FBI, I'll take that as a compliment." A snippet of steel drum, backed by undulating Spanish rap rhythms, came out of nowhere. Enrique fished his cell phone off his hip and hit a button as he held it to his ear. "*Hola, son Enrique, ¿Quién es?*"

As Enrique listened to whoever spoke at the other end of the line, Chase mouthed, *Latino rap?* He'd have put the man's musical tastes anywhere but with the hip-hop generation. A couple strikes against, twenty for—okay, a guy couldn't be perfect. Hell, God knew, Chase kept a few stupid preferences and bad habits in his own back pocket.

"Yeah, no problem." Enrique paused to flip Chase off. "*Una hora, hora y media, y podemos allí. Por favor.*" Then he tugged a small notepad and pen from his back pocket. Flipping it open, he scribbled a few lines. "*Sí, gracias, Senora.*" He hit disconnect and slid the phone back into its case on his hip. The butt of his gun flashed under the tail of his shirt. If Chase hadn't been eyeballing for a shot of Enrique's ass, he never would have seen it in the booth. Oblivious to Chase's perving, Enrique switched to English. "The psychic, the guy at the Botanica set up Fuertes with, she says she has time to talk to us in about an hour." He banged the table with his fist before snatching up the notepad. "Come on. It'll take us that long to get over there. The place is in Whittier, off the 605." Enrique started to slide out of the booth then paused. "I guess we're taking my car, 'cause yours will be tied up for a few days."

Crap. That was one of those stupid habits in Chase's back pocket. "I guess." He hated being a passenger. It left him too much time to think. And, with Los Angeles, it was fucking scary not to be in control on the freeway. "You drive okay?"

"I'm a cop." Enrique scowled. "I drive in LA all the time."

"Holy Christ," Chase downed the remainder of the roll of antacids in one gulp. "I don't know if my insurance covers that kind of risk."

Enrique glared as he headed out of the hotel's café. Chase stopped just long enough to log his room number and a tip on the check and then jogged after him. Following Enrique outside to the parking lot, Chase caught site of his BuCar and a tow-truck. Shit. He was so going to get hell; the Bureau goons could run for years on something like this.

Enrique's "Hey!" yanked his attention back and he headed to the Nissan. Given that someone was out looking for them, using Enrique's personal vehicle wasn't a bad thing. The little sports car without special plates would blend more into the background than the big American-made sedans favored by law enforcement.

More Latino rap echoed through the speakers as Chase clambered into the car and buckled in. Enrique rolled his eyes when Chase reached over and twisted the volume down. He'd barely slammed the door before Enrique threw the hot rod into reverse and gunned out of his space. Chase tried not to be obvious about grabbing the Jesus-bar on the door as Enrique swung out onto the roads. Masking his nervousness, he stuffed a piece of Juicy Fruit gum into his mouth. Damn Jason for getting him stuck on the stuff.

Almost accustomed to the slide and glide on surface streets, Chase bit his tongue when they hit the freeway. Time and time again, Chase stopped himself just short of slamming his foot on an imaginary brake. Enrique drove like most cops; traffic laws didn't necessarily apply to them.

Finally, after forty-five minutes of Chase living with his heart in his throat, Enrique took the exit off the 605 and headed into Whittier. Along the main drag, old homes rubbed elbows with taco stands and discount marts. There really wasn't any difference between residential and commercial as far as Chase could tell. They passed rows of single-family homes, the courthouse, a Botanica, more homes before turning onto the street they sought.

They pulled up to the curb. In front of them, off to the left, a large wooden sign announced with red letters: *Master Psychic Mistress Sienna! Reunites lovers! Removes bad karma! Aura and Chakra Balancing! Tells past, present and future! Palm and Card Readings! No problem is too small or too complex to benefit from my help!* A pair of huge disembodied eyes glared at their car. Sepia stained sunlight added an odd cast to the colors, washing the scene with the patina of an old photograph. Chase shuddered as he clambered out of the car.

Enrique looked over the roof of the car at Chase. "I guess she's really serious with all those exclamation points."

"No shit," Chase shook his head and spit the well-chewed piece of gum into the gutter. "Do you think she does windows?"

"Only if they need their auras cleansed." Enrique slammed the car door as he headed to the sidewalk. A little pink house squatted behind two six-foot-tall wooden jack-o-lanterns. The day glow orange and black pumpkins mocked motorists whizzing by on the five-lane boulevard. Their grins said we know things you will never comprehend. Black awnings emblazoned with suns, stars and moons, gave the house the same jeer as the fake pumpkins in the yard. Chase folded another piece of gum into his mouth before falling into step with Enrique. When he worked, Chase ignored the clawing of booze need at the back of his skull. So long as he was busy, filing it away didn't bite him. As they walked up a concrete sidewalk to a concrete stoop, Chase pulled his wallet from his pocket. Enrique hit the landing first and pressed the bell.

A tall woman wearing a floral wrap dress met them at the door. Full lips pressed into a thin line and arms crossed over an ample bosom she looked them over, hard. "Yes?" A faint accent tinged that one word, drawing out the s at the end.

"Mistress Sienna?" Chase flipped open his badge and held it up. "Chase Nozick, FBI."

She pushed her heavy black hair behind one ear. "Yes." A large silver hoop dangled against her neck. "Well mostly. My name is Analisia Del Carro. Professionally I use Sienna." Blunt-cut bangs gave her a severe, stern edge.

"And professionally I use Chase Nozick."

"Miguel from the Santorio De Luz Botanica called." Stepping in, Enrique pressed against Chase's back and placed his hand on Chase's shoulder. His voice sounded apologetic. For a second Chase became completely aware of Enrique's body. How close he was. Warmth spread from the faintest contact at shoulder and hip. Chase's breath hitched in his throat. That spicy cologne drifted off Enrique's skin to flood Chase's senses. So overwhelming, Chase almost missed Enrique's next words. "He set up the appointment. We have a problem."

Sienna ignored him. Instead she looked Chase over. One long-fingered hand, nails cut short, reached out and ran along his forearm. "You're tense."

Chase was beyond tense. "Excuse me?"

"You're tense, holding your body all wrong." She ran her hand up his arm and latched onto Chase's bicep. "Especially right around your neck. I know a good Naturopathic Doctor, the supplements he has could do wonders for you. Maybe acupuncture. There's pain there."

"Thanks for the diagnosis, but we came here—"

"I know, come in." Her smile opened up her whole face as she pulled him inside. "You have questions." The interior of the house caught Chase off guard. After that last comment he expected some form of New Age purgatory. Instead, Chase stepped into a fairly normal home. "And, my spirit guide says something happened this morning."

Pictures, some of people who might have been ancestors or family, shared wall space with religious paintings of saints. Over every doorway and window crosses were nailed. "Really?" Enrique sounded a little nonplussed by Sienna's comment.

In one corner a narrow, white wicker chair with a huge fan back and a sea blue cushion cradled dolls, beads and toys. Anywhere else and Chase might have thought it a collection of children's toys, but the display was far too perfect for that, like an altar or shrine. Sienna touched a few of the objects reverently as she passed. "Yes," she paused then turned and smiled at them. "We'll talk about all of it."

Moving over to make room for Enrique, Chase bumped the TV. A ceramic statue of a woman robed in white with a gold-edged red cloak brandishing a sword in one hand and goblet in the other rocked on the top. Chase grabbed the castle base of the statute before it could fall. "Yeah," he righted the figurine. "We have a few things to talk about."

"Come with me." Sienna led them back into a room that may have once been a small bedroom. Now a round table of pickled pine and four matching dining chairs took center stage. "My guide says I must help you. It is very important. Both your chakras are of the warriors…warriors on an important quest. There are evil forces chewing at your aura, Agent Nozick. Although," a reassuring, almost motherly expression blew across her face, "you have someone from beyond looking out for you, someone who respected you a great deal."

"Your guide?" Pale blue lace curtains, sea foam green paint and white trim calmed Chase's nerves. That, in and of itself, was amazing. Especially considering Sienna babbled about spirit guides, auras and people from beyond. "He, she, told you that?" Another wicker chair, the match to the one in the front room, presided over the scene. Rows of crystals and colored bottles cluttered the sill of a long, thin window on one side. A larger picture window faced out to the front yard.

"Yes, my spirit guide, Nezahualcoyotl." Sienna closed the door, stepped around the table and seated herself. Behind Sienna, a large tapestry of a nude woman dominated the wall. Her face seemed secretive and her lips turned slightly in a Mona Lisa smile. Strings of tiny copper beads made up the woman's hair, and a white clamshell crown with a blue heart graced her serene countenance. Each outstretched palm held a cowry shell. Waves danced at her feet. It had to mean something. Chase just couldn't figure out what.

The shuffling of a deck of cards grabbed Chase's attention back to Sienna. "He was an Aztec priest buried alive by the Spaniards because he would not convert to Christianity." A blue five-pointed star had been painted on the top of the table. Each point led to a chair. "Go ahead and sit down." Sienna smiled and set the deck in front of her. "I use the twisting path for readings."

Chase wasn't sure what she'd just said. "Twisting?" he repeated as he pulled out the chair on her right and sat. Enrique took the one just to her left.

"Yes," Sienna folded her hands over the deck. "The spread provides insight into the path ahead of you and the choices you must make. When there are many pitfalls and problems that face you, this path will lead you in the right direction."

Realizing Sienna was talking to him like they'd come for a reading, he snorted. "I don't need my cards read."

"Everyone needs their cards read. You have questions, everyone does." She paused and cocked her head, as though someone whispered in her ear. "Especially after what happened this morning."

God, they were going to have to humor her if they were going to get any information at all. "Why me?" He leaned across the table and slapped Enrique's chest with the back of his hand. "Do Enrique."

Sienna studied Enrique for a moment. Then she shook her head. "No, you need it more."

Enrique chuckled and Chase rolled his eyes. "Fine," he mumbled. "Why don't you do a reading for me, then we can discuss our case."

"These are Voodoo cards." Sienna wrinkled up her nose. "Really, more Santeria than Voodoo. The images, I mean." With one elegant hand, she turned the first card, placing it near her body to the left of the table. "Congo La Place." An emaciated man, dressed in white cotton pants, stood on the pillar of a cross made of light. "This card," she tapped the face, "represents the first decision you must make." Water poured from the man's palm across a machete's sharp edge. "The knight of cups. Shango." Her hands circled inches above the table. Slyly, Sienna glanced at Chase and then at Enrique. "He is water become fire." She smiled and dropped her eyes to the table. "Shango is as strong as the rushing river. The essence of passion and romance. Charming, handsome, but remember he is a creature of intense extremes."

Sienna turned over another card, farther left than the first. "Yaguo." Staff held high in one hand, a bow and arrow in the other, a woman stood before a red-painted door. At her feet, a skull grinned. "This is the first false path. The page of coins embodies the strength of the mountain. She teases you with material wealth, pleasures of the flesh. But she rewards your hard work and goals. She often portends a new job or promotion. It is something you must work for. Whatever Yaguo gives, it is not given lightly. Many, many things may try to sway you from your path."

Another card went down. Reversed, Chase dredged the import of an upside down card from somewhere in his mind. Red flames leapt about a large crocodile. In its arms a man struggled. "This is the second decision you must make." Sienna placed it in the middle of the table. "Simbi La Flambeau warns you not to rush. You are moving very fast and you must hurry some. There are only days to do what you need to do. If you do not act quickly, someone will be hurt. But you must remember that if you are impatient you make poor decisions about everything. Do not jump into the unknown...go with haste but not without reason. Think before you act."

Sienna drew another card and placed it higher still, the stair pattern of the cards became evident. "Beware of the second false path." Water swirled about a nude and pregnant woman. One brown arm rested over a full belly painted with flowers. "Balance and harmony during upheaval...Olofi. She is a dance—two steps forward and one step back. When you think you have found your path, you may have to step back to move again. I do not know if this is a change in how you do your job or a change of jobs or where you do them. Olofi is speaking to two problems at once."

The final card Sienna placed above the others. It also was reversed and it took a bit for Chase to make it out. Two warriors stood side-by-side, metal shields held before their bodies. Oddly enough, both wore mirrored shades. The image hit him hard—*Muertos*. They looked just like Garcia's thugs, but without high-powered weapons. "This is one possibility of your future. Somebody is after you, wants to hurt you. You must be calm in the face of this threat. You grow through pain. It is how you meet it that determines who you are, who you will become."

"This is all a path of caution in the face of danger. Stay true to who you are and what you know and this will help. Yet you cannot be wedded to influences from outside you. It is what is in the core of your being, what your heart tells you is right. Let this," she leaned in and pressed her index and middle finger against Chase's breastbone then moved them up to the center of Chase's forehead, "guide this."

A gentle warmth spread from her fingers. For a brief moment, things twisted into sharp focus. And that focus centered on the man across the table from him. Chase could almost hear Enrique's heart beating in time to his own. The slow, warm smile hid in his dark eyes and teased an upward turn in Chase's mouth. So subtle, yet there at the edge of his senses, the smell of sex, cologne and gunpowder overwhelmed Chase. He blinked. Like windblown smoke, the sensations drifted off and left Chase wondering what he'd really experienced.

"Now," Sienna smiled at Enrique, "there is something on your mind."

"*Sí.*" He shrugged and offered a sheepish grin to Chase. "I think someone cursed us."

"Why do you think so?" Her voice held the monitored, inquisitive tone of a doctor.

Chase snorted. "Slaughtered poultry doesn't normally come standard on Federal assigned vehicles."

That earned a raise of both her eyebrows. "Slaughtered poultry?" Her tone, however, remained clinical. Somehow Chase doubted this was the oddest conversation she'd had.

"Someone sacrificed a chicken on the hood of Chase's car."

"You know it was sacrificed?"

"Middle of Hollywood, pins and beads…all the marks of black magic."

"Yeah, I'm no expert." Chase had to bite his tongue not to comment on that bit of truth-shading by Enrique.

"But it looked pretty ritualistic." Enrique shrugged. "If somebody wasn't actually trying to curse us, they went to a lot of trouble to freak us out."

Instead of commenting, Sienna grabbed and shuffled the cards. She dealt three down each side with one in the middle forming an H. Along the left, a woman seated on a porch faced away from them. Below her a man banged a drum and below him, Yaguo's card appeared again. On the right, a gaping whale rested above an upside-down card with an old man standing on one foot. Again the bottom card was a repeat—the two warriors wearing sunglasses. The crossbar card sported two figures, a man and a woman, with their legs and arms touching.

"This is a spread of partnership." Sienna smiled, her eyes darting between Chase and Enrique. "You must work together to overcome this curse…it is not something I can do for you." Chase suspected that she knew. Knew about them. Some little comment or action must have given it away.

Breaking into his thoughts, she rested her hand on Chase's arm. "You search for a kindred soul. This is something you think you lack, and maybe you do. It is a hole inside you."

"Why are you focusing on me?"

"The dead bird was on your car. It's your curse." Considering all the weirdness Sienna spouted, that made a twisted amount of sense. She tapped the cards with her fingers, drawing their attention to the spread. "The last cards were about movement and action. These cards, how you overcome this curse, are about how you are tied to Enrique. You work together, but the cards say it is deeper. In the coming days your partnership will be tested, maybe broken or strengthened." This time, Sienna didn't name the cards. Her hands floated above them like she tasted them with her fingers. Why it was different, Chase didn't have enough clues to solve.

"The cards only give direction. They offer information. It is your job to use it wisely. You see this person in your life," Sienna nodded towards Enrique, but didn't take her focus from the cards, "as having it all, the things you feel you lack, but that they take them for granted. But you also trust him and you're not sure why. Trust is not easy for you. You find yourselves drawn to each other like magnets." Another smug smile flashed. "Don't try to resist, it is too powerful."

"Now, Chase, you feel Enrique is brave, honest and you sense he trusts in you as much as you in him. But to make this happen, there are sacrifices and you may not be willing to make them. If you do only what others tell you is right and do not listen to your heart…that is your choice. And this person, who trusts you, worries about you. Some things are not in his control but are in yours and they harm you." Sienna turned to Enrique. "It is a sickness you see. My guide says he drinks too much, yes?" Enrique opened his mouth as if to speak. Instead he swallowed and looked at Chase. Sienna seemed to read the answer in his face. "This is not the time to fix it, but your presence helps more than you know."

Focusing back on Chase, Sienna added, "What you must do, to set the balance back to right, is believe."

Her last comment to Enrique rattled Chase more than he wanted to admit. And then here she was telling him to *believe.* "Believe in what?" He managed to stutter the question out.

"Many things. Believe what your heart tells you is right. Believe what your eyes see and your ears hear. Your mind may not wish to accept, but you must. If you try and rationalize, if you don't believe and take it at face value, it could kill you. To find this girl you must believe."

Suddenly suspicious, Chase ran his tongue along the inside of his cheek. "We didn't tell you we were looking for a girl."

"No, Nezahualcoyotl told me at the door this is why you were here. And Miguel from Botanica Santorio De Luz told me when he called." The second explanation went down far easier for Chase. "Also her brother came to me; he was worried about her and himself. They both had reason to worry. I tried to help him, but there wasn't much I could do. So I sent him on to someone."

"Did he tell you where she is?" Enrique's question was the obvious one. Chase figured they both already knew the answer.

"No, I don't know that. Nezahualcoyotl cannot see it either; she is very well hidden. I am going to send you to see someone, Dr. Jonas. For two things—your neck, Chase, he can help. Also, Rodrigo Fuertes and Carmen too, I sent them to the same man. I do not know if they went, but I hope that they did."

Enrique, hand drifting over the cards, asked, "You didn't follow up?"

"No, I only put people on the path. It is their choice to follow it. Although, I think they would have. They were running out of time. Carmen, she kept saying that she must be free by the end of October or it would be too late."

Mentally thumbing through the days, Chase hit on the date—October 26. "It's almost the end of October now." Fuck, already Friday.

"I know. She was scared to death of not being finished by then. They came on a Friday...she said she only had two left, this is one of them." Sienna placed her hands flat on the table and stood. "So, Dr. Jonas sees walk-in patients tomorrow morning. It would be easiest to see him then. He's only in Los Angeles for another week, I think." Again, like she was listening to her unseen guide, she grew quiet. Then she smiled and turned. Walking out the door, she called back, "I'll get you the flyer."

Chase shook his head, trying to clear the bizarreness spinning 'round his brain. "She could have told us that before we went through the whole spook show."

"What did I tell you," Enrique glared. "Respect, supplication. It wasn't that bad." Then he flashed one of his wicked grins. "Besides, I saw the price list on the door on the way in. You just got two, hundred dollar readings for free."

Chase snorted. "What a deal."

CHAPTER NINE

Latin rap rattled in the back of Chase's brain. The syncopated rhythms, almost lyrical the way the words wove into the drums, wormed into his skull and made a marginally uncomfortable home. His head didn't hurt, but it sure didn't feel right and the ghosts of Enrique's play list didn't ease the situation. Still, Chase found himself drumming his fingers against the LAPD unmarked car's dash in time to a phantom beat. Hanging out with Enrique got him stuck on the stuff. Somehow each of the partners he'd connected with foisted one of their habits on him; Jason and his damn Juicy Fruit, Enrique's music. Chase even found himself flipping through channels on the hotel satellite looking for a little salsa-tinged patter.

Ahead of them, the 110 freeway split around a brownish hill. Above the road, signs announced that the freeway ended in three quarters of a mile and offered the option of continuing onto the Vincent Thomas Bridge and into Long Beach. Enrique didn't even bother to look over his shoulder before cutting left across three lanes of traffic.

"Man," Chase grabbed the edge of his bucket seat and tried not to panic. "Can you just, I don't know, drive better?"

"I'm driving like I always do." Slender scaffolds and long-necked gantries rose from the mist on the driver's side. Out the passenger window, all Chase could see was sunburnt hill.

Three deep breaths and then Chase growled out, "That doesn't mean you don't have to drive better. The Bureau would kinda like to get me back in one piece."

"You're hungover again." Enrique chided him.

"I told you." Chase stared out at the passing foliage. At least along the coast smoke from the raging wildfires blew back inland. Of course, smog and fire-haze was replaced with fall fog. "I don't get hangovers." At least the air only smelled of diesel fumes and fish. Winds off the ocean pushed back the smoke from the fires raging farther inland. It meant a nice change from the taint of smoke.

"Right," Enrique snorted, "and the 405 doesn't have traffic."

Chase turned and glared. The bones in his neck grated and pinched. "Fuck off." He would have yelled, but embarrassment prevented him. Enrique hit it a little too close to home. Chase, most times, admitted to himself his drinking equaled a problem. Admitting it to other people, well that he wasn't quite ready for.

Whether he was ready or not, Enrique pressed. "You need to lay off the booze, Chase." Not as much judgment as Chase expected seeped through Enrique's tone. It was there. A lot of other things warred with it. Some of them echoed harsh. Most didn't. "*Mofuco*, it's bad shit."

"Look, Daddy." Chase sighed and rationalized. Enrique was just a guy he worked with on a Special. Nothing more than that—well that and a fuck-buddy. One that smelled real good and made a mean cup of coffee, but just a guy he fucked and worked with, and who had a good sense of humor. Chase physically shook the thoughts out of his head. "I can handle myself." It felt like someone else's head had been tied to his shoulders with shoelaces, and rather loosely at that.

"Check it before you wreck it, dude." Even Enrique rolled his eyes at the lame use of slang. "And you keep calling me daddy and we could go to a whole 'nother kink there."

Trying to redirect Enrique's train of thought, Chase grunted. "Fuck my personal problems, what are we looking at here?" He tapped the manila file in his lap. Sheets of dot matrix printing, crappy photocopied photos and some handwritten notes spilled out of the sides. It contained the quick and dirty profile he and Enrique had wrangled together on Rico Padilla a.k.a. 'Dr. Jonas.' Aside from a few busts for selling snake oil or a run-in with the city for running an unlicensed business out of a house, Dr. Jonas almost squeaked with clean.

"Dr. Jonas operates as a spiritualist doctor." Enrique flashed a smile across the car at Chase, telling him something they both already knew like a lead-in. "Some things you should be prepared for: the place will be very chaotic, almost unorganized...don't let that fool you. Everyone knows exactly what is going on. Also, probably he'll have a real altar, not like the shrines we've seen so far. There's liable to be a lot of sick people there. His people said..."

Chase damn near choked at the thought. "He has *people?*"

Ignoring him, Enrique continued, "His people said he'll talk to us or he won't. They can't guarantee anything. We show up, if the right signs are there he may talk right away. Otherwise we put our names into the draw and if he gets to us, he gets to us."

"That's an awfully loose way to run a police interview there, Enrique."

"Well," that sly smile Chase was beginning to recognize as Enrique being cagey crept across his mouth, "I figured we'd try cooperative and pleasant first. Then if that didn't work, we'd get insistent."

Damn, that smile hit Chase in all the right places. Because they were right...they were wrong. He did not want Enrique under his skin like that. To cover the obvious pause, he snorted out, "Devious mind you have there."

Enrique rolled his eyes. "Layer on the false compliments, why don't you?"

"No seriously." He may have been trying to deflect attention from his personal demons, but the praise was sincere. "It's more than your usual, or at least the usual I expect from cops. I've worked Specials with a lot of departments, a lot of officers, and most have an *I'm better than you* attitude." Chase drummed the dash. "A lot of this is underground...not illegal, but looked down on. You always come at it from the 'let's be respectful' angle first. You've been batting a thousand so far."

"Lucky, I guess."

"No, cagey." The car dipped around the off ramp and brought them straight into a stop at a two-way intersection. A massive concrete pedestrian bridge swept over their heads. The wonders of the 110—dead-ending on surface streets at both ends. They followed the left-hand sweep of the road. "My grandma always said 'luck is working your ass off to be in the place where luck happens.'" Industrial buildings mixed uneasily with residential homes as they eased into San Pedro. "People who plan, scheme, reason things out and work toward them…they're lucky."

"Well," first Enrique offered a sly glance at Chase then he made an overt show of checking traffic, "there are some things that are just dumb luck."

Unimpressed, Chase drawled out, "Like what?" Absently, he rubbed the back of his neck. The pain seeped through the general malaise of too much to drink the night before. It pricked nerves all down his spine, layering on its own brand of discomfort.

"Like you and me ending up in the same bar, looking for the same thing that night and then getting on the same assignment." Back to his normal erratic driving, Enrique gunned the car and shot through a right-hand turn at the intersection just ahead of the red light. "Explain to me, FBI, how that is anything but fate?"

"Give me a bit."

"Not possible." Enrique cut him off before Chase could even think. "I don't disagree with you. People make their own luck most of the time. But once in awhile lightning strikes from above and you get hit upside the head by fate."

"Okay, some really random things happen." Chase nodded. "I'll grant you that."

Enrique shrugged. "And sometimes you're meant to be someplace. And no matter what, there you are."

That had to be one of the more convoluted sentences out of Enrique's mouth. Chase mulled it over a few seconds and still couldn't figure out where he was going with the thought. "What do you mean?"

"That night. I wasn't going to go out. This friend of mine, her car broke down in the restaurant across the street. She calls me. I went to help, still in my work clothes. So I'm right there and I think, what the hell, I'm here already, I'll just have a drink. I ran into someone I haven't seen in ages, who doesn't even live in LA anymore...one drink turned into two. And then, my friend bails, I'm walking out and there you were. I was going to just pass you by, but this dude almost ran me over and I did not want to wear his drinks. I backed up against you and I decided to flirt a bit. There you have it...fate, luck in action."

"And it was love at first sight?" Chase teased.

"No it was, 'damn I want to get into those jeans' at first sight." Enrique dished the teasing right back. Chase held his laugh. You had to really appreciate someone who could take it and throw it right back. Most people didn't pass snappy patter 101. It worried Chase, slightly, that Enrique possessed that quality. One of those *things* Chase always looked for, a slightly snarky sense of humor. In a more serious tone Enrique added, "But, you know, then the next day, we run into each other at work. We're going to be working close...I knew at that point deeper things were going on."

"You're scaring me there, Enrique." On more levels than Chase wanted to admit.

For a bit, Enrique just navigated the soft undulating drops down towards the shore. Houses shrouded in bougainvillea and shaded by palms and pine trees lined either side of the five-lane road. Mid-morning sun burned the mist off the water in the harbor. It glittered bluer than blue had a right to at the edge of Chase's vision.

"Look," Enrique blew out his breath, "sometimes you're just meant to know someone. You're supposed to be with them, even if it's only for a while. That's what I figured. Maybe it's only that you and I will work good together, be a great team for this. Maybe it goes beyond work. I don't know, but I ain't gonna fight fate."

There wasn't much Chase could say to answer that. Well, there was a lot he could say and all of it would take him places he didn't want to think about. Enrique just, well he felt too good, too right. Chase never let fate get the upper hand. To give in now—no, it wouldn't happen. Another left swept them into a mixed-use neighborhood. Chase watched houses turn to offices and back to homes.

Finally, Enrique pulled the car to the curb. Black painted numbers on the concrete indicated the address they sought. A tan box squatted up against the sidewalk where an alley met the street. Four flat windows punctuated two doors. The second floor door led to a white metal fire escape, its raw form the only thing really disturbing the symmetry of the building. Not even window boxes added a touch of life. Chase figured it was the damn creepiest building he'd ever seen; nothing that sterile had a right to inhabit the earth.

Both quiet, subdued, they clambered out of the car. Chase rolled his shoulders and popped his neck. The familiar grind settled into the normal bone-weary bitching of an uncomfortable car ride. Dull, but there, it reminded Chase just why he wanted to nail Garcia to the wall. Enrique stepped ahead of him and pounded on the door. Someone on the other side responded without opening. A brief, quiet conversation in Spanish flowed and then the door opened. Chase killed time by grabbing another stick of gum. Well, at least it was a better habit than smoking. That's how Jason got stuck on it.

The short hall Chase entered smelled musty. Having half a dozen people crammed into the space didn't help matters. Their nervous sweat mixed with a hospital smell that slid like jelly down Chase's spine. The place felt like some low-rent clinic. A woman, her brown skin set off by a white nurse's uniform—the kind nurses wore in nineteen-fifty—waved at them to follow her. Her posture was as starched as the white cap on her head. Thick, black hair wound tight into a bun at the nape of her neck. The only thing that broke the image of some stern ghost sixty years gone was the pair of Nike track shoes skimming quickly across the carpet. Of course the red swooshes on the white leather matched the red cross on the woman's cap.

She paused before a white painted steel door at the end of the hall. Silently, she pushed it open and stepped inside. Just ahead of him, Enrique twisted to look back and gave Chase a half-hearted smile. Then he too disappeared into the gaping maw. Chase reminded himself that this was just a junky old building filled with pretentious people. He took a deep breath and followed.

The tiny room they entered was marginally better than the exterior suggested. Red paint on the walls only slightly jarred with the industrial blue carpet. At one side resided the ever-present altar. When Enrique had said to expect an altar, well Chase had expected an *altar*. Something out of the movies with big stone benches and torches would have done it. This was a converted entertainment center, one of those cheap discount store types, with shelves at random points and covered in fake wood laminate.

Multi-colored bandanas draped off the shelves. Plaster statues of saints, Chase recognized Mary and St. George slaying a dragon, which stared at him with gaudy, painted eyes. A Mermaid fashion doll lay on a bed of fake flowers. Soup tureens wore necklaces of beads. The dishes could have come from any old lady's garage sale. Dolls heads, toy animals, pieces of jewelry were scattered among pieces of candy and sparkly bits.

The tableaux barely rated a glance from the nurse—Chase didn't have anything better to call her. Her sneakers whispered across the carpet. She hit the door to her right with the flat of one palm, yanking the handle down with the other. The lock gave with a leaden crunch. It reverberated deep in Chase's gut, driving chills down into his fingers and toes. With a grunt he shook off the feeling and pushed through the door behind the nurse.

The next room was large, not quite cavernous, but an industrial space. Light came from overhead fluorescents flickering dimly against unpainted cinder block. Throngs of people hugged the walls, some visibly ill, grotesque boils or deformities twisting their bodies. Others seemed well enough. All watched the center of the room.

White sheets draped a dining room style table framed under the guttering light. Beside it, a man stood, his left hand resting on the belly of a toddler. Steel gray hair was pulled into a short ponytail and heavy sideburns swept across the line of a square face made of folded leather. He seemed stern, yet somehow tender, like the mask of someone else's expression rested just on top of his own. The child, dark eyes wide, barely moved. Only the tiny chest rose and fell in a regular rhythm.

The man's right hand cradled the side of the child's skull. Slowly, his leathery thumb swept up across the swell of the cheek. "Shh, *liebling*." He cooed through full lips cracked by sun and time. "Soon it will be over." A guttural accent, almost Germanic, flavored his English. Neither language seemed appropriate to the man or the situation. Since he held court and tended a patient, Chase figured the man at the center of attention was the fabled Dr. Jonas.

According to the brief bio, the good doctor had been born and raised in little Havana. Nothing remotely Teutonic lurked in his ancestry. Yet mutterings in that chopped, strong language slipped out of his mouth. Dr. Jonas pressed his thumb into the inside corner of the child's right eye. A wet, heavy sucking sound echoed and then the child's eyeball rested on its cheek.

Chase fought the bile erupting up into his throat. By Enrique's choking gag, he battled the same issue. Nurse wasn't fazed. She pushed through the onlookers and headed for the doctor. Only a quick glance was spared for her, then Jonas reached to a jumble of instruments on the table. Out of the pile he pulled a common butter knife. With a quick flick, he wiped it on his sleeve. Then he rolled the eyeball so that the back, with veins and nerves stretching in a damp red cord into the socket, faced him. Chase could make out a sickly yellow mass clinging to it.

Nurse stepped up holding a paper cup. Jonas nodded at her then smiled at the child. Only a sniffle answered him. It wasn't the reaction Chase expected of a toddler with his eye strung out across his face. Jonas slipped the dull blade under the fatty mass. Slowly, precisely, he peeled it back. Mouth puckered in disdain, Jonas held the growth between his finger and the metal and momentarily studied it. Then he dumped it into the cup.

Rolling the eyeball a bit more, Jonas seemed to check whether he'd gotten everything. With a satisfied grunt, Jonas shoved the eyeball back into the socket. The toddler blinked, but still didn't cry. It wasn't until Nurse picked the child up and deposited her into her mother's arms that the baby began to wail. Jonas rolled his eyes. Nurse quickly ushered the pair between Chase and Enrique and out the door.

Chase turned back to find Jonas directly in front of him. He started back. Damn, he hadn't heard the man move. Jonas set the back of his hand against Chase's jaw. He pushed to the side and Chase hissed as pain snaked down his neck.

"Ja, I can help you." Jonas slid his hand to Chase's shoulder. With a bear trap grip, he pulled Chase toward the table.

Snake oil and charlatans Chase didn't need. "Look," he protested as Jonas shoved him toward the table. "You got a lot of sick people. I'm okay. Deal with them."

Jonas glared. "Take off your shirt." He ordered as he rolled up his sleeves. "You are next."

Looking for salvation, or at least diversion, Chase glared at Enrique and raised his eyebrows. Enrique spread his hands in a what-have-you-got-to-lose gesture. Damn, he was caught in that whole respectful, play along game they had going.

"Shirt," Jonas repeated the order. "Take it off."

Fuck. Chase relented and began to unbutton his shirt. What was the worst that could happen? The guy would poke around, maybe pull some chicken blood and fat from his sleeve and everyone would think it was magic. The stunt with the baby's eye…it was an illusion. Had to be. No child would put up with that abuse without protest.

Hooking his fingers under his jacket lapels and the tethers of the jackass holster, Chase managed to pull the butterfly rig off with his coat. He rolled the fabric around the gun and placed it on the table within easy reach. When Chase's shirt slid off his shoulders, Jonas slapped his chest. "You," his hand smacked the table. "Lie here! Stomach down."

It was a vulnerable position. Chase didn't like it one bit. Still, Enrique watched his back. A little voice in the center of his brain whispered that Enrique wouldn't let Jonas actually hurt him. Put on a show, yeah, but if the guy actually harmed Chase they'd have to scrape him off the concrete. No rational reason backed up his belief. Still, Chase knew it better than he knew his own name.

Chase unhooked the *collare* as he eased himself onto the table. With a last searching glance for Enrique, he slid onto his belly. Folding his hands above his head on the heap of jacket, shirt and gun, Chase dropped the beads on the pile and tried for relaxed indifference. Given everything, Chase figured he missed it by a mile or six.

Thick fingers prodded the skin at the base of Chase's skull. They probed down each vertebra until one bumped one of those spots. Chase hissed and tensed.

"We have found something." Clinical and detached, Jonas' voice seemed to come from both above him and below him. Chase chalked it up to the bizarreness of the situation. The whole atmosphere screwed with his senses.

A clear, glass bowl appeared before Chase's eyes. Nurse must have set it there, although Chase seemed to have missed the actual action. "We will remove it." Jonas muttered. "These metals are dangerous where they are." Chase snorted to himself. The scars must have given it away. Thick, yet somehow raw, puckering dotted the skin of his neck where Garcia's shattered bullet had ripped into his spine. If the projectile hadn't clipped the mirror first, the fucking hollow point would have mushroomed through Chase's spinal cord. Thank God for small favors and bad aim.

Jonas rubbed Chase's neck between his thumbs. It wasn't pleasant but it wasn't awful, just a ham-handed massage. With each stroke, pressure built. Heavy glass marbles seemed to roll up his spine. Chase found himself drifting under the touch. Acupressure, possibly, put a little feel good relief in with the fakery and you'd have yourself a happy room of patients. Now if Jonas would just move a little left, across his shoulder, hit that knot, Chase figured he'd survive.

A cool, thin object lit on Chase's spine just between the shoulder blades. Slowly it drifted up and down his neck. "I must see the bone." Jonas' voice cut into the drowsy state his touches brought on. "The metal must come out," he whispered.

Molten glass shot through Chase's veins, radiating out in a spider-web fracture from the tip of Dr. Jonas' fingers and whatever the goddamn cold thing was. Chase hissed, "Holy shit, what the hell?" and pushed up from the table. He was in the wrong position. Too vulnerable like this.

"You must be still." The hands never left his neck. "Do not fight it."

Threaded shards of pain wormed through Chase's left shoulder. "Fuck you!"

Dr. Jonas set his hand between Chase's shoulder blades and pushed him down, hard. He banged the table with a thump. "Make him still." The man was stronger than he looked. Chase's sternum turned to lead. Tiny, electric touches floated across his flesh. They came from everywhere and nowhere at once. His muscles trembled as all the surface of the table sapped his strength like a sponge.

Where was Enrique? Chase couldn't move. He could barely breathe. He tried to yell. Only a small cough broke his lips. Wet trails, Chase couldn't see them, but he assumed it was blood, ran down his skin and pooled at the nape of his neck. Where the fuck was Enrique? The asshole cut him! He needed to go down.

Dr. Jonas clicked his tongue as he probed in Chase's neck. The pressure split Chase's senses, but the pain dropped back to a dull, leaden ache. "There is too much blood. I can see nothing." Dr. Jonas grumbled. "Stop the blood." Chase had no clue if that were an order to him and how the hell he'd comply anyway. The damp tendrils faded and dried on his skin. Above him, below him, almost in Chase's own skull he could hear Dr. Jonas muttering, "Here is metal." Like the sting of a wasp, a burning sharp pain dug in inside his neck. A second later it vanished. The chink of metal hitting glass snatched Chase's gaze to the bowl. Tiny, dull and twisted, a small fragment of lead spun at the bottom.

Another sting was followed by more metal shards. "And here as well." It felt as if someone were pushing Chase's vertebrae along his spinal cord like point counters above a pool table. Back and forth, the slithering sensation of things moving in a way they weren't designed to filled Chase with dread. If he tried to call out, nothing but coughs or hard breaths sounded. And he couldn't move. Not a finger responded to his brain's screaming to make it all stop.

Jonas kept mumbling as he worked, filling the bowl with bits of metal, some dull and brass-colored, others lines of melted silver or blackened drops. "We must find it all. All must come out." Hours seemed to drip by as Dr. Jonas searched and plucked and tossed bits in the bowl. Finally, he grunted. "That is all." Dr. Jonas' hands wrapped around Chase's throat, index fingers cupped along the line of his jaw. Chase wanted to scream. The pressure of Dr. Jonas' thumbs pushed the skin along Chase's spine. Heavy and deep, his flesh felt like it was melting into itself. "We are done with this." Dr. Jonas' voice sounded satisfied.

Chase drew in a huge breath of air. He still couldn't move, but he was alive—sore but alive. It was some kind of drama for the audience. Maybe a form of hypnosis, Chase rationalized. Not like he could do more than cycle it through in his head. None of his joints responded to his pleas to move.

Dr. Jonas' hands swept the back of his neck twice. Then the touch moved down. Oh shit! Not more. Instead of the hard determined prodding, Dr. Jonas' just stroked down and down. The light touch drove the anger and fear from Chase's body. He couldn't have held it in if he'd tried and he tried like hell. He wanted to be righteously pissed at Dr. Jonas, break his head in, but it just didn't seem all that important anymore. Finally, Dr. Jonas stilled over Chase's low back. "You have another problem here, *Hepatomegalia*. I cannot fix this. You must stop drinking. It may fix itself now if you do. You will become very sick if you don't."

He patted Chase's shoulder. "You may get up." Slowly, Chase's muscles began to respond. Good thing it was slowly or Chase still might have come off the table and wrung Dr. Jonas' neck. He was too shaky for that. He pushed himself up and swung his legs off the edge of the table. Nurse, efficient as all nurses, appeared at his side and helped him stand. Dr. Jonas handed him his shirt and *collare* from atop the pile of jacket and holster. "Stop drinking. I think it will kill you if you do not." The man's face seemed sad.

The bitter accusations died on Chase's tongue. Silently he took his shirt and shoved his arms in the sleeves. Nurse moved behind him. Chase heard the rattle of the metal against glass. He spun. "No wait." He grabbed her arm and earned a scorching, derisive glance. "I want to keep that. I need to keep those fragments."

If he kept the fragments, he could prove it a fake. Chase's mind spun, pulling the threads of the why and the how together in an instant. They'd be nothing more than bits of copper and tin scavenged from someplace. Dr. Jonas knew they were coming; he had their names. He could have Googled Chase and found the accounts of the shooting. It made national news. Dr. Jonas had at least a day to prepare. For a good con artist he wouldn't have needed that much time.

Chase glanced up to see Enrique crossing the room toward him. Now he took action; well, it probably hadn't looked any worse than the trick with the baby.

Surprisingly, Dr. Jonas shrugged. "If you wish. Margarita will get a bag for you." Chase expected him to deny the request. So easy to prove that the fragments hadn't actually come from Chase's body. Of course, by the time Chase verified it, Dr. Jonas would be long gone and none of these people would care.

Enrique coughed, gaining the Doctor's attention. "Dr. Jonas, we would like to talk with you about one of your patients."

The worn leather face split into a smile. "I know. But you must wait while I see to these people. It will be some time."

"We'll wait." Chase sneered in a cop's growl. Then he realized he still hadn't buttoned his shirt. He probably didn't equate to awfully intimidating at that point.

CHAPTER TEN

Dr. Jonas, Rico Padilla, sat at a scarred laminate table drinking Cuban coffee from an espresso cup. On the other side of the door supplicants waited for their turn with the Doctor. "Carmen." Sans affected accent, Dr. Jonas pushed the name around on his tongue. "Carmen Fuertes."

Chase perched on the edge of his chair. He felt disconcertingly relaxed, like he'd slept better than he had since he could remember. The sensation started shortly after he'd clambered off the table back in the treatment room. The smothered blanket feeling in his temples had drifted away. Even the ever-present ache in his belly faded. No matter how much Chase fought it, he couldn't shake the almost dreamy state. "Yeah, Carmen Fuertes. You saw her and her brother, Renaldo."

Dr. Jonas stared over his scarred, meaty hands. They completely engulfed the delicate espresso cup. Hands like that hardly belonged to a surgeon; they hardly belonged to anyone outside a meat-packing plant. Thoughtfully, the Doctor mumbled, "I saw her?" as he blew the steam from his coffee. Dark eyes seemed even more intense with the deep purple circles under them.

"Yes." Enrique slid Carmen's photo across the table. "This girl."

Drawing Dr. Jonas' attention down to the glossy picture, Chase tapped the corner. "Mistress Sienna sent her to you." He flipped Renaldo's photo on top of it, the old mug shot from his file, not the post mortem from the morgue. "Both of them."

The doctor shrugged. "She sends many people to me." He made it seem as though it were no big thing, the passing back and forth of clients for fleecing.

Chase froze the smile that threatened to slip. Neither Dr. Jonas nor Mistress Sienna would call it a fleecing, con or scheme. And really Chase didn't care what these people thought they were buying into. What he cared about was finding Carmen and then nailing Garcia to the wall. "Renaldo Fuertes brought her. She was sick. Sick in a way Mistress Sienna couldn't help."

One hand cupped his chin as Dr. Jonas set his cup on the table. "Why are you looking for them?" The flesh of his face sagged around his fingers, making him look like a weathered bulldog.

Enrique caught Chase's eye. The barest jerk of his chin asked the question and Chase answered it with only a nod. "Not them, just her." A partner's groove, he didn't have to ask Enrique to know what the next words out of his mouth would be. "We already found her brother shot in the LA River." The words weren't what Chase had known, but the content was. The unspoken question was *how much should we tell?*

"Murdered?" Dr. Jonas rolled the word around in his mouth for a while, like it was something that didn't taste quite right.

"Final word on that hasn't come out." Chase rocked his chair onto its back legs and laced his fingers behind his head. The seat protested. His back, for once, didn't. "Sure didn't look like a suicide though."

Dr. Jonas petted the photo, stroked it, and traced the line of Carmen's face. His eyes drifted shut and he licked his lips. A subtle shudder ran down his frame. "We remember this girl. Very frightened. Very, very frightened." The accent returned as he spoke. He shook his head wearily. "There was nothing I could help her with. She was scared for her brother. His sickness originated without his body. Someone caused him to be sick." Like ice water, the words coursed down Chase's neck, raising every hair in their wake. "I can heal a body, I cannot cleanse a soul. His soul was tainted by his past, owned by another man. Because of this, someone found a way in and used this to hurt him and her, and make him very sick to punish her and bring her back to this person. This is not something I can help with."

Swallowing down the willies, Chase tried for a calm, reasonable question. "Are there people who could help with that kind of sickness?" Given the situations lately, that was as calm and reasonable as he could manage. Two and two seemed to be adding up to four-point-five these days. The world seemed slightly south of true.

Dr. Jonas smiled and sipped his coffee. "Your friend knows of them." He used the cup as a pointer, swinging in it a general arc to indicate Enrique.

Enrique smiled and prompted. "I do?"

"I would hope you do." The harsh rebuke snapped across the table.

Quick on the recovery, Enrique quipped, "*Santeros?*" It rang of less a question than a need for Dr. Jonas to confirm something Enrique already knew. The man was a master of the quick save.

"*Ja.*" Dr. Jonas glared.

Well, Chase could take the heat as the dumb white cop. "Did you send them to a *Santero?*"

The glare he rated was slightly less poisonous. "I advised Carmen and Renaldo to seek the advice of the *Orishas.*"

Chase spun his coffee mug in his hands. "Any *Orisha?*"

"Any *Santero* or a special one?" Enrique added.

"Any *Orisha* that felt they might help." He answered Chase then turned his attention to Enrique. "I told her of Joseph, Joseph De Vaca, he is a *Santero*. I do not know if they sought him out."

"You didn't check up on them?" Chase wasn't sure of the protocol of the faith healer and gullible schmuck relationship. He assumed they'd keep tabs on the people who came to them. Keep the suckers, and their money, coming back. As yet he hadn't seen anyone at Dr. Jonas' ask for money. They probably accepted *donations* in specified denominations, maybe handed off to the nurse since Chase hadn't noticed a cash box anywhere.

"No, he was my suggestion, but they may have known another who they felt could help them more." He smiled at Chase. Almost double-exposed, Chase had the sense of someone else's face hovering a millimeter over that of Dr. Jonas. It was, at once, the most comforting and disturbing smile Chase had ever witnessed. "I cannot tell you to stop drinking. I can only say I see it is bad for you and that it would be best if you did. You take my advice or you do not." He shrugged. "That, I have no control over."

Chase shook off the image and reverted to his training. When all else failed—still drunk from the night before, scared shitless by a gun shoved in your mouth or just off your game for any reason—years of practice led you through what needed to get done. He didn't even have to think to ask the right question. "Do you know where we could find Joseph DeVaca?"

"*Ja.*"

Chase waited for more. When nothing was forthcoming, he prodded, "Can you let us know?" The unease drifted away as Chase fell into the routine of an informational interview; how and where can we find someone? It was the bread and butter of an investigator's life.

"He can be found through the *Botanica Christo Del Rey.*" He stood and walked to the sink. Depositing his cup, Dr. Jonas turned on the faucet. Almost distracted by the simple chore, he muttered. "They will know where he will hold services and when."

"What do you remember about Renaldo's illness?" Enrique fished for more information. Chase would have rather not gone back to that topic. It left him uneasy and unsettled.

"His stomach, that bothered him. She had headaches sometimes and so did he. Mostly it was that their luck was bad." Dr. Jonas turned and waved absently in Chase's general direction. "Like yours, but much worse."

Chase shifted, rolling his neck out of habit. "What do you mean like mine?"

"You have a dark cloud over you. A curse has been laid on your head."

Mistress Sienna likely told him that. All these charlatans traded information. Chase wished they wouldn't bother. He didn't need to be impressed. He just needed to find Carmen and then Garcia. He drawled out a noncommittal, "That so?" Why they kept bothering him with this shit, well they all had to be attention-hounds. Or maybe they bought into their own line of bull. Spout it for so long, you might start to believe.

"It hovers, not so strong as his." Almost like dance moves, Dr. Jonas' hands spread and twined and twisted in front of his body. "This girl, Carmen, many things she saw and did or did not do, they poked tiny holes in her soul...like pinpricks. And these pricks left her weak, allowed the evil to seep in and take hold of her. Renaldo, he did not want to tell me, but it was much deeper for him. I think he gave it away and regretted."

"Like witnessing drug deals, hearing about murders," Enrique added. "That would tend to taint your heart."

"Sounds like cops," Chase snorted. "They all must have little charred nuggets for souls." God, Chase didn't even want to know what his soul, whatever that was, might look like.

"No, not so much." Now, the doctor folded his arms over his chest and propped his butt against the counter. "Not the good ones." That comment got a sly wink as punctuation. After a heavy sigh, Dr. Jonas continued his impromptu lecture. "The ones who challenge the evil of men. It is very hard to see, day-by-day, these evil things and not be damaged by them. It takes a very strong heart to resist and keep fighting. And many things can cause these holes and allow bad things to seep in." Dr. Jonas' dark gaze zoomed in on Chase. Once again he had the feeling of being studied by two sets of eyes. "Anything that weakens you, your strength, your judgment..."

"I get it," Chase snapped, dredging up annoyance to keep the willies at bay, "I need to stop drinking. You can get off that highway now."

"When I look at you," Dr. Jonas held out his palm as if to block Chase's face from his view. Slowly, he slid it down, like he was wiping glass. "It is a film, like grease, over you, but it does not touch you. With Carmen and Renaldo it reached inside," mimicking his words, he reached out and balled his hand into a fist, "became part of them so that they were cursed. Whoever cursed them already had a hold on them. They'd given it to this person. The one who cursed you did not know you. Because of this, it is very common and not very strong."

Chase drummed his fingers against the scarred table. "Not strong?"

"You have to know people to curse them." Dr. Jonas' smile grew tight. "Or have something of theirs, something they value, that means something to them. This creates the connection. I feel the connection, but as if it is light through a window. It is as warm and as bright, yet not the same as if I stepped outside." With a deep, introspective sigh, Jonas added, "Something you care about connects you. I feel it. But what he has is not yours. I don't know. The pull is still strong enough that you should be concerned."

CHAPTER ELEVEN

"I so do not get all those people's faith in Dr. Jonas." Chase stripped his jacket, holster rig and tie before collapsing on the micro-couch in his suite. He fished the various stuff from his pockets—cell phone, gum, wallet, badge—and tossed them on the table with the clothing.

The badge spun on the wood, the number catching the faded afternoon light. Jason's badge had been nearly the same as his, the last two numbers transposed. They'd joked about the synchronicity. The weight of the memory hit Chase hard, especially after the day he'd been through.

Shit, he was tired. Traffic had been a nightmare straight out of Dante's Inferno. Of course it was Los Angeles, traffic was always purgatory. Add the crawl through the downtown slot at two hours before rush hour and Chase would have preferred a stint in the fiery inferno.

Wandering past, Enrique laughed, catching Chase off guard with a response. "What do you mean?" He dropped his own coat on Chase's head and moved around the island into the small kitchen.

Chase yanked the jacket off. He would have glared, but Enrique wouldn't see it from where he was. Instead, Chase took a moment, brought the fabric to his face and inhaled. The wonderful, spicy scent of Enrique swarmed his senses. Before Enrique could catch him, Chase balled the coat and tossed it onto the chair across the room. Just in case, he grumbled. "How gullible can they be?" Go offensive instead of being pushed into a defense, Chase took that tack more times than he could recall. "The man's a snake oil salesman."

Enrique leaned over the breakfast bar and snorted. "How's your neck?"

"Fuck off." Even as he said it he couldn't help but smile up at Enrique. "I'm just getting laid a lot more than usual." He minimized, justified and explained away all the stuff he really didn't want to think about. "I'm relaxed."

"Even when you're asleep you're not relaxed, Chase."

Chase banged the half-wall behind the couch. "Come here and I'll show you how not relaxed you make me."

"Tempting me, huh?" Enrique laughed and walked back into the tiny living area. Settling into a true cop stance—feet spread wide, arms folded over his chest—Enrique licked his lips. That pretty much ruined the whole cop image. "In the middle of the afternoon no less."

"Hey," Chase reached over and bumped Enrique's thigh with his fist. "We've been up since the butt crack of dawn. We got a little down time coming." Then he ran his knuckles over Enrique's crotch.

"A little going-down time?" Enrique teased and pushed into the touch.

The prick trapped in those slacks was getting harder under Chase's touch. "A lot of going-down time."

"You are a dirty-minded bastard." Enrique hissed and stepped closer. "You know that, Chase?"

Chase stared at Enrique, daring him with raised eyebrows and a wicked grin. He jerked his chin toward Enrique's crotch. "Like you're complaining?" The hard bulge hovered just inches from his face.

Enrique snorted and unzipped his pants. "Nope." His own smile just as evil, Enrique pulled himself free and closed his eyes, raw sexual energy rolling over his features. He tilted his head back, his hand sliding over his stiff prick, teasing Chase with the sight. The man was beyond sexy. Every move he made, every sound, it whispered sex.

Every time he saw Enrique, Chase remembered how fine that dick was, so large and dark, the heavy vein pulsing along the shaft. Chase reached out and grabbed it. That hot cock felt so good in his hand. Chase stroked Enrique's hard prick with slow, steady strokes, savoring the warm skin sliding against his own. He squeezed just to hear Enrique groan.

Chase wanted to suck his dick like nothing else. He got off on sucking dick. Always had. Chase used the grip on Enrique's cock to pull him to the couch. He leaned over and stuck out his tongue. Looking up into Enrique's deep brown eyes as he licked around the head of his throbbing cock, Chase hit heaven. He wet his lips then took the full length of that magnificent cock into his mouth. Chase fought with his own slacks. Trying to yank down a zipper one-handed was a bitch. Still, Chase managed.

Enrique's hard meat tasted so good, felt so good against his tongue. Chase already savored the bittersweet salt of pre-cum. It wouldn't be too long before Enrique shot his load down Chase's throat. He could already feel the heat building. Chase fished his own prick out of his pants. A cock in his mouth, a cock in his hand, life didn't get much better. For a brief moment it pushed the flavor and want of other things out of Chase's mind.

Chase felt Enrique shift. He lowered himself, bracing one knee on the arm of the small sofa. Chase sidled over to keep the contact, keep that fat prick between his lips. Then Chase hissed as Enrique's palm wrapped over Chase's prick. Chase released his own grip and moved his hand to Enrique's ass. He opened his throat and took Enrique's thrusts. Chase wrapped both arms around his hips and pulled Enrique close. He closed his eyes as he took all of that thick prick. He slid his lips along Enrique's hot shaft. Enrique moaned loud as Chase squeezed his ass and sucked him.

Enrique slid one hand against the back of Chase's head. He groaned again as he wound his fingers in Chase's hair. Fucking Chase's mouth, stroking Chase's prick, Enrique's moans rocked Chase to the core. Pinpricks of desire frosted Chase's belly and thighs. Nothing compared to making someone else go wild. Around the mouthful of prick, Chase whispered, "Cum for me!" He wanted to taste everything. "Cum in my fucking mouth!"

Enrique slammed his mouth, his cock banging the back of Chase's throat again and again. Chase felt the shudders start in both of them. "I'm cumming..." Enrique's hoarse whisper pooled heat in Chase's prick. One more long groan and hot cum hit the back of Chase's throat. He milked the cock in his mouth for all he could get.

When Enrique's breathing returned to more normal pace, he pulled back. "You're turn, *Compa*." The wicked grin was back.

Enrique's fist flew over Chase's rock-hard cock. Chase bucked into Enrique's hand. Pleasure wracked his body. Chase's balls grew tight. He dug his fingers into Enrique's hip and moaned. The shot snapped down his spine as he blew. Chase couldn't manage more than to breathe out, "Fuck!"

Enrique chuckled and shook the spunk off his hand. He twisted and dropped down next to the couch, his head lolling against the arm. Chase wrapped his arms around Enrique's warm body and pulled him against his chest. Not a bad day by Chase's reckoning. A possible lead and a heady session of sex, life didn't get much better. He rolled his neck and nothing popped, for once. "I think I need a drink after a lay like that."

Chase pushed Enrique up and eased off the couch. Yanking up his pants as he moved, Chase headed into the tiny kitchen. He fished a glass out of the cabinet and popped a few cubes of ice out of the tray. When he turned toward the island something was missing. "Where's my bottle?"

"Your what?" Enrique didn't sound as mystified as he should. In fact his tone was rather cagey, like he was hiding something.

The post-sex haze evaporated in an instant. "My JD." Chase snapped. He wasn't in any mood to play games. "You were in here last. Where did you put it?"

After a heavy pause, Enrique huffed. "I, ah, poured it."

He did not just say what Chase thought he said. "You fucking what?" In denial, Chase pulled open cabinets. Panic welled in Chase's chest, wrapped ghostly steel fingers about his heart and squeezed. "Where the fuck did you hide it?" He looked up to find Enrique leaning on the lip of the counter and zipping up his slacks.

"I dumped it." Enrique flipped his fingers toward the trash. "Look, Dr. Jonas is right, you need to cut back."

He dumped it! The raw hint of JD mixed with bile flooded Chase's mouth. "Fuck you!" Growling, Chase fished the bottle out of the bin and stood. The tiniest bit of amber liquid swirled at the bottom. He swung on Enrique, using the empty bottle as a pointer. The panic he'd felt a moment before billowed out of his mouth as anger. "Not your right! What made you think that was okay?"

"Maybe, I don't know," Enrique spat back, "'cause I like you?" Defensive, he folded his arms over his chest and glared. "Call me crazy, but I'm even starting to care about what happens to you. That *mofuco* is fucking up your life."

Chase slammed the empty bottle into the can. "Go to hell!" The shattering of glass punctuated his yell.

"What?"

"Get out!" Chase advanced, using his bulk to push Enrique out of the kitchen. "Fuck off! How fucking self-righteous." He slammed one hand into the center of Enrique's chest. "Get the hell out!"

Enrique backpedaled, almost tripping over the coffee table. "You're this pissed off because of booze?" He grabbed his jacket from where Chase had tossed it. As he shoved his hands through the arms, he yelled back, "You're putting that shit over us?"

"What us, Enrique?" Chase bellowed. Who the fuck cared who heard? Where did Enrique get off thinking he could do that? "We're doing a Special. This is easy for both of us." Chase grabbed his crotch. "Nothing more than that. A few weeks of casual fucking and we're both good."

"If that's all you want out of your life, that's fine." Enrique's voice dropped low and menacing. Chase swallowed, but he'd be damned if he'd back down. "I thought, maybe, here's somebody who can understand me, know what I go through every day. Somebody who treats me like an equal, a man, a real partner." Enrique shook his head and stalked down the short hall. Over his shoulder he yelled, "But hey, you want that fucking bottle more? You go right ahead. Drink yourself to death for all I care." Chase didn't bother to follow. If he followed it meant Enrique was more than a casual fuck. Nobody was more than a casual fuck. Enrique's final comment slapped him just before the door slammed. "You're too good for that, but if that's what you want, you can have it!"

CHAPTER TWELVE

Chase pushed away from the keyboard. Lines of information scrolled across the screen. He'd read it and re-read it at least five times before he'd realized it. Some email about logistical transfers and resource allocations, and beyond that Chase couldn't concentrate, not even enough to figure out why he'd been included on the list. He'd go back later and sort the information.

Standing, Chase stretched. The grinding pops in his neck seemed conspicuous by their absence. Maybe he just needed to get a bed like the one at the hotel. He mulled the possibilities vs. probabilities of causation. The stiff mattress and thin pillows might be the reason his back felt better than it had in ages. Maybe he just slept better in Los Angeles, the climate agreed with him even if the sky smelled of smoke. The ache in his gut hadn't vanished, however. If anything, it was at record levels this morning.

Chase tossed the last of the junk memos and half-finished reports on the borrowed workstation. Then he headed to find something vaguely resembling caffeine, or a danish, or both. Anything with the capability to distract him would serve. If he made it through how today was shaping up to be…

A horrendous pit of self-loathing lived just below his sternum. His hands shook and his head felt too big for his neck to support. Some nights were bad. Last night had been bad. After he'd tossed Enrique on his butt, Chase stalked to the nearest convenience store. In the space of two-and-a-half hours he'd downed a fifth and played dial-a-drunk with his mom's answering machine. Sunday afternoon and into the night he'd done it again, except for the dial-a-drunk episode. Chase was amazed he hadn't poisoned himself.

Of course, he almost wished he had. Easier that way.

Every misdeed and stupid move, whether real, marginal or wholly imagined, came swelling back in the early morning darkness. It wove a net of deceit through his mind so tight reason couldn't worm its way through. Whisky-tainted sweat sucked his soul out through his pores. Chase spent the small hours before dawn wrestling down the desire to swallow his gun.

By the time he'd given up on sleep and hauled his ass out of bed, his brain was a muddled mess, like his thoughts were being sieved through a filter of chocolate pudding. A shower and coffee managed to raise him to a semi-functional level. He grunted hellos; luckily he didn't actually know any of the home agents beyond a nodding acquaintance. A lot of people would excuse it as a typical Monday mood, even if they didn't know what his typical Monday was like. When he sat down, all he did was futz with the computer. If he succeeded at any actual productivity this morning, it'd be a fluke. And all the work he'd been neglecting for this Special piled on his mind. A weight so crushing Chase couldn't even sort the mess. Prioritizing seemed beyond him. Instead he worked things as they came. Nothing handled, but the fires dimmed back to smolder level.

Chase shoved his hand in his jacket pocket, searching for the pack of antacids he always kept. Instead he found the baggie with the metal fragments. There was a manageable project. Of course he didn't know the routine at this office. This was the FBI, the routine here wouldn't deviate much from the routine of a hundred field offices spread across the nation. Chase just had to locate the local key to that routine.

It took a bit of searching, but Chase managed to both identify the person who could help and actually track them down. Agent Craig, his alleged point of contact for "anything he needed," grudgingly pointed him in the direction of an Agent Doheny. Locating Doheny proved the more difficult of the two tasks. After a few wrong turns, Chase poked his head into one of the warren of cubicles.

Fake cobwebs stretched across the add-on shelves and draped over a bowl of mini candy bars. A woman, brownish hair pulled into a conservative bun, studied her monitor. Two pens and a thin highlighter stuck out like hair ornaments from the tightly wound 'do.

"Hey." Chase called softly to let her know a visitor waited. Like all the others, in countless field offices, furniture made by the lowest bidder filled her micro office. Small mementos of the occupant's life dressed the space up. When she turned, he smiled. The smile almost hurt. "Chase Nozick, I'm on the Almandeto Famosa-Garcia Special."

"Ally Doheny." She smiled back and held out her hand. "To what do I owe the pleasure of your dropping by, Agent Nozick?"

"I'm led to believe," gingerly, Chase accepted the handshake, "that you are the only person capable of getting some bullet fragments run and compared for me." Doheny's firm grip made Chase wince. Not because she was overly strong; the pressure just shot up his arm and pounded on the back of his head. Quickly as he could manage, without being offensive, Chase pulled back his hand. To mask the abruptness of the move, Chase fished the pack of gum from his suit pocket and held it out. "Juicy Fruit?"

As she spun her chair fully around to face him, Doheny shook her head. The pens clacked together when she moved. "There's a ton of people who could have helped you with that."

"Like I said," he grinned and laid on the flattery as he dropped the pack back in his pocket, "I was told you were actually capable of getting it *done*." Even agents needed ego strokes, especially the backbone operational types. All a field agent's savvy meant shit if you couldn't trace a latent or match a set of fibers to put a suspect at the scene. Chase fished out the baggie. "I need a rush put on these."

"A rush?" Doheny held out her hand and Chase handed her the bag. "And who shot which president?"

"No, seriously." Chase pushed. Like any government job, resources got stretched, juggled and prioritized. You had to know how to fit your needs into the grand scheme. "A witness turned them in. Claims they were pulled out of a body that Garcia shot shortly after he shot a known hit." Chase's line— this was important but not resource intensive. If he could convince Doheny of that, it might actually get done before the next presidential election. "There's no way we can prove it's a Garcia hit, but I need it run through NIBIN and DRUGFIRE as soon as possible." He wheedled. "All the known Garcia hits have ballistic records in the joint ballistics databases. If it comes back positive, I can at least link a circumstantial chain and put the son of a bitch near a local."

Doheny held the bag up to the light. Squinting at the remnants, her face went sour. "Shit, where'd these come from? They're in a freaking sandwich bag…one that, I think, had sandwiches in it once."

He crossed his arms and leaned against the edge of her cubicle. "A back-alley cutter." Chase shrugged.

That earned him a roll of Doheny's eyes. "The guy licensed to practice in any third world country?" She dropped the baggie in her lap before reaching off to the side and a shelf filled with forms and manuals.

He'd won at least the first round. Chase smiled as a small bit of the pressure eased off his shoulders. "Not that I know of."

A few forms got teased from the general jumble of paperwork. "The last refuge of the truly desperate then." She pulled one of the pens from her bun.

"Yep. Can you do it?" He still wanted her to say she would. Just because Doheny acted cooperative, didn't mean she actually was. "I just need to know if they're a likely match to anything Garcia has used. Cross check them against the Jason Olhms murder. I know they're in the database for that. There's no way I can make a connection stand up in court. The cutter won't testify. But I'll know, and Garcia won't, and I can use it as leverage."

Rolling closer to the desk, Doheny asked, "No independent forensic firearms review?"

"Nope, don't need a human set of eyes, just a print out of likely matches will do." Chase made it as easy as possible. Easy meant it might actually get processed. "The chain of custody is blown on this evidence anyway. I have no idea where this guy kept these."

"Looks like his lunch box." Doheny teased and tapped the bag still in her lap. Then she began to scribble on the form. "I'll see what I can do. Maybe a few days, possibly a week, if I can squeeze a quick favor."

"That's fine." Chase breathed a muffled sigh of relief. "We don't even know where Garcia's at yet. Once we bring him in, we'll worry about whether the report's done."

"You got it then." She smiled as she glanced up. "I'll forward it on to your desk."

"Thanks, I owe you."

"No problemo. I'll get it started with the FTU. Give me your routing info."

Chase rattled off the information Doheny needed for the form. Based on that, the Firearms-Toolmarks Unit would process the fragments, load them into the system and let it run for matches. NIBIN searches turned up anything logged in the FBI or BATF databases. The DRUGFIRES, regional and state versions, hadn't yet been fully integrated, but that work was ongoing. Still, the FBI should be able to access the only one Chase cared about—Florida.

Then the question was, were the bullet remnants identifiable at all? If they'd actually been under Chase's skin for five years, the pieces might be degraded beyond recognition. "Let 'em know a good possible is enough. Even if they can't state for certain." He reiterated, "I don't need this to hold up in court." *I just need to know it for myself.*

As he walked away, chalking up one success in an otherwise sucky morning, Chase's cell rang. He fished it off his hip. Glancing at the screen, Chase didn't recognize the number, it carried a 213 prefix marking the number as central LA. He hit the button and barked, "Nozick."

"Well, it lives." A warm voice with the edge of a Spanish lisp hit him. Enrique, fuck. Why did Chase have to give *him* his cell number?

Chase cast about for a bit of privacy. Ahead one of the assortment of random conference rooms seemed dark. He hissed, "Fuck off, Enrique," as he ducked into the dim room.

A heavy pause lingered on the line. Finally Enrique spoke. "What, you want me to put in for someone else to take over?" Irritation and worse things crackled over the connection. "Then you can look like a screw up with them and not drag me down."

"Honestly," Chase leaned against the wall and banged the back of his head on the plaster, "I don't need anyone else to make me look bad. I am perfectly capable of making a total ass of myself."

"No shit." Enrique's voice snapped. Even through a crappy cell connection, Chase heard the anger. "So you still on this case, FBI?"

Enrique was mad. Chase knew it from the first words. He was also hiding behind talking about work when his voice said he wanted to be slicing Chase's gut open. "Let's be clear about something Enrique. You're a good cop. I'm okay working with you." He jumped in and passed over the knife. "I'm liking the other part of our partnership, too. But you don't own me. What you did wasn't your right. Do you get that?"

More silence. Chase hated silence, but he waited it out. Finally, Enrique huffed, "I don't want to see you like that, Chase."

At least they were talking about what needed to come out so they could do their jobs. "Do you understand?" Given the stakes, and the prestige of a Special Assignment like this, everyone from the director on down would be suspicious if one of them tried to bail.

Another huff, then Enrique mumbled, "Yeah, I get it."

Well, he still sounded pissed, but not the *I'm going to kill you* kind of pissed. "Okay." Time to play the contrite card. "Look, I'm sorry I yelled at you. I probably overreacted a bit. We good now?" Part of Chase didn't want to apologize. It wasn't his fault. Enrique overstepped and got shot down. Still, the smallest little bit of him didn't want to see Enrique mad, especially not mad at him. And that felt really odd. Chase usually didn't give a rat's ass what people thought of him personally.

He cared a shitload about what they thought of Special Agent Chase Nozick.

"We're okay. I'm not sure I like taking second place to a bottle, but I get the feeling you've been with that whore a lot longer than me." Chase could almost hear the shrug. "I can live with it."

"Great, but I'm guessing you didn't ring me for relationship debriefing 101." Chase headed out of the conference room. It wouldn't do to have people thinking Chase hid personal calls. Hell, he was on the line with Enrique, his LAPD liaison. That wouldn't matter much to a rumor mill jabbering about furtive calls in dark rooms. "Tell me what's up."

"We're good."

Maybe Enrique had wanted to just talk about them. "Yeah, you said that." Strange and warm, a lump snuggled into Chase's chest at the thought.

"No." A different level of irritation seeped through Enrique's voice. "I said *we're okay*, but the *investigation* is good. We're hooked up with the next ceremony. Joseph DeVaca, they'll be in Simi tonight. You up for it?"

"Yeah." Chase stifled a yawn. He still hadn't managed to rustle up any coffee. "Great."

"You don't sound like you're really up for it." Enrique chided. At least he didn't sound like Chase's mom when he did. "I can go scope it out, do the interview thing."

Enrique would not leave him behind. "No, I'll be fine. I'm going to cut out to my hotel then and catch some z's."

"Hit it too hard, did you?" Again with that track. If Enrique didn't sound like a concerned partner, Chase would have cut him down.

Instead Chase growled. "You make a lot of assumptions there, Enrique. Especially for a guy whose mom still does his laundry."

"Tell me I'm wrong." Enrique ignored the jab. "Look, *Compa* if you look as roached as your voice sounds, people are gonna think you've been converted to a Voodoo zombie." He snorted a laugh. "I bet you're scaring the secretaries."

Chase found himself laughing at the bad joke. "I'll catch you tonight."

"Great, I'll swing by around seven. You should have slept it off by then."

"Fuck you." Chase's obscenity wasn't half as cutting as the same statement two nights earlier.

Almost sultry, Enrique purred out, "We'll see."

CHAPTER THIRTEEN

A decent nap marginally improved Chase's mood, although he was still pissed when Enrique swung by the hotel. The ride along the maze of freeways to the 118 had been strained. Everything either one of them said came out like bitter poison. Finally, they'd just stopped talking.

Chase wished he knew what to say to make it all better. He just sucked at the whole relationship gig. Not that they had a relationship. A friendship, with benefits, and they worked together on this Special. If it hadn't been for the assignment, Chase probably would have just blown Enrique off. A small, nagging section of his brain told him maybe not.

Once off the freeway, they'd wound into the bone-dry foothills. Wind buffeted the sedan. After a few miles, Enrique pulled to the lip of the road near a jumble of sandstone boulders. Ahead and behind, cars in various states of disrepair lined the dirt road. Enrique slid out of the unmarked. Before slamming the driver's door, he reached back onto the seat and grabbed a paper bag. Then he was off.

Chase shut his own door with a little less force. He jammed his hands in his pockets and picked his way down a dusty, not-quite-gravel drive. Every so often he'd catch the glimpse of a building between the boulders or through scraggly branches of scrub pines. At the first bend Enrique paused. A few candles in tall glass jars painted with the now familiar images of saints flickered in the shadows of early evening.

Scattered across a small stand of boulders, cracked china held crumbs of food and drink. Enrique pulled a small bundle of paper, two candy bars and a small bottle of rum out of the bag. The bag he tossed to the side, before he handed the candy and booze to Chase. Then he unwrapped a bit of meat and bread that looked saved from a lunchtime sandwich. Crouching on his heels, his fingers moved from forehead to heart and then touched each shoulder. With that he tossed the leftovers onto one of the plates. He stood and began to walk farther up the path.

Chase jogged after him. "What was that for?" Curiosity overwhelmed his fading anger.

Enrique shrugged and answered. "Feeding the dead." He didn't look back.

"What?"

With a huff, Enrique stopped and turned. When Chase caught up, he answered. "We must feed the dead to keep them away. Honor them."

"With leftovers?"

"And cracked plates." Enrique offered up a half-smile. The moon flooded his features with a soft, mystical light. It took Chase's breath away. "They must be fed, but we can never let them forget that they are dead…the world of the living holds nothing for them."

Chase desperately wanted to know exactly how deep into this whole Santeria thing Enrique was. A cop's knowledge-base from studying up was one thing. This, this was a practicing man's familiarity. Instead he bounced the two candy bars in his hand and waved the bottle in the air. "What are these for then?" They didn't have time for philosophy. And, like politics, probing someone's devotional ideology could get you into a mucky, too-much-information discussion. Chase would stick to what he needed to deal with the ceremony they headed toward.

"For Eshu." Enrique turned off on a side path.

Chase stopped dead in the road. "Eshu? Didn't you say that Eshu was like the devil?"

Enrique snorted, "I don't ask him for things very often, but when I do he knows it's important." Then he stopped and turned. "Do you believe in the devil, Chase?"

"I don't know."

"Not knowing is okay. If you did not believe then you could not come with me. It would harm the offering." The world was black. "I think that you are a spiritualist," delivered with satisfaction, "You have the signs."

"What do you mean signs?"

"You don't make fun of my religion or say it's sick. There's no way in hell I'd let someone from the station follow me around like this...I mean, where I'm actually somewhat participating." Enrique kicked the dust at their feet and jammed his hands into his pockets. It made him look like some nervous kid, especially without his sidearm. "You just know which things, people, should get respect. You seek the balance and trust of the people you talk to. And they trust you." He paused, took a breath and shrugged. "You have the right light over your soul."

"You see a light around my soul." Although Chase tried not to be judgmental, each word got its own emphasis.

"Sometimes," Enrique nodded and then continued in a rush, "when I'm not looking for it. It is very bright and blue-white. It is a good light." He added before walking away.

Chase had no idea what could be said to a statement like that. Not cop talk, that was for certain. It was unsettling and comforting all at the same time. Yeah, Enrique basically admitted to seeing things, but they were good things, a positive influence emanating from Chase. Nothing really seemed appropriate to say, so Chase just followed Enrique. Silence ate up the space between them.

Sand skidded beneath their shoes as they stepped off the drive and took a foot trail that dipped down into a wash. White plastic gone to yellow, pinks and blues faded to almost gray under the moonlight, a cheap child's playhouse squatted in a grove of scrub. First Chase thought it was a dumpsite. The area about the plastic hut was strewn with toys and beads and bottles. When they were closer he realized it wasn't trash. Melted wax covered the stones around the warped structure. Candles in painted glass holders flickered among bottles of rum and plates bearing offerings of sweets. Deep in the recesses of the house, a ragged devil mask presided over an altar of stones. The flames made its eyes dance and wink at them.

Enrique knelt, motioning for Chase to do the same. Chase started to speak and was halted by Enrique's fingers on his lips. Fishing a broken bit of candle from his pocket, Enrique lit it with a sputtering taper stuck on a rock. Wax pooled on another stone as he twirled the candle in his dark fingers. Then he jammed the votive into the wax. Enrique motioned for the candy and Chase handed it over. With little ceremony Enrique opened the chocolate and tossed the wrappers aside. Both bars were stacked below the candle.

"*Eshu, mi padrino*," Enrique mumbled the words with reverence of a prayer. "I need your help…only you can help me. Someone has taken a girl. Maybe this girl thought the man she was with was a good man. Maybe he was a good man once. But whoever he was when she first met him, he's not that man now. And she's in trouble." Still, Enrique's tone was friendly, like he was speaking with a lover or a friend, not a god. He turned and took the bottle from Chase. The crack of the seal echoed loud around them. "We need to find this girl, help her. We want to bring him to justice and we need her to do it. He has done many bad things, and many voices cry to you for your help. I believe in you. I need you. I know you can help me." Now he started to wheedle. "See what I have brought for you, rum, good rum, the best I could buy. Have a drink, Eshu." Enrique poured a bit of the bottle at the base of the rock.

The stench of rum hitting earth rose about them and Chase's mouth started to water. From his shirt pocket Enrique pulled two wallet-sized prints. "This, this is a picture of the girl Carmen." He rested that against the candle. The other he slid under the candy. "And here is a picture of the man we think is keeping her. So you will know them. So you can find them. So we can find them." Six candles were set in a circle, each one lit with a new match. They surrounded the first candle, candy and the photo printouts.

"And I brought the candy, something sweet. My friend, he bought them for you." Enrique turned and smiled up at Chase. "He is a good person, a very nice person." Now Enrique gave his attention back to the little, plastic hut with the flames dancing about. "If you need something, *padrino*, you can count on him for help." Chase took two steps back. Maybe if he got far enough from the circle, the devil wouldn't see him. It was an insane and stupid feeling, but strong all the same. Enrique had better not use his name. The last person, thing, god, he wanted calling on him for favors was the Prince of Evil himself.

Enrique stood, wiping dirt on his thighs. He spun on his heel, striding towards Chase and grabbing him roughly. "Walk away. Don't look back, FBI. We just go back up the trail." Chase scrambled after him. When they made the main path again, Enrique stopped. "What did you want to ask, Chase?"

"That…" he pointed back where they'd come from, "that was a shrine to the devil."

Shrugging, "Yes and no, Eshu is not the devil. Bad things can come from Eshu if you do not treat him with respect. So you must keep Eshu happy so that he does not cause problems." He waved back towards the shrine. "If he has his sweet things there, then he will not come into the house," Enrique pointed toward the house above them, "and make the ceremony go bad. He also knows the evil of men." With a huff, he started walking again. "If you are a good man, and you want to find a bad man, you ask Eshu for help."

A fairly plain ranch-style house hulked on a rise at the end of the drive. Light spilled across a beaten dirt yard from an open doorway at the side of the attached garage. Chase dropped his voice to a whisper. "Do you believe in this stuff?" Okay, polite social boundaries and work were heading to a four car pileup. It was time to just bite the bullet and ask.

"Do you believe in God?" Enrique's voice echoed the softness. It was as though neither wanted to offend anyone living, dead or otherwise. Their footfalls crunched in the gravel. It was a very lonely sound in the night.

Chase thought, really thought about the question. He'd done church with his parents. He couldn't wrap his mind around the concept of all powerful, all knowing and pretty ambivalent beings. Still, the universe was damn big. Finally, Chase admitted, "I don't know."

"Neither do I. I have seen some very strange things. I know enough that this is special to me, that I will respect it, this part of me. And, most importantly, our witness believes and circulates among groups of believers."

The closer they got, the more fear nestled into Chase's chest. He felt naked and exposed without his gun. Enrique claimed the Santero insisted they come unarmed. It would disturb the saints, the ceremony. Chase grudgingly obliged and hoped to hell he didn't have occasion to regret it.

"Why, exactly, are we here?" There was the strange and unusual that the FBI prepared you for. This wasn't it. Each step though this investigation ended up weirder than the last. And given the performance at Dr. Jonas' clinic, Chase doubted he'd be at all prepared for any of this. "Couldn't we have just arranged to talk to DeVaca?" He winced at the whine in his own voice. Last thing he wanted was for Enrique to think he was a wuss. Damn, the man already had him pegged for a drunk. A drunk with no balls meant a liability in any crises. Hell, either meant a liability; the combination could be fatal.

"He said we needed to come tonight. That we didn't need to talk to him. We needed to consult with the Orishas. They will tell us what we need to know." Enrique took a breath and smiled back at Chase. As if he sensed Chase's nervousness, he added, "It's okay. Think of it like a holy roller service or something."

For a moment, Chase tried to make the connection. He failed and sputtered out, "Holy roller?"

"Yeah, you know." Enrique damn near whispered the last of it as he stepped to the door. "Flopping on the floor, speaking in tongues."

"Does that happen?" Chase hissed the question back.

Enrique shrugged. "Sort of." Further discussion was cut off as a short, wide, blonde woman stepped up. "DeVaca," Enrique anticipated a question that didn't seem to have been asked. "He told us to come tonight."

She smiled and pointed to her left. Men filled benches made from boards stretched between cinderblocks. Chase opened his mouth to thank her, but stopped when she raised her finger to her lips. Pointing to the front of the room, Chase realized the ceremony already had started. A whip-thin man dressed in a white shirt and slacks spoke in hushed tones.

The altar at the front of the converted garage was grander than the one Chase had seen before. It was no less haphazard. Here, however, the entire congregation obviously worked to make it impressive. Wedding cake tiers rose from the floor. Beaded shawls, lace curtains and embroidered tablecloths in various colors covered wood planks strung between cinderblocks. Large statues of saints, some plaster, others cement, were arranged between lidded bowls. Huge *collares* in every color spilled over their lids and bases.

Enrique pulled Chase near the front. Chase would have preferred the back, but there weren't any seats. As they settled onto a bit of bench, Enrique pointed to the man, "That is the Santorio," he whispered. "DeVaca." As they moved through their quiet entreaties, Enrique fed Chase bits of what was happening.

First Eshu received his offering. A young man, his gut spilling out from under a white shirt, appeared with a plate of corn tortillas. Waddling in behind him, an older woman cradled several bottles of good rum.

Chase licked his lips. His mouth watered. Damn, he could use a belt.

The Santorio, DeVaca, placed his hand on the food and drink, blessing it. He entreated Eshu to guard the gate and not let the ceremony be disrupted. Then his assistants, heads bowed, went out into the night with the offerings. Just how they would find that dark little path to Eshu's hut, Chase had no idea. He also had no doubt that they were headed there.

With a low rumble, the drums began to talk. Chase jerked. He hadn't seen the men sitting on the floor. Several had large cone shaped drums cradled between their knees. Another held a huge gourd, its belly wrapped in a net of beads. Dark and light hands beat out a rhythm. In Chase's mind, it called up the threads of the Latino rap Enrique listened to. From the door where the earlier assistants had come, a row of dancers, all women, slipped into the room. Black, white, brown and every hue in between; Santeria, at least the Los Angeles version, seemed an equal opportunity religion.

DeVaca started a chant praising God. His voice boomed about the room as he raised his hands to the heavens. The dancers chimed in with silken, shrill voices. Clapping their hands to the rhythm of the drums they circled counterclockwise around him. The next chant went up to Jesus. Chase only understood by the name that was shouted out. Otherwise, his minimal Spanish was overwhelmed. And the words didn't really sound all that much like Spanish.

At the sound of DeVaca's call, the drums and dancers changed pace. They switched direction, waving their hands in the air, clapping their palms together and sounding the beat with their feet. The Blessed Virgin and the saints all got their prayers as well.

Hymns for God and Christ were repeated for Olorun, the creator and Olofi, the creation. Chase recognized a few of the refrains, the names chanted over and over. With each new prayer the tempo altered, the emotional cadence switched and the dance reversed. But the dancers, the drums, the rattle of the beads against the gourds, the singing never stopped. Supplicants crawled from the crowd to kiss the drums before scurrying back to their seats. The pace changed and swelled. Burrowing into the bones of the congregation, the building swayed to the rhythm. Each Orisha was flattered with the song of his saint.

Again the beat changed. Faster, harder the *batas*, what Enrique called the drums, began taunting. DeVaca's voice went from respectful to mocking. His songs teased and insulted, coaxing the spirits down into his flock. The dancers' moves turned seductive. Hips rocked in counter-tempo to shoulder rolls. Breasts shook. Women's hair came loose as they whipped around. Even the ground rocked with the rhythm.

A man next to Chase groaned, tossing his head back. His companions pushed the man's face between his legs. Sweat drenched his shirt as he twitched, shivered. Someone grabbed his arms and crossed them behind the man's neck. A woman blew on his ears. His friends pulled him off the bench, almost running over Chase, as they hurried him out of the room.

Chase shifted on the bench. People prostrated themselves on the floor, kissing the concrete. They clapped in time to the beat with faces turned to the sky. Entreating voices followed the Santorio's song. A woman across the room screamed, stood and fell limp on the ground. The air suddenly felt heavy and charged. It flared about the room, licking the hair up from Chase's skin.

The dancers whirled about the Santorio in a cyclone of sound. Then one girl stumbled. The dancers hardly seemed to notice her as she reeled from their midst. She stood and shook her head. Moving back to the circle of dancers, she tried to regain the beat. A turn. Then another. Her legs would not obey her. Again she fell. DeVaca caught her. The other dancers kept stomping out the beat of the drums. She scratched at her body like ants swarmed under her skin. Although he held her, the Santorio did not try to restrain her.

The drums worked into Chase's blood. It was hard to breathe. He needed air. He needed to get out. He had to get out now! The rising tide of panic swelled and his mouth went dry with need. God, he wanted a fucking drink, something had to pull the feelings back—drown them out. Chase stood and stumbled to the door. Enrique followed.

Enrique's hand was warm on Chase's clammy skin. "Are you okay, Chase?"

"Yeah." He gulped down the scent of the desert beyond. "I think. I just needed some air." Not as good as a hard shot of whisky, but fresh air would work for now, even if it tasted of the fires still tearing through the hills.

"Air is good." Enrique's fingers worked on the back of his neck. "Just stay inside please." Concern wound in his voice, "It's not safe to go outside, not alone."

"Sure." No shit it wasn't safe. They were in the middle of the freaking desert in Simi Valley. It wasn't someplace you wanted to take a stroll among the rattlesnakes and coyotes. Chase palmed his face and then turned and smiled at Enrique.

Bracing his back on the frame he said, "I'm good. This is just, well more than I'm used to dealing with." Pointing towards the girl writhing on the floor. "That's just freaky shit." Older women fanned her with their skirts as a large man grabbed her under her arms and pulled her toward the rear door.

Another stroke on Chase's neck was meant to calm him, "She is being touched by the Orishas. The god is riding her." The words did anything but calm Chase. "But she is not initiated; they will take her away from the drums."

Chase felt a tug on his slacks. Startled, he looked down to see a little girl with a cherub's face. Thick, black hair was French-braided in twin tails down her back. Purple ribbons fastened into bows held the ends. Crochet insets on the chest and sleeves of her simple cotton dress transformed it into something exotic. Another gold ribbon drew the material in at her waist. She let go of his pants and patted a vacant space on the bench. With her gap-toothed smile, she beckoned Chase to her side. It would be nice to take a place farther from the chaos at the altar, back where he could breathe.

Chase sat down, heavily, next to the child. Ropes of alternating black and white beads, others of brown and still more of maroon draped over the front of her bright white dress. She touched his hair, sweeping her finger across his blue eyes, before lighting on the beaded collar the *Curandera* had given him. Pure laughter floated about them. Tiny hands cupped his ears as she pulled his forehead to touch hers. She whispered something. With the drums so loud, Chase couldn't make out the words.

Her skin smelled like jasmine.

Her hair smelled like soap.

Her hands felt like fire on his skin.

Chase jerked back. He blinked. The child became a woman, a beautiful black woman with almond eyes. "You are a warrior, but not Ochossi's warrior." Her fingers laced into the *collare* about his neck. With a honeyed laugh, she ripped the necklace from Chase's throat. Turquoise and brass beads scattered across the floor. "You are for me. I protect you." The voice was ages older than the girl who spoke. "Remember he will never be faithful, but you will always be first. You alone will have his love." She slipped one of her *collares* over her head. Maroon beads clicked as she fastened the short length around Chase's neck. Unable to even scream, he fell backwards off the bench. White light tore through his body. Chase felt himself ripped apart and thrown back together a hundred times over.

Enrique's arm slipped about his shoulder. "Do you see her?" he hissed.

"Yes." Both of them were breathing hard. Chase thought his heart might rip itself loose and careen about his chest.

"So do I."

The woman/child dropped to her knees, trembling and swaying in time to the drums. Two older women appeared at her side. Chase hadn't seen them approach. One took the girl's hands, rubbing them with her own. Voice heavy and thick, Enrique whispered in Chase's ear, "It is Oyá, Shango's lover." The other woman blew cigarette smoke across the girl's face and shoulders. Her small body jerked, twisted then stilled.

Enrique began to shake. He stood, stepped away and stumbled toward the altar. Chase twisted to his knees. As he watched, the dancers parted, allowing Enrique into their circle. Every inch of his body trembled. Brown eyes rolled back until nothing but white showed. A shrill scream, trilling up and over the scale, broke from his throat. His body arched, bowing, until his black hair swept the floor behind him. It was as though giant hands held him at the head and feet, pulling.

Chase jumped up, and found himself pinned by the child. "No," the old/young woman's voice warned. Her arms were a vice around his waist. She couldn't have weighed more than fifty pounds. Yet she restrained him like a mule chained to a plowshare. "Don't." She hissed, "The Orisha is seating himself." Futilely, the hands of the old women clawed at her fingers where they dug into Chase's skin.

Snapping upright, Enrique screamed. He leapt into the air. Feet landed heavy, already pounding out the beat of the drums. The women circled him. Their bare soles added to the intensity of the rhythm. Dust rose in a cloud around their legs. Enrique's hips started to rock. A shudder passed through his frame. Another followed on the heels of the first. Skirts twirled. An undulating rainbow swept across the floor. Every time the fabric brushed his legs, Enrique jerked like he'd touched an electric fence.

As one, the children fell to their knees and extended tiny arms to the heavens. Men prostrated themselves on the floor. Women threw themselves, weeping, onto their sides, arms flung over their eyes. A chant began, rising over the throb of the drums. Cries of "*Kabiesile!*" and "*Oba ko so!*"

"What are they saying?"

"Praise the King," the girl whispered, her breath burning across Chase's skin. "The King is not hung!" Chase wrenched himself out of her grasp.

A man bundled the little girl into his arms, dragging her from Chase's side. Quickly, he picked her up and headed to the front. DeVaca stepped forward to intercept them. Hushed tones, heavy expressions; the way they conversed told Chase they were scared. Something was wrong. Two older men and a young woman rushed to them. They wrapped the child in a shawl and slipped through the door from where the dancers had come, leaving DeVaca to control the confusion.

Another woman began writhing. Pulling at her hair and screaming, she ran into the middle of the dancers. DeVaca caught her and spun her off into the arms of an elderly man. Gently, he slapped her face and she went limp. The man slid her to the ground out of the way of the whirling dancers.

The drums became even more urgent. Possessed by God knew what force, Enrique spun and jumped. His heels never ceased to stomp out the rhythm. Women crawled from the crowd to kiss the ground where his feet had landed. They threw themselves on him to be caught up in a rough, gyrating embrace and then tossed away. From every mouth came screams and yells.

Chase crept along the wall. When he found the corner, he wedged himself into it. With his back against something solid maybe, maybe he could make it through the night. The drums pounded in his head. He bit his bottom lip to keep them at bay. Drawing his knees to his chest, Chase prayed to stay safe. The skin on his arms crawled. The drums, the dancing threatened to pull him under. The air was charged. If someone lit a match, the place would explode.

Drum beats throbbed down Chase's spine. He couldn't stop. His muscles twitched, trying to rise, to dance with the drums. Chase locked his fingers into his arms, dug into the skin with his nails, using pain to fight the lure of the drums.

Every inch of his soul rattled in time to the shush of the beads over the skin of the gourd. His heart only beat when the dancers' feet hit the floor. It reached into his gut and tugged, enticing him with sweet lies of rapture, forgiveness—in a moment of chaos, finding pure clarity. The shrill, repetitive cadence of song broke in waves against his senses. Like heavy surf, it rolled him in its fist until he lost his sense of up, down or even self. 'Come lover, come dance,' the collective voice coaxed.

Sudden, shattering, the drums stopped. An agonizing crescendo of silence thundered about Chase. Dancers dropped to the floor like marionettes with cut strings. Mournful, DeVaca's voice rose in an accapella wail. Enrique, eyes wide, slumped onto his hands and knees. He shook his head.

As DeVaca's slow chant pulled the fingers of tension from the room, two older women ran to Enrique. One, thumb pressed half-over the mouth of an old style soda bottle, sprinkled him with liquid. The other woman knelt, cupped Enrique's face in her hands and blew across his forehead.

When Chase stood, he thought his knees might give. He managed to stagger to the front on rubber legs. As he dropped next to Enrique, the scent of Juicy Fruit gum hit Chase hard. The sense that Jason was with him welled up in the smell of cinnamon and flowers. He could almost see his former partner rolling his eyes and folding the gum into his mouth.

God, what would Jason think of him now, drunk almost every night, fighting the demons in his head? Chase had been the squeaky clean, oh-so-proper agent then. Well he'd been gay, but Jason knew and hadn't cared and hadn't talked. Chase's secret went to the grave with his partner. With Jason gone, Chase's security in the closet, confidence in his skills and sense of self slipped inch-by-inch. His breath caught and he shuddered from the almost physical sense of *presence*.

A hand settled between Chase's shoulders and he jerked. It took a moment for his brain to process that someone other than the invisible specter of Jason Olhms touched him. He glanced up and caught the edge of worry etched behind the eyes of the Santorio, DeVaca. "How is your friend?" DeVaca's deep and comforting voice vanquished the eerie feeling of a ghostly visit.

"I don't know." Chase pushed the hair out of Enrique's fevered eyes. His skin felt clammy under Chase's touch. "How you doing?" Actually, Chase couldn't be certain whether it was himself or Enrique with the clammy skin. That brief feeling of Jason being there next to him had shaken him more than he wanted to admit.

Enrique palmed his face, catching Chase's hand in his own. The barest tremble carried through the touch. "I feel very rested and a little fuzzy. Okay, I guess."

Moving closer to Enrique, DeVaca placed a thumb below the detective's eye, pulling the skin down. He studied Enrique for a moment before announcing, "You are not initiated."

"No." Enrique started to stand. Both Chase and DeVaca helped him as they gained their own feet. "I am not." There was a little bit of shake in Enrique. Chase sensed it through the hold he had on Enrique's left arm and shoulder.

"You should be." DeVaca patted Enrique's other arm before releasing his own supportive grip. He frowned and stepped back. "The Orishas rode who they wished tonight, taking those they should not have."

"You mean this isn't normal?"

"To have people mounted, yes, if the drums do their job. But they are those who have been trained to receive them. Sometimes they miss and try to take someone who has not received the *Ekles*. We take those people away from the drums and it stops. Or we chase them off."

Chase did not like the tone in the Santero's voice. "So, it's not supposed to be like this."

"No, not like tonight." DeVaca crossed his arms over his chest and scowled. "And there are problems."

Holy crap, problems? Chase had a problem with everything he'd seen, heard, felt. He wanted to go back to the hotel and drink the feelings into submission. Instead he asked, "What problems?"

DeVaca glanced toward the doorway where they'd taken the little girl. "She will not leave until she speaks with you."

"Who won't leave?"

"Oyá, she will not leave the little girl until she speaks with you." If anything the scowl became more intense. "It is not good for one so young to be ridden by an Orisha."

"What do you mean?" Chase squeezed Enrique's bicep. It gave him something tangible, normal and comforting to hold on to.

Enrique spoke up. "They should not seat themselves on children."

Blowing out his breath, DeVaca unlaced his arms and ran a hand through his graying hair. "Sometimes," he explained in the patient tone of voice that priests, doctors and teachers cultivated, "the Orishas do not pay attention and we drive them out. She will not go. You must speak with her."

Chase looked to Enrique, who shrugged. What harm could there be? Maybe the girl was just as freaked out by the whole thing as Chase. It might help her let go of her fear. She'd seemed fixated on Chase and maybe needed that one last contact to settle down. Chase nodded and indicated with a wave of his hand that DeVaca should lead them.

The Santero turned and hurried through the rear door. Chase headed after him, fast enough not to lose sight but slow enough to make sure Enrique could manage. They followed DeVaca into a laundry room and then a short hall. A door opened to the left and DeVaca disappeared into the opening. Chase and Enrique stepped in behind. Floral prints and cheap furniture overwhelmed a tiny bedroom. The little girl sat in the middle of a printed field of roses and vines. Her tight braids had come loose and her thick, black hair fell across her shoulders. Multi colored strings of beads rested in her lap. She ran her fingers through them as though they were precious jewels. One of the old women from the other room sat in a rocker off to one side.

With a grunt, DeVaca eased himself to his knees onto a worn area rug woven in pinks and golds. The colors jarred with the blue carpet beneath. Enrique followed suit. Not knowing what else to do, Chase knelt as well. When the other two men pressed their foreheads to the floor, Chase didn't go that far down.

"You've brought him." Like he was a willful child, the girl smiled at Chase with tight lips and narrowed eyes, the sort of look women gave precocious and spoiled children who misbehaved. Ignoring DeVaca and Enrique, she held her hand out to Chase. "Come sit with me, pretty man."

Pretty wasn't a word he would have used to describe himself. Beat up, mature, aging not-so-gracefully, maybe a bit of the *daddy* thing going on, but pretty...no. "You are Oyá?" Chase hoped that he didn't mangle the pronunciation of the name. As Chase eased himself up off the floor, he added, "Look, I'm here." Enrique grunted as he stood and Chase reached down to help. Looking annoyed, Enrique waved him off. Chase turned his attention to the girl on the bed. "The ceremony's over. Why don't you leave this little girl alone?"

Rolling her eyes, she held her hand out. Slowly curling fingers beckoned Chase. "Listen to me and I will." Eons of command no child could know echoed in her voice. "I do not desire to keep this child."

Chase eased himself onto the edge of the bed. The hair on his arm, the one close to the girl, prickled. "Why did you take her then?"

"Because she was close to you, silly pretty man." Oyá chided with a world-wise woman's tone and little girl's voice. "Remember this," she reached out and tapped Chase's forehead with tiny fingers, "will overcome this," the touch drifted down to settle briefly against the empty holster rig on his belt, "always."

If that's what it took, Chase would do it. "Okay, talk to me." For the life of him, he couldn't figure out why she creeped him out so much. She'd just become overwhelmed by the drums, like he'd almost been.

"You look for a girl." Oyá took Chase's big hands in her tiny ones. The sense that thin, elegant fingers gripped his skin beyond that of the actual contact crawled over Chase's soul. "She cries out to us, we hear her. The *Endoki* are about her."

"*Endoki?*"

DeVaca whispered, near his ear. "Ghosts, dead who have been bound to serve a *Palero*." Chase started. He hadn't realized how close the other two men had come. DeVaca knelt at the edge of the bed.

Enrique's thigh pressed against Chase's leg as he took a seat beside him. "*Paleros*, followers of the paths of *Palo Mayumbe*." As though the word had a bad taste, Enrique scowled. "It is like *Santeria*, but not like *Santeria*. *Palo* uses the dead. *Santeria* does not. The dead know nothing more than they did when they lived. To ask them for help is to ask a blind man for directions. But, the drums and some things are the same, used by the followers of *Palo Mayumbe* to control the spirits of the dead, make them serve them. They take things from the dead. Sometimes bones, sometimes something special to them and force them to do what they say."

"Are we talking black magic?" Chase tried to pull his hands from Oyá's grip and couldn't.

"Sometimes." This time DeVaca answered. "Magic only is...the man who uses it makes it bad or good."

"I can hear her." Oyá snapped, cutting off further explanation. "She is in a place she has been to many times. There she saw things, did things. I think that she was one of them. Those who guard her are men who are no longer men. Someone you know is with her. He is not happy and wants you to find them. But he knows only what he saw, not what he sees now. The numbers add up the same he says, remember that." Chase tried to wrap his mind around what she might mean. "In her brother's car, she had a book. She drew things in this book, kept her thoughts in it." Almost pleading with Chase, she leaned in and dropped her voice to a husky whisper. "The men who took her, I think they must have left this car before they could find it, because she says you must find this book. If you find it, you will find her." The grip on his hands was a vice.

"Where is the car?" Chase couldn't believe he asked that. How would she know?

"Not far from where her brother was when you found him." She shook her head and closed her eyes tight, as though she were shutting out something she did not want to see. "I think you already have it, but you have not connected it to him. I see it with many, many other cars."

"If you can see the car, why can't you see her?"

Her eyes flew open. Intense, she stared at Chase. "Silly man," Her rebuke cut him sharp for his doubt, "I can see her. I see dark walls and tall grass. Rocks and trees and a red dirt road. I smell smoke, much smoke. But I do not see enough to tell you where she is."

"No street signs?"

Again her voice slapped him. "Don't tease me, silly man. I protect you, even if you do not wish to believe. Find the car and you will find her." She leaned in. "You only have a few more days. He's waiting for the souls to come home. That is when he will take her."

CHAPTER FOURTEEN

"There's freaky and then there's freaky." Chase rubbed his temples and tried not to stare at the miniature altar above the bookcase. After the night he'd had, the little bits of religion, even the *collare* he still wore seemed odd and tainted with power. He didn't understand it. Didn't want to understand it. Creepy, spooky, the world had expanded an inch in every direction. Chase wished he knew how to force it back down into the comforting little box reality had been before.

Ice rattled in a glass by his ear. "So this was freaky then?" Chase looked up to find Enrique smiling down at him and holding out a glass of amber liquid.

"Yeah," He blew out some of the angst burrowing into his chest, "Just a bit." Reaching up to take the drink, the cool glass and Enrique's warm skin against his fingers reminded him that there were still bits of sanity in the world.

Enrique flopped onto the couch next to him. "Why do you think it was freaky?"

"I mean, there's all these people that were so intent on believing something was going to happen that things got weird." So weird that Chase hadn't wanted to spend the night alone. He'd almost begged Enrique not to leave him. God, and now surrounded by a normal house with stains in the carpet and holes in the sofa, he felt like such a wuss. Chase rolled his eyes and downed a belt. The burn felt oddly disquieting.

Enrique mumbled. "Like what?" Sounded like he was half asleep already.

If Chase could just stop jangling, he figured he'd have been at that state. "What do you mean like what?" Bone weary and amped all at once. Even the booze didn't seem to damp it. "The little girl all pretending she's some goddess and everyone's buying into that. And then you're jumping around like some tweaker on PCP." Maybe another two or three might push Chase into the I-don't-give-a-fuck state so he could sleep.

"I don't remember it." The sigh sounded frustrated. Whether it was because Chase kept talking or because Enrique thought he should recall events and couldn't, Chase couldn't figure out.

Instead, he picked. "You don't remember it…any of it?" He knew he didn't want to go to bed yet. He wasn't half hammered enough to forget everything enough to sleep.

"I remember the little girl and her eyes while we were back in the benches near the door." Enrique roused himself enough to sit up and glare at Chase. "And then I remember being on the floor and wet and you're asking me if I'm okay. I felt odd, like I overslept or like when your head's all fuzzy because you have *la gripa*. But I also felt very calm, peaceful. After that I remember talking with Oyá."

"I'm sorry I'm bugging you." Chase shrugged before polishing off the last of his drink. "I'm just trying to get a handle on it all. Understand it, you know, rationally."

Enrique nodded and patted Chase's thigh. "There is no way to understand it, Chase." Leaning in, sliding his arm around Chase's shoulder, he added, "Just accept that something a little bigger than us happened."

The contact felt good. Better than the booze and that said a lot. "But things like tonight," Chase protested more for his own ears than Enrique's, "they don't happen."

With a shift, Enrique pulled Chase a little closer. "They don't happen because people refuse to believe they happen." His fingers tightened against Chase's leg, adding another small bit of comfort. "Things just as strange and wonderful occur every day and we're too busy to see them. That's all it is."

Chase couldn't believe it was all that easy. "Something took you over. Doesn't that frighten you?"

"I know," Enrique's warm, tired smile said more than his words. "And no it doesn't frighten me. I feel very small right now, a little overwhelmed, but not scared. Because this is a faith

I believe in." He patted Chase's leg. "Would a Holy Roller be frightened if they started speaking in tongues during a service? Nothing like this has ever happened to me before. But I accept that it does happen, so that it happened to me is not so scary." Then he leaned in and nuzzled Chase's neck. "Come on, *Compa*, let's put those monsters back in the closet. I'm tired. Come to bed." As he stood, Enrique took Chase's glass and set on the table. Walking away, he shucked his shirt, only pausing at the door to the bedroom, as if to make sure Chase followed.

With a groan, Chase rose from the couch. Damn, his knees didn't like him anymore. They weren't bad. They just chose to remind him by popping and creaking how long ago it'd been since he'd seen the backside of twenty. "So, you're ready for sleeping huh?"

"Or," Enrique's voice called him into the bedroom, "maybe something before sleeping."

"You know," Chase yanked off his tie and began to unbutton his shirt, "I've had more sex in the past month than I think I've had in the prior year." The *collare* rubbed against his collarbone. Chase reached around and unhooked it, dropping it into his shirt pocket.

Enrique's shorts and slacks hit the floor and he stepped out of them with a salacious grin. "Complaining, old man?"

Damn, Chase just stared. Every time he saw Enrique, it just rocked him. He could imagine waking up to that body for years to come. For once, that thought didn't knock the wind out of him. Instead, he eased out of his shirt and shot the leer right back. "Nope, no complaining here." Fighting with his belt buckle, Chase stepped to the bed. When it finally came undone, he dropped onto the mattress and wriggled out of the rest of his clothes.

Enrique stood above him, his prick already half-hard. Chase thought about thirty ways to get him the rest of the way there. "Man, Chase," Enrique teased as he headed to the nightstand to get what they needed. "You look like a fish just flopping about doing that." First he set his own *collare* on the wood, where it couldn't fall to the floor. Then he dug out and tossed the more sexual paraphernalia on the sheets next to Chase.

"Shut up and get that ass over here."

"Grumpy old man," Enrique straddled Chase. "Getting pushy with me." He bent down, hands to either side of Chase's chest, and ground their hips together. Then he moved closer still to devour Chase's mouth in one of those demanding, burning kisses that shoved the night's events from Chase's mind.

Pushing his tongue between those sensual lips, Chase ran his hands back to grip Enrique's tight ass. For a guy in his thirties, Enrique had the butt of a twenty-year-old. He pulled Enrique's cheeks apart, kneading them with his hands. Firm and fuckable, just needing to be pounded. Letting go with one hand, Chase felt around to find what he needed.

Enrique's prick slid against Chase's stomach. Little trails of wet heat burned up his abs with each thrust. It damn near distracted him from getting ready, not an easy job one-handed, even without the humping. And Enrique wouldn't let him breathe. Their tongues twisted around each other, ramping up the sensations. Finally, he got it open and rolled down.

Enrique, like he sensed it, broke the kiss and pulled away. He scooted back the few necessary inches. That dark body all tense and waiting, smoldering dark eyes, and a fat cock up and begging for Chase, fuck, Enrique just had everything Chase ever wanted. He was falling for Enrique, in a desperate and needful way. Damn, to be this fucked up for a guy he'd met not a few weeks ago…it didn't make much sense. Life rarely made much sense though. Sometimes you just ran with it and figured things out later.

Chase used his hand to steady his prick, center it just right. He brushed Enrique's hole and hissed. Then, slow and easy, Enrique rocked himself down. Tight heat swallowed Chase's dick and he let go, figuring Enrique could manage from there. Instead he let his hands wander across tense thighs and belly. Enrique's skin was so warm, covered in a sheen of sweat with a layer of hard muscle hidden by just enough softness to make it comfortable. A working man's body, a cop's body, not a gym rat. And the way Enrique moved, it was like he knew just how to rock Chase hard.

Chase hissed. "Damn it."

"What?" Enrique managed in between little satisfied moans.

"I need you too much." It was hard to talk, but if he tried any time but now, Chase wouldn't ever get it out. Sex stripped his inhibitions better than scotch. "I don't want to finish, leave LA." Enrique shifted and a groan welled up out of Chase's chest. When he could manage again, "Don't want to leave you."

Enrique stilled, their hips pressed together, Chase's prick buried inside his body. How sexy he was, that cock straining, his balls resting heavy on Chase's skin. "*Compa*," Enrique panted, "you ain't the only one. Something says, you and I, we'll manage."

"Yeah." A smile twisted Chase's lips and he reached out to give Enrique's prick a stroke. "Okay, enough talking, huh?" Twisting Enrique's cock through his fist made the man shudder. That shudder lit fires all through Chase.

Enrique snorted and leaned over again. "Yep." He growled and began to rock. With this position, Chase could help instead of just lie there and let Enrique ride. He bent his knees to get some purchase and then began to pound. Their hips slammed together. Chase pumped the cock in his hand. With everything, he wasn't certain it helped much, but he loved the feel of stroking a guy's meat while he fucked them. That it was Enrique sent him soaring.

Chase swam in the rolling tide of pleasure sweeping from his balls to toes. His whole body tensed. For a moment he forgot how to breathe. Ecstasy pumped from his soul and out through his prick. When he could focus again, Chase found that Enrique's fingers had replaced his. The muscles of Enrique's stomach danced as his hand flew over his cock and he bounced on Chase's dick. Chase grabbed his hips and gave Enrique what he had left, pounding while aftershocks slid over his nerves. Enrique shuddered and spunk spilled over his fingers.

They both panted hard. Chase wormed his fingers over the cum-slick head of Enrique's prick and Enrique shivered under his touch. "Damn," he managed to wheeze out, "that was a work out."

"For you?" Enrique slumped onto his chest and Chase's softening dick slid out of Enrique's hole. "*Compa,* all you did was lay there. I did all the work."

Chase nuzzled Enrique's sweat damp hair. "Okay. Next time you can fuck me."

The snort blew warm across Chase's skin. "And I'll probably end up doing the work then, too."

"Well." Heavy, the day settled onto Chase's shoulders. "You young'uns gotta take care of us old fogies." With a yawn, he added, "Or maybe I just got to take care of you some. Make sure you remember I'm around."

"Couldn't forget that if I tried." Enrique mumbled. "I've gotten a little too used to you, Chase." Enrique slid off his body and ran a hand through his dark hair. "Nice not to have to explain my life to some idiot who's never worn a badge." He leaned back and offered a quick kiss as Chase pulled the condom off. Taking the used rubber from Chase, he stood. "Be back in a minute. Don't go to sleep without me."

Try as he could, Chase couldn't help drifting off into dreams of fire-eyed women, shuffling hoards and two warriors—one dark, one light—wearing sunglasses as they strode through hell.

CHAPTER FIFTEEN

Finally back to a BuCar and driving, Chase swung off the 5 onto the 134, missing traffic only because it was between rush hour and lunch. Enrique's e-mailed directions told him to stay in this lane. He'd be taking the exit for San Fernando Road immediately. "What have we got?" He spoke loud enough for the microphone fob on the headset to pick it up over the whine of the wheels as they bumped from transition ramp to freeway to off-ramp. One of these days he might actually spring for a Bluetooth, move into the twenty-first century.

"Well," Enrique's voice answered him, "Oyá's comment got me thinking…"

It took a moment for the name to register. When it did, the reference still didn't make much sense. "You mean the little girl?" The interrupted cloverleaf brought the car to a broad industrial road. Across the way hulked scrap yards and warehouses, all rimmed by concertina wire fences. Stretching both directions, on Chase's side of the road, smaller industrial buildings, upholstery shops and auto detail places didn't do much to up the ambient character of the neighborhood. Hell, with the smoke-backed sky, Chase felt like he was driving into a post apocalyptic movie set.

"I started thinking about what was around the place where we found Fuertes." Enrique rattled as Chase drove. The right turn headed him toward Burbank. Glendale proper would have been left and somewhere along the way little tongues of LA snaked in. "If the car ended up in LA city limits, we'd know." Chase started counting streets, looking for Senora so he could cut down to Flower and the official tow yard. This was the industrial no-man's land of urban sprawl. "So that left Glendale, the other side of the river. We ran Fuertes through DMV, got the registration, make, model and license for his junker. Could have been hotwired and stolen, since he had his keys. That just didn't feel right. So, anyway, had Glendale run their recent impounds. They pulled it on a roving tow."

"Roving tow?" Chase hadn't heard that term before. It sounded slightly disreputable. A left on the correct street pulled him farther into fading business parks.

"Yeah, the tow contractors in California can just notify the PD and tow if they see a car parked in a fire lane or such." When Chase swung right onto Flower, he caught sight of Enrique leaning against his unmarked talking into the air. A wry smile twisted up the corner of Chase's mouth. Man, he looked fine. Dark jeans and a red polo shirt hugged everywhere just right. A holster rig sat on his hip conveying instant authority.

All of it reminded Chase of the other night and what that body looked like out of clothes. Apparently, not yet aware of Chase's proximity, Enrique kept talking. "That or parking'll notify them to go grab it, since it qualifies as a hazard they don't have to ticket first. *Tipo* left the ass end of his Hyundai three inches in the red."

Chase tapped his horn and Enrique looked up. As Enrique's eyes rolled, the line went dead. After parking along the opposite curb, Chase simultaneously eased out of the car and his jacket, then tossed the coat into the back seat. After grabbing his search gloves, Chase jaywalked across the street.

Enrique'd warned Chase to dress for a search. Unfortunately, in the Bureau, that still meant a suit and tie. "So the police had it." Chase smiled and resisted the urge to kiss that sensual mouth. Instead he adjusted the jackass rig so that his holster rested more comfortably against his ribs. Then he pulled the ever-present pack of gum from his pants pocket.

"Yep, it's been sitting at the yard here in Glendale the whole time. You could almost see this place from where we found him." Chase followed Enrique's gaze east, toward the river. Or toward where the river lay hidden behind industrial sprawl. Chase figured Enrique wasn't being literal. "The DA got us impound and search warrants so we could take custody, although the initial inventory search went down a few days ago."

"And…" Chase folded a piece of gum into his mouth, "so we're in Glendale not Los Angeles."

"And, we're going to re-search the car *in situ*." Enrique turned and led him back into a crammed garage smelling of dust and oil. At least it was a change from the taint of smoke still hovering in the LA basin.

Walking behind Enrique gave Chase ample time to appreciate all of that firm body. Chase dreaded the hammer falling from his admission the other night. It still hadn't come. No backlash. No overly emotional scenes. It just seemed that Enrique accepted it as far as it went. He wouldn't push, but he wasn't pulling back. Chase's words were as close as he'd ever gotten to a declaration of love. And while he might whisper that four-letter word to himself, Chase doubted he'd ever actually utter it. Too many hurdles stood between them and a workable solution, least of all Chase's home agency being Jacksonville, Florida and Enrique as LAPD. Three thousand miles of continent and two careers contrived to put a damper on even exploring a future.

They made their way through the indoor lot. Cars in various states of repair lined the spaces, some two and three deep. A few had been stripped, headliners and door panels missing, upholstery torn to shreds and anything removable, removed. Whether it was a legal tear down for evidence or a stolen, then dumped shell was hard to tell on some of the vehicles. Getting a car back from police impound didn't always mean you got it back in one piece.

Enrique shrugged as he ducked into a more private area. A light green two-door Hyundai Accent sat in a cleared space, waiting for them. "The tow disturbed some shit anyway. They didn't flatbed it. The custodian did the regular inventory search of glove box, under the seats, trunk and such. I've got the guy's log book from that search." Enrique tapped a small spiral notepad resting on a large tool case just off to the side of the car. "No diary in the trunk, under the seats or glove box."

Chase stared at the car for a moment before rolling up his sleeves. As he stuffed his hands into his TurtleSkin gloves, he asked. "What did they find?" Flexing his fingers settled the leather and specialized liner onto his hands.

"Trash and a paperback in the door pocket." Enrique read from the notes as he worked his hands into a different, but similar brand of gloves. Nothing could guarantee you wouldn't get cut or stuck, but search gloves came damn close. A cheap hypo would bend instead of puncturing the thin, but tough, liner. Razors, glass and metal shanks might cut the leather without reaching skin. "Center console cup holders held change, car charger for a cell phone, three cassette tapes..." he snorted, "does anyone use those anymore? In the little drop space they found playing cards, car air freshener spray, pen, superglue. The glove box had a bunch of maps, screwdriver, multi-use tool, receipts and a party invite that was about three years old. In the passenger side pocket, two music CDs and the owner's manual. The trunk had a backpack, hiking boots, two blankets, a big first aid kit, jack and a flat spare."

"Typical crap." Chase looked over the target car. The molded body held a few dings and scrapes. Nothing out of the ordinary. "No diary or anything huh?"

"Not on the list."

Walking to the car, Chase smacked Enrique's shoulder as he passed. "Damn, couldn't be easy huh?" He'd rather have grabbed his butt, but this wasn't the place for it.

Enrique fell into step beside him. Their footsteps echoed empty through the building. "Never is."

"Dual search?" Second opinion searches; two sets of eyes independently searching were more likely to catch something.

"Best way not to miss anything." Enrique nodded. "You want to follow me?"

There were basically two ways to do a second opinion search, have one person thoroughly search the car then the second person repeat the entire search. Chase opted for the other option. "How 'bout I start at the back bumper and you at the front." It resulted in the same amount of search, in half the time. You just had to be real careful not to get sloppy during the small bit of crossover.

A wicked grin blew across Enrique's face. Puckering his lips, he teased, "Kiss in the middle?"

Chase smacked the back of his head and headed for the aft end of the Hyundai. "Shithead." Kneeling behind the car, Chase began his search by running his hands over the rear bumper. You never knew where people could hide stuff. A little tape or wire, or hell, if they were motivated, a welded-in box might secure small shit under the bumper cover. A series of clunks from the front of the Hyundai indicated Enrique'd started on the engine. "Person who finds the prize gets the blow job?" Chase leaned around the rear of the car and caught Enrique mirroring his move at the front.

"I'll do that bet." He snorted before disappearing back under the open hood. "You like being on your knees huh?" Enrique's voice was muffled.

Damn good thing the garage was deserted or they'd both be in a world of shit. "I like seeing you on your knees." Chase teased back as he slid his fingers around and in the exhaust pipe. At least he didn't need lube for this tailpipe excursion.

"Just search the damn car." Enrique shot back.

Chase popped the hatchback. "Bitchy, bitchy." Running hands along the sides of the frame, he wiggled anything and everything that might have give. Tears in carpet, panels and the headliner all received scrutiny. Dome lights got popped out. They tugged up the floor panels and pulled out the seats to crawl around with flashlights, peering into the body cavities of the car. Any place something could be stuffed or hidden was explored.

Whatever items they turned up, no matter how seemingly insignificant, Chase and Enrique logged with as precise a description of location as humanly possible.

A few hours later, Chase slid down onto the concrete. The large toolbox acted as a rather uncomfortable backrest. Chase dropped his hands between his bent knees and watched Enrique amble over. "So what we got?" When he peeled back the gloves, Chase noted the black layer ended abruptly at his wrist. Running his hands through his sweat drenched hair only succeeded in redistributing dirt. He'd need three showers to get the smog-edged grime out of his pores. The shirt—between the pit stains, the oil stains, and whatever that yellow-brown tarry substance holding down the trunk carpet was—merited the incinerator.

"I'd say about five bucks in loose change," Enrique grabbed a spot of floor next to Chase. A dark V marred the back of his polo shirt. Although most of the filth Chase discovered was black, every bit of light-colored dust had attached itself to Enrique's dark jeans. With a weary huff, Enrique added, "A couple old charge receipts, an old insurance card for a 1997 Cadillac El Dorado outta Arizona with a C. Fuertes as insured, three business cards, a broken necklace, a pencil…and a blow job."

Too tired to do much more than roll his head in the general direction of Enrique's voice, Chase mumbled, "Excuse me?"

"Well, it ain't a book, but it's almost as good." Enrique held up a sleek cell phone with a red and silver case. A dime-sized, red crystal heart tethered to the phone by a short length of gold chain bumped the back of his hand.

"How do you know it's hers?"

"Guessing, but guys don't usually bling their cells out with big crystal bangles and glue on jewels. Especially ones that spell out the initials C.R.F., Carmen Reloso Fuertes if I'm not mistaken." The large display screen cycled to life as Enrique swept his thumb across the white button inset in the keypad. Little box icons with rounded corners floated like bubbles over a glittery set of puckered lips on a black background. The words *Kiss Me* sparkled an invitation. "A BlackBerry Pearl with a bPhone display option." Enrique pointed out the features like a mall-kiosk sales pitch. "Email, phone, IM, text, camera, personal organizer and media player. Too bad she didn't wait around, she could have gotten a Pink."

"You know way too much about the damn things."

"My phone," Enrique shifted and pulled a black version of the same phone off his hip. Holding them together in comparison, he added, "Her phone."

"So you know how to use it."

"Damn straight." His phone went back on the snap clip. "Although I think mine is the generation before Carmen's. It should be about the same." Staring at the phone in his hand, Enrique ran his teeth over his bottom lip. "Now the question is why was Carmen's phone in her brother's car?"

"You mean 'cause a chick who tricks out her phone like that probably has it welded to her ear."

"Her generation, more likely texting calluses on both thumbs." He grinned and aped pressing the buttons with his thumbs. "And that'll be some problem. The cell companies don't store text messages anymore than they store your phone conversations. Well, actually, any she received may be in the Blackberry's memory if she hasn't deleted them out for space. Unlike e-mail, there's no law requiring texts to be saved on an outside server."

Chase resisted the urge to take Carmen's phone and study it. It was the closest link he'd had to her. Without gloves though, he risked mucking up any prints. "Maybe Carmen was with Renaldo the day he got popped."

"Might explain his behavior at the restaurant." As if thinking or just tired, Enrique shut his eyes and pinched the bridge of his nose. "If he got a call from his sister to come get her or something? Maybe she did something stupid or thought Garcia found her? Or dropped it last time she rode with him…it was wedged up under the passenger seat."

"Well, if she called her brother, the number'll probably be on her phone still. Most people don't delete the dialed calls log right away."

"We'll want more than just the numbers." Enrique twisted his wrist and cracked open one eye to glare at the LED display on his watch. "One-fifteen. Damn, we worked through lunch. But, let me see if I can get a hold of the DA. If we get real lucky he might be able to slip a warrant for the cell phone's information under the judge's nose when the court comes back from noon recess."

"The quicker the better. We've lost a lot of days already." Way too many days, each minute they'd spent was one closer to the reality of not finding Carmen alive.

Enrique eased up from his position on the floor, using the toolbox to help him stand. "Too many maybe." Fishing a plastic evidence bag out of the clutter, he added, "Unless he really liked her."

"I don't think Garcia liked anyone that much." Chase took a deep breath and blew it out. "Garcia, however, is one sadistic motherfucker. He might keep her around just for the jollies of torturing the hell out of her."

"Is that good or bad?"

"Good for us." Both knees popped as Chase clambered to his feet. Getting old blew. "Would suck to be her though." As they walked from the garage, Chase voiced the thoughts that had been chewing at the back of his brain. "And I've been thinking about what the girl said. How he needs her and the *Palo Mayumbe* ceremonies. Halloween's coming up...witches, death and shit, that's a big day. What about in Palo?"

"No. But for Santeria, Palo, Vudun, two days later would be."

Pushing through an exterior fire door, Chase shot a comment over his shoulder, "I don't get you." Then they were outside, the graveyard of cars behind them.

"All Souls Day." Enrique stared up at the smoke-tinged sky. "November second. For Mexico, *Los Dias de Los Muertos*. But still they are syncretic religions. They borrow from Christianity. If he was going to capture her soul for a *prenda*, it would be an auspicious day to do it."

Chapter Sixteen

A sea of digital photos spilled across a table old enough to be classified as an antique. Most of the prints fell into that grainy, snapped-by-a-cell-phone category. Sheets full of logged calls, stacks of credit card receipts, and transcripts of stored text messages lay scattered in piles. A jigsaw of information and they had to put the pieces together to find Carmen. Maybe, if he stared hard enough at it, the bits would arrange themselves.

Enrique's cough caught Chase's attention and he looked up.

Eyes narrowed, Enrique stared hard at a flat-screen monitor resting on top of an outdated computer. He claimed reviewing the electronic version of the data was easier on his eyes. Behind him, a support pillar, several five-drawer file cabinets and a few cardboard boxes inked with people's names formed a wall blocking off the chaos of the detectives' bullpen.

The whole damn interior of Parker Center looked like it hadn't been redone since the 60's. Cork bulletin boards interrupted walls of stained plaster. Overflowing bookcases went almost to the height of the dropped acoustical ceiling, which badly needed replacing, orange-brown stains spreading over the pitted tiles. Retrofitted electrical ran through exterior conduit while overhead fluorescents threw a callous light over everything. Mismatched file cabinets ate up every inch of available space.

Chase loosened his tie and returned to studying the photos. Sweat ran down his back, sticking his shirt to his skin and causing the butterfly straps of his jackass rig to chafe. Over the space of the last four hours, five separate calls that Chase'd overheard pleaded for maintenance to turn off the heater and start the air conditioning. No one had yet to respond. The janitors didn't believe that Los Angeles stayed hot through October. Of course, according to Enrique, LAPD Brass didn't believe that their detectives needed voicemail.

Everyone in Los Angeles apparently lived one step to the left of reality.

Several of the shots took place in spring. Carmen's phone date-stamped the photo files and LAPD technicians had printed them on the hard copies. Many were backyard shots of dogs playing or knots of friends, a few of whom Chase recognized as known associates of Garcia. Other than smoggy skies and a mountain range, Chase couldn't get a real idea of where they'd been taken. As he flipped through the images, one photo caught Chase's eye. He flipped it around to see a date in mid-May scribbled across the back. That was back when Carmen and Garcia were still on good terms. They posed as a couple in the shot, which looked like Carmen was holding the phone at arm's length to take the picture. A midday scene, colored by the sepia ambient light of the Los Angeles basin, taken at some outdoor table. What caught Chase's interest was the barely visible signage in the background.

He tugged at his coat, draped over the chair back. From the inside pocket, he fished a pair of reading glasses. As he settled them onto the bridge of his nose, Chase realized Enrique was staring. "Don't say a damn thing." He growled the warning.

"Wouldn't dream of it." Enrique choked back a laugh. "See something interesting?"

"I think. The smog coupled with palm trees in the background is suggestive of this being an LA shot. I'm guessing, since she was still with Garcia at the time this was taken, it may have been around where she is." He peered at the photo. "Ever hear of *Devil's Ink*? Looks like a tattoo shop, looks like the place next to it is *Juan Moore Mexican Restaurant.*" Both groaned at the lame joke. Pulling the glasses down, Chase looked over the lenses at Enrique. "Ever hear of that place?"

"No." Wiggling his fingers over the keyboard, Enrique teased, "But I have Google-fu."

"You all don't have voicemail, but you have Internet access?"

Enrique rolled his eyes, conveying ultimate exasperation in one simple gesture. "On some computers."

"Okay, then, let's narrow our focus a little." Chase pushed the photos off to one side for the moment. "We should examine Carmen's credit card and bank statements from April this year through the end of June. That's when Carmen contacted us."

The clack of keys told Chase that Enrique had returned to typing. "Thinking they'll be more centered where she was staying?" As slow as the sounds came, Chase knew he did the one finger hunt-and-peck of someone not used to full keyboarding.

"Yeah, people tend to do their regular shopping close to home." He rifled through the loose papers. "If we're lucky, it'll give us a focus, a home range. Then maybe some of these casual shots might lead us to a neighborhood."

"True. Want me to help?"

"No, you keep sorting through the strings of LOLs and TYLs." Chase tapped the stack of credit card statements. "I'll see if I can make heads or tails of this mess."

One baggie got swept aside as Chase reached for the receipts. Then he came back to it—a party invite unfolded, flat and encased in thick plastic, rested inside. A skeleton, robed in blue with a crown on its bony head and roses clutched in desiccated fingers, jeered at him from cheap cardstock. Candy, cigarettes and playing cards made up the background. Words in the heavy old-English script favored by gangs spelled out words in Spanish. Chase muttered, "*Santisima Muerte,*" as he read it.

"Saint Death."

Looking up from the card, "What?"

"*Santa Muerte, Doña* Sebastiana." Enrique shrugged as he continued his hunt and peck typing. "She's Mexican."

Chase twirled the bag by one corner. Saint Death laughed at him as she spun. "Why would a Cuban have an invitation with a Mexican saint on it?"

"Well, Los Angeles has lots of crossover." Stretching, Enrique swiveled in his seat to face Chase. "The *Doña* is the patron saint of thieves, prostitutes, drug dealers and cops. I know a patrol officer who carries a Sebastiana medal."

"This is a Catholic thing then?" With a scowl, Chase placed the invite on the table, interior side up. A prayer in Spanish ran down the left. Typical party information—date, time, place—filled out the other side.

"No, she's a folk saint. Not recognized by the church. Why?"

"The party invite in the car. It has this robed skeleton on the front and a date of November 2 three years ago. What does, *Cumbacha para Carmen satisfacer a su Santo*, mean? I don't understand *Cumbacha*."

"It's a big party, like a wedding reception or confirmation, so Carmen can meet her saint. The marigolds! *Shinga, son medio estupido!*"

"You're half-stupid?"

"I'm not thinking straight." Finger pointed at Chase's face, Enrique warned, "Don't say it. Carmen's dedicated to *la Doña*. That means she carries some of the saint 'in her.' She could evoke *Santa Muerte*. And that cult is moving from the Mexican gangs into other Latino populations. Marigolds are her flower."

After waiting for Enrique to continue, "And..." Chase prompted.

"In *Palo Mayumbe*, you use human bones for a *prenda. Paleros* have pots they keep their spirits in and one of the things that must go in them is human bones. For the good ones, it's supposed to be the bones of your ancestors and they help you. Bad guys, bones of the tortured, the insane...those go in the pots used for black magic. A *Tata*, head priest, plays with the *prenda* to make the spirit inside do what he wishes. They feed them blood daily. The bigger the animal, the more powerful the *prenda* becomes. And a *prenda* to Saint Death would be very powerful."

"He's going to kill her..."

Rubbing his temples, Enrique looked like a ball-buster of a headache was brewing, "On the day her saint came down on her."

"And put her in a pot."

"Her bones." Two quick passes through his hair with his fingers and Enrique added, "Skull and maybe a few others. He may give some of the small bones to other *paleros* who do dark magic. Probably bury her and dig her back up in a year."

"Holy shit." Hollywood should make movie scripts so twisted. "We got to find her quick." In a movie, the answer would land in their laps, completely obvious and with a couple cold drinks in its hands. Unfortunately, both knew quick in police time meant slogging through the information they'd gathered. You couldn't cut corners.

Twenty minutes of ringing phones, snippets of conversation, and one suspect led past them spewing hate passed while Chase thumbed through reams of bills and statements. Notes scribbled on a yellow pad and a few removable-tape flags marked information that he wanted to return to. About the time Chase started doubting whether he could digest any more information, Enrique spoke up. "Hmm, would lucky be an address?"

"Yeah," Chase pushed his reading glasses to the top of his head and rubbed the bridge of his nose with his fingers. "That would be lucky."

"Well, I've got a number and a street." Enrique almost crowed. "It's in her sent emails folder from the phone. There's no city, but it looks like she was telling someone where to pick her up." Spinning his chair around, he crossed his arms over his chest and grinned at Chase. "Sent May 21 this year."

Shit, maybe they'd lucked out and were filming the next blockbuster. "Maybe we should go play the lottery?" Probably nothing that Perry-Mason, but Chase could always hope.

"The thing about luck," the grin dropped to a wise-ass smirk, "is knowing when not to push it."

"Very true." Chase cracked his knuckles and stood. "I think I've got a handle on this. At least a quick and dirty one." When he stretched most of the other bones in his body popped, too. The only thing that didn't feel natural about that was his neck. Yeah, it was sore, but not as much as it should have been, as much as he was used to. "I'm looking at the San Fernando-Sylmar area. You have a street map with block numbers on it that we could look at?" Chase shoved the papers he thought might be useful and his recent notes into his working file.

"Best bet would be the BFD."

Chase raised an eyebrow at the name. It couldn't mean big-fucking-deal.

Enrique caught the look and added, "Bunko-Forgery Division. I think I heard that they were working an elder abuse scam up there. Come on," Enrique almost bolted out of his chair. Both of them had been sitting too long. "If we're nice, they may let us borrow it for a moment."

Twists and turns through the crumbling building brought them to a set of dark double-doors. Someone had tacked two grinning paper pumpkins to the wood. Enrique pushed through into a small conference room. The place seemed as jammed as everywhere else in Parker Center. A large street map pinned to a framed corkboard leaned against the windowed back wall. The other end was propped on an old table, a twin to the one Chase had been using. Enrique ducked between bookcases and file cabinets, disappearing through a door in the right hand wall. After a few seconds, he returned with a portly detective. Like most of the conscripts in that day's LAPD gulag, the man had removed his tie, rolled up his sleeves and still had sweat stains over most of his shirt.

Chase stepped up, smiled broadly and held out his hand. "Chase Nozick. Hate to bother you when everyone's dealing with no air on top of a full caseload." Preemptive strikes worked best.

"Fairpark." The man grunted. Almost like an afterthought, he took Chase's hand then quickly dropped it. "Ochoa here says you want to borrow our map? Doesn't the FBI have a budget for that kinda thing?"

Ah, hell, a man into sandbox pissing. Unfortunately, Chase didn't have the time to probe into whether it was because the detective was territorial or because he'd been burned before. Chase took a deep breath. "Yeah, but it would take me five months and twenty forms to get it. Look, Ochoa," he switched to the habit of calling people by their last names. Last thing he wanted to do was come off too familiar with Enrique. That might muck things up big time if the guy thought Enrique might be brown-nosing the Bureau. "He says you're a real stand-up guy and could help us out of a jam. We got a girl who's missing, every second counts."

"If she's dead, it doesn't."

"Call me optimistic." Chase shrugged. "Actually, call me a realist. The guy we think has her is a sadistic creep. If he just pops someone, that's usually business. This gal was going to roll on him. Normal perp would whack her and dump her in the Angeles Crest. This guy is more likely to put her through hell before he does it...sort of a lesson to anyone else who wants to cross him. Take his sweet time ripping every inch of skin off her body kinda thing. And, we have some info that he may be waiting for November second. It's a significant date for him."

Fairpark chewed on his lip for a moment. Oppressive heat wouldn't improve anyone's disposition, least of all someone already with an attitude. The options seemed to flow like molasses through Fairpark's brain. Finally, he grunted again and jerked his chin toward the propped up board. "It's over there. We're done with it, but don't damage it." Without even saying *good luck*, Fairpark trundled back into his cave.

"Okay then." Enrique's face went tight with suppressed mirth or anger or a mixture of both. "Let's take real good care of his map."

"They got any pins?" Chase scrounged for a moment and came up with a sad box of map pins in various colors. Beggars couldn't be choosers. Gingerly, he moved the box in front of the map, trying to keep the sides from crumbling. Then he dropped his notes down next to them. "These are the ten places Carmen shopped on a regular basis. More than three charges. Okay. So we've got this," he ran his hand over the map, searching for the street then following that with his finger to the block he needed. "Target and a Vons." Modern TV crime dramas were light years ahead of reality in terms of technology. LAPD didn't feel much like it ever left the Dragnet era. Chase searched for the next address. "Maria's salon, that's all the way over here." He shoved a pin through an area down and left of where the others were. The nearest city label read La Cresenta.

Enrique stared at the lone pin. Then he shook his head and snorted. "Women are choosy about their stylist. They'll follow a good one halfway across the city."

Chase'd never pegged Enrique for fem. "How the hell do you know that?" He tugged the ever-present pack of gum from his pants.

That earned him another snort, this one more of a *you don't know what I put up with* type. "Three older sisters."

"Okay." That made sense. After offering the gum to Enrique, who took it, Chase fished out another pin. "We have two different drug stores, a 99 Cents store, bakery—Cuban, I'm guessing by the name." By now, a small cloud of tacks was forming in San Fernando. Enrique returned the pack of Juicy Fruit. As he talked, Chase stripped the foil from a stick. "Gas station, Ross and a Mom and Pop convenience store." Chase stepped back, folding a piece of gum into his mouth as he moved. "The address from the party doesn't fit in, but that was three years ago."

"Well, here's our address from the email." Enrique picked up a pin and stuck it near the others. "Not a residential place."

"Wouldn't Garcia hole up in a residential place?" Chase flipped open his folder and drew out one of the FBI printouts. "I'd think he'd live large."

Passing the file over to Enrique, Chase grabbed another few markers. "Here, read me off the address of his known LA associates." As Enrique rattled them off, Chase stuck the pins in place. When they were all marked, Chase drew an imaginary circle around the main cluster with his finger. "We got guys in Chatsworth, Altadena, San Pedro and one boy in San Fernando—Franco Pale." That made him smile. "He's right in our nice little cluster of pins on Dominguez Ave."

"Robbery, extortion, drug trafficking, money laundering. A regular MBA of the criminal world." The file hit the table with a smack. Enrique moved in close to study the map with Chase. "Think he's got her there?"

He so needed to back up about two inches. With as close as Enrique was, Chase became overwhelmed with his scent. The heat ratcheted it up, throwing a sexy, musky overlay to Enrique's cologne. Salt and mint and warm skin flowed through Chase's senses. It hit his body with a shudder and landed between his legs. Chase'd rather be doing something that didn't require clothes than staring at a bunch of dots on a map.

Blowing out a breath, Chase stepped to the side and adjusted himself. It wasn't much, just enough to not be so completely taken by Enrique's presence. "Don't know," Chase mumbled and nodded to himself. It fit. It just fit. "But it's the best lead yet." Turning to Enrique, he smiled with a dare lighting up his eyes. "So how are your stake-out skills?" What better way to spend the next few days, cooped up in a car, smelling Enrique? "Let's call it in to the brass. We want to jump, we only have two days…maybe only one."

CHAPTER SEVENTEEN

Enrique stretched in bed, his hands high above his head, brushing the headboard. That whole lean brown body went tight, white sheets falling in around his legs and outlining his ass. Even at too-fucking-early in the morning Chase thought it was a damn fine way to wake up. "Morning sexy." Once again waking up in Enrique's house, damn, he could have saved his expense account if he'd have known this would happen. Why was he kidding himself? He'd have kept the hotel room as cover. No sense advertising. Still, he kept his carry-on stuffed with a change of clothes in the trunk of his car—just in case.

Somewhere on the other side of the bedroom wall, another day of stakeout waited. Hours sitting in smog, without air conditioning or even a convenient trip to the can, could cool its heels a little longer. That last one was the worst any more. Forty turned him into a wuss who had to take a leak every hour. An extended trip to Hell needed tempering with a bit of Heaven first, and yesterday's four hours of sitting in a BuCar while kids in costume raced by sucked. And it hadn't done his back much good.

Chase slid one arm around a sheet-wrapped middle and nuzzled into the soft fur under Enrique's arm. The smell of guy and recent sleep surrounded him. He licked across the space from chest to arm and Enrique hissed. "Damn, *Compa*, you're going to make me all excited before my coffee."

With a laugh, Chase reached out and grabbed Enrique's opposite arm. Pulling it across his body, Chase moved their fingers between his own legs. His not-quite-hard prick swelled under the combined touch. It felt so damn good. "Already headed that way." He blew the words against Enrique's skin. Then he kissed a trail to one hard, brown nipple and sucked it into his mouth.

Enrique shifted, turning a bit and Chase had to switch to the other pec. Now that Enrique was occupied, Chase burrowed his hand under the sheets, searching for Enrique's cock. He swept his hand over a hip and thigh before cupping a soft package of dick and balls. Kneading and tugging, Chase felt Enrique come alive under his hand.

As he rolled his head back, Enrique came down for a kiss. It started off slow and sensual and quickly turned to damn near desperate. The stroking woke them both up fast. Enrique cupped Chase's balls and squeezed, making Chase groan into their kiss. Two could play at that game. Chase ran a tight-fisted grip up Enrique's shaft and chuckled as the other man shuddered.

There wasn't much talking. More of a mutual humping, stroking and heavy petting session. That suited Chase damn fine. He loved to touch and be touched. He could explore every inch of Enrique's stubble-covered neck. Enrique licked around the margins of his ear, shooting shivers through Chase's frame. They met the heat welling up from his groin somewhere in his belly and mixed into a heady dose of need.

His hand flew over Enrique's now hard cock and he humped Enrique's fist. Then Enrique let go. Chase was about to protest when he felt that strong grip slide across to his butt and pull them together. Oh, yeah, he could do that. A little reluctant, he let go of Enrique's fat prick and wrapped his arm across Enrique's middle.

Bumping and grinding, pushing their dicks together again and again, Chase savored the heat. Enrique's skin tasted of salt and he smelled like sex. Their juices mingled, adding delicious friction to the rub off.

Almost desperately, Chase pushed Enrique onto his back and rolled on top. Then he began to hump in earnest. Fists tangling into Enrique's hair, Chase pillaged that hot mouth for all it was worth. Enrique's fingers tore up the skin along Chase's spine. They grunted and swore under a sheen of sweat until the whole room smelled of lust.

It wasn't until Chase shook that his body let go. He buried his face in Enrique's neck as spunk pumped between their bellies. Enrique's fingers clawed into his shoulders and he hissed out, *"Shinga,"* as he joined Chase in ecstasy.

"Fuck yeah." Chase rolled off Enrique's frame and lay, panting, next to him on the bed. "That might get me through today."

Enrique's warm chuckle filled the room. "Okay, *Compa*, I'm going to wash the spunk off my skin." He shifted on the bed so he could view the bedside clock. "If you want to hose down, you probably ought to join me. We're running late."

"Ah, work." Chase sat up and ran his hands through his hair. The world seemed awfully bright and shiny for some reason. It took Chase a moment to fathom why. Getting the approvals, resources—mechanical and human—and logistics in place for the stakeout ate up yesterday almost to midnight. They'd hit Enrique's place, barely bothering to shuck clothes before they crashed. Nowhere in that scenario did getting a belt sneak in. Shit, Chase hadn't seen the sober side of a morning in ages.

"So?" Enrique's one word question caught Chase's attention. Something resembling amusement cracked Enrique's otherwise stern face. "You coming? I plan to use up all the hot water."

Chase stumbled out of bed, dragging the sheets part of the way towards the bath. "Sure."

Enrique just shook his head and disappeared into the small room. The clatter of old plumbing heralded the spray. Chase ducked in after Enrique and hot water needled his senses. God, the man looked like some skin-rag shoot, water cascading over a toned brown form. It ran in rivulets as it traced the lines of his body to flow like a waterfall from the tip of his prick. Enrique was ten times hotter than any glossy porn model. And he was real, right in front of Chase.

Still, after the morning's calisthenics, there was no way Chase could fire the engines back up. Chase settled for a lot of soap-coated caresses and deep kisses. It felt so good not to move to fucking. The touching. The stroking. The sucking on Enrique's tongue. Those were ends unto themselves. And,

Chase marveled, they ended up reasonably clean, even with the distractions.

After toweling off, Chase left Enrique to shave as he made a pot of coffee. Enrique's mug sat in the sink. Chase rinsed it and searched the cabinet for the one he'd started to consider *his* cup. Again the normalcy hit him. He was becoming domesticated. Worse, he liked it.

He passed Enrique at the bedroom door, exchanging a mug of coffee for his turn at the sink with a razor. Play it while it lasts, he reminded himself. An agent's life never got settled. Even if you established yourself somewhere, made a home, the Bureau had a habit of transplanting you as soon as you started to put down roots. Chase buttoned himself into his agent persona with his clothes. Sliding his arms through the straps on his rig, Chase wandered out into the living room just in time to find Enrique pulling a beer from the fridge.

"Okay." Chase paused and tried to make sense of things. "Look, I can put it away, but even for me, five-thirty is pretty damn early."

"*Cundango,*" Enrique glared at him and slammed the refrigerator door. "I have something I have to do real quick." From the counter, he picked up one of those small candles in a glass jars you could buy at any discount house. Several huddled behind a large orange and black bowl, settling in the corner between the wall and appliance. Two full bags of candy, bought in anticipation of hoards of miniature ghouls swarming the neighborhood last night, rested nearby.

Chase stepped up, dropped his empty mug on the breakfast bar and spread his hands, indicating he was game. Besides, curiosity had him by the balls. "Let's go." He'd have tortured Enrique to tell him what was up. Inviting himself was far easier and less messy.

Enrique twisted the cap off the beer as he disappeared through a door at the back of the kitchen. Chase scrambled around the island, darted through the door and found himself dropping down a ragged flight of metal stairs.

They ended up on a flat little strip of land underneath the stilts of Enrique's porch. Hardly enough dirt to call a yard crawled toward a cinderblock fence. Several small boulders or large rocks formed a knee-high pile on one side. Some had been painted in red and white with the geometric butterfly pattern surrounding Shango's little shrine in the house. A few forlorn husks of candy bars rattled in the light morning wind.

Enrique didn't say anything before he poured the beer on the ground. The wet stain formed a cross. On one side he placed the still half-full bottle. On the other he set the red candle in its glass jar. After lighting it, Enrique stepped back and spoke. "My father, Shango. Our paths have been tied. Help me. I beg you to accept this humble present from us. Take it and open our way." After a moment of silence, Enrique turned and grabbed the candle to blow it out. He scrambled back up the stairs with Chase following. When they reached kitchen, Enrique poured himself another cup of coffee. Offering the pot to Chase, he took a swig and leaned against the counter.

"That's it?" Chase took the pot and used it to point toward the rear door. "The other god got rum and candy bars. You begged like a guy trying to get laid." He filled his cup before setting the pot on the counter. Hooking his thumb into one pocket, Chase settled his butt against the opposite Formica lip. "With Shango, who if I get it right, is like your patron saint or guardian angel?" He downed a steaming gulp of coffee and continued. "With him it's, here's a beer bud, need your help."

Choking on his own coffee, Enrique wiped his mouth with the back of his hand. "Shango is not as fussy as Eshu."

"Is that why you keep hanging around me, 'cause you're not the fussy type either?"

"Shut up and drink your coffee, we have to hit the road." Enrique dumped the rest of his cup down the sink. Chase took another swig before doing the same. They both grabbed coats and headed out the front door.

As they buckled into Chase's car, a thought hit him. "Why did you call me FBI up on the hill that night?" He twisted the key in the ignition, threw the car in reverse and, with his right arm looped over the seat, backed out onto the street. "You haven't done that in days."

"Didn't think you'd really want Eshu to know your name." The way Enrique said it, Chase realized he probably really didn't. "Orishas who know who you are might ask for favors. You don't want Eshu asking for favors."

"You used my name for Shango."

"Oyá knows who you are." Enrique waved it off with one hand like it didn't matter. "If Oyá knows something, she would tell Shango anyway."

Chase let the statement weigh on his mind for a bit. They dropped out of the hills of Silverlake heading towards the I-5, the most direct shot into San Fernando. Finally he risked a quick glance across the car. "You really believe in all this."

"Yep." Enrique's answer was delivered in a clipped, no-nonsense manner.

"And it doesn't," Chase drummed the steering wheel, "bother you to be a cop who practices what, you know, a lot of people think of as a cult?"

Enrique snorted. "Catholics believe that wine turns to blood when a priest prays over it. They believe that a cracker turns to flesh. Does that make them bizarre? If they pray, are they sane or are they crazy for believing that it actually helps?"

"It's just faith."

"And mine is just a different faith." With his slow, warm smile, Enrique seemed to try and ease Chase's doubt. "It's just a prayer...done a little different, but that's all it is." He kept his tone even, not offended. "My religion uses drums instead of some big organ. They have priests, we have priests. They light candles to saints for blessings, I light candles to Eshu for blessings."

Weighed down by his thoughts, Chase let it go. "It's not that different, I guess." It really didn't matter what Enrique believed or didn't believe. He was a good cop. He was a good friend. Hell, he didn't hock lugies in the bathroom sink, snore too bad, or use towels to wipe his ass—the *Santeria* stuff paled in comparison to some of his former lovers' bad habits. Even the whole mom doing laundry and sis cleaning his house; they were a little juvenile, but Enrique didn't live in his parent's basement or anything.

The roiling plumes of smoke tarnished the sky and matched Chase's turbulent mind. Bone-dry grass covered the hills. Even the trees seemed to fade with the heat. The suffocating possibility of failure settled onto Chase's shoulders. They had to hit pay dirt today.

Tomorrow might be too late.

CHAPTER EIGHTEEN

"How many hours have we been here?" Chase ostensibly mumbled the question to Enrique. He neither expected nor cared for an answer. Sitting in silence, however, grated on his nerves. It gave him too much time with his thoughts. Right now, his thoughts revolved around how screwed they were. That, and how uncomfortable it was having his back glued to his shirt which was glued to the seat.

October baked them in their little four-door oven, and gave Enrique's response a drowsy, almost drunken slur. "Too long." Although most of the twenty-three wildfires were out or largely contained, thick smoke still stained the horizon, made it seem hotter than the thermometer indicated.

Traffic whizzed by on the five-lane boulevard. All the road trip games—license plate bingo, slug-a-bug, or red-car-green-car—useful for passing long hours on blacktop as kids were denied to stakeout participants. "And if you ask again, I'll pop your ass." Despite the rancor of the statement, the words were delivered with an aura of resigned boredom; nonsense filling time. You sat and you watched, and sat and watched until your butt went numb, your legs ached and you had to piss like a Russian racehorse.

TV always used a good stakeout as a plot device for deep heart-to-hearts between partners. Reality meant sitting and not talking, at least about anything of any importance, for seemingly endless stretches of time. Conversations distracted you. "You pop ass good." Trading barbs kept you alert and awake. "If we don't die in this hot-box, maybe I'll let you pop it tonight."

Chase always wondered what aura of invisibility surrounded a stakeout car. After all, two men wearing business casual and parked in a four-door sedan...well it wasn't late night on Santa Monica Boulevard. They'd popped the hood like the car'd broken down. In an era of cell phones and the Auto Club, the situation strained the bounds of credulity. But still, nobody really looked twice. Chase figured it was part survival and part self-centeredness. People generally didn't stick their noses in where they really didn't want to know. Busybodies were a rare breed and tended to earn Darwin Awards. Most folks walked around so wrapped up in their private lives, they wouldn't notice a naked cowboy roller-skating past.

They did get a few breaks here and there. Nothing major. Just enough to head down the street a ways and maybe duck into the can. Enrique would go take a walk around the block. He'd return, they'd sit some more and then it would be Chase's turn to stretch his legs. Chase shifted in his seat, pointedly ignoring the sucking sound of his back separating from the upholstery, and refocused on the warehouse across the way. Their target brooded on an off-angled corner of visibility. If they'd parked where the front entrance was easy to view, they'd be discovered. Rule of thumb—if you can see them, they can probably see you.

Especially in a navy four-door monstrosity sprouting a few too many antennas.

Deep in the middle of a heat-induced yawn, Enrique's, "So what does Garcia look like?" caught Chase off guard.

Reaching for an energy bar, Chase mumbled, "You've seen the photos." Why couldn't they have gotten one of the better locations? Like the guy up on the roof down the street. Or Hungwell, who was playing attendant at the gym with full frontal view. Or even Wyatt, reliving her high school career as a coffee slinger at the donut shop.

"Humor me." Enrique slung his arm over the seat, his body half-turned to face Chase. For some reason, a soft, sexy smile played across his lips.

Chase took a bite of the not-quite candy and grimaced. "Kinda stocky, short." He mumbled around the overly chewy and not half-tasty-enough wedge. They didn't want to starve while they were stuck. Greasy fast food, like in the movies, didn't do more than give you heartburn and stink up already close quarters. But shit, they could have at least packed something edible. "He's got that whole Napoleon complex going on." Folding the package back over the uneaten part, Chase tossed the remains into the door side-pocket.

"Scar on his nose?" Enrique ran his hand over Chase's shoulder, lingering along the collar of his shirt. Chase froze. What the hell was Enrique thinking? For all the suggestion in his face and moves, Enrique's voice was all business. "Going gray?"

As Chase started to turn, Enrique stopped him with a deceptively subtle touch to his ear. The touch might seem gentle, the pressure behind it wasn't. "Scar, yeah," something was up. "I would assume he might be a little gray by now, why?"

Although he faced Chase, Enrique's eyes watched something behind the car. Damn it. It took all of a second before Chase processed the solution. He rolled his neck and glanced at the rearview mirror. Heading towards them, cell phone jammed to his ear and accompanied by two of his *Muertes* with their black T-shirts and mirrored shades, Garcia looked like some hip Hollywood wanna-be. Of course, the movie industry types all tried to look like thugs and gangsters these days.

Hand still near Chase's ear, blocking a good view of his profile from behind, Enrique asked, "Would he know you, what you look like?" He scooted an inch or so across the bench seat and slid his fingers down Chase's neck.

"He looked me right in the eye and tried to blow my head off." Hopefully, Garcia didn't have a clear memory of that. Chase figured Garcia hadn't spent weeks memorizing his features. Then again, someone recognized him enough to tail them, try and run him over, rear-end a car and find his hotel. Fuck! "He might recognize me."

Enrique tugged on his neck, pulling Chase close. "Kiss me." He hissed.

"What are you...?" Chase sputtered.

"Shh, *Compa.*" Enrique leaned in. As he pressed against Chase's body, he whispered, "Play along." Then Enrique's lips settled against his own.

Damn it, on a stakeout, on duty and fucking making out with Enrique. "Shit." Chase managed to mumble as a half-hearted protest. For all of two seconds it was a ruse. After that, Chase barely managed to remember exactly what they were supposed to be doing. He opened his mouth and teased Enrique's tongue with tentative licks. Enrique's firm grip wrapped around the back of Chase's head. Chase cupped Enrique's chin in his palms and drew him close. If they got any nearer, they'd be in each other's laps. Chase wouldn't mind that one damn bit.

Enrique pulled away just enough to break the kiss. He pressed his forehead against Chase's and whispered. "Just look at me and talk to me like it's really intense, okay."

"Pretending like its intense is not a problem." Chase managed not to break up while saying it. "Tell me exactly why you did that while we're on duty?"

Hand still around the back of Chase's neck, Enrique squeezed hard enough to pinch. "So you wouldn't blow our cover."

"'Cause we're being obvious?" Checking the rearview netted Chase a view of open street. He managed a quick glance at the side view. Nothing in the mirror, but the barest glimpse of a set of black jeans pinpointed the trio. With as casual a movement as he could manage, Chase moved around to blow in Enrique's ear. He might as well have a little fun while ducking for cover behind Enrique.

"Yeah," shivering, Enrique muttered, "sort of, because if we're this damn obvious, we can't possibly be two cops on a stakeout. This way, if Garcia kinda recognizes you, he's not going to *recognize* you."

"Bastard." With words and kisses, Chase teased. "I hate it when you might be right."

"Get used to it." Enrique shot back. For another few moments, he let Chase taste his skin. Then a swift nod punctuated, "Okay, they're crossing the street, heading for the warehouse."

Reluctantly, Chase gave in as Enrique pushed him away. A few seconds of terror welled up; what if someone on the team had seen them, mentioned something? Then he blew out all the fear of reprisals and questions. They had a cover story and Chase would go to his grave defending it, along with suffering some teasing and throwing a little around himself. You had to walk a fine line between defensive, humored and embarrassed to pull off the lie. Chase had done it before.

Enrique grabbed the radio and transmitted their information. "Ochoa on the Code 5, primary OBS near Denver 58 proceeding toward our target." Hopefully the open hood would block most of the view.

"Fuck, don't you guys use plain speak? Lot easier to say Garcia's heading toward the building."

"Yeah, but it's not as fun." A bright grin mocked him. "No cloak-and-dagger that way."

The radio crackled, "Denver 58, 10-23. Other units reporting in."

Shit, it'd been way too long since he'd used 10 codes. "Refresh my memory."

Enrique laced his hands behind his head and leaned back into the seat. "We wait."

"Why did I not see that coming?"

CHAPTER NINETEEN

Fists balled and supporting his weight on a rickety table, Hungwell filled them in. "Team Bravo saw one of Garcia's associates, the one who owned the house, shepherding the target, Carmen Fuertes, out of the location about thirteen hundred hours." Enough paramilitary gear to arm a third world army hung off his body. Chase wondered whether he'd washed out, or missed out, on joining the Marines. "They'd shaved her head. Looked like either cuts or tattoos on her scalp. She was wearing a red sack dress, like the kind gals wear to the beach as cover-ups."

Beyond himself and Enrique, Team Alpha consisted of Special Agent Donaldson, Hungwell, Wyatt and a few other agents, LAPD and San Fernando PD. You had to invite the home team to the game if you wanted to play on their turf—all three square miles of it. Detective Sergeant Hill headed up Team Bravo at the Dominguez Ave. address. That mix of law enforcement had tailed the group of three *Muertes*, one guy they pinned as Franco Pale, and a woman identified as Carmen to the warehouse. Now they all crowded in a briefing room at the San Fernando City Police Station.

"They're *called* cover-ups." Wyatt's voice cut ribbons into the other detective without even trying. Hair pulled back like before, but dressed in a raid uniform of jeans and a T-shirt, she strode into the group of agents and cops like she owned them. With little preamble, she tossed the donut shop smock on a table and picked up a bulletproof vest. "Your big, bad-ass cop lingo is somewhat stilted on vocabulary." Chase remembered why he liked her. Any law enforcement officer who could use badass, lingo and stilted in the same sentence rated high in his book.

"Okay," Donaldson smiled. He and Detective Sergeant Hill coordinated pretty damn well. "San Fernando PD pulled the plans on the warehouse." His stubby finger traced the areas on the blue prints as he laid it out. "We got a bottom floor with a bunch of small offices. Enter through a reception area, you can go right into a small storage area where the freight elevator is or left into a warren of cubby offices. At the very back is the warehouse. One stair up to the right." Black lines on white paper never really conveyed the size or lack thereof of the real place.

"At the head of the stairs you have a bullpen and four decent-size offices. Two overlook the warehouse, the others the front street." His thick finger jabbed at a small box on the plan. "The elevator opens into the front left corner office. We won't risk that entry unless it becomes absolutely necessary. Roof access is here." Another swipe of Donaldson's hand pointed out a stairway adjacent to the left back upstairs office. "We'll send a team there to clear. Only windows are at the front and all barred over, even on the second floors." He grimaced and crossed his hands over his chest. "There you have it."

They'd left Enrique and Chase as a team, something that Chase appreciated immensely. He'd come to rely on Enrique. Nobody else could watch his back.

"We tailed them to the old warehouse pegged as Garcia's." Hill strode in at the head of a wave of SWAT. "We estimate maybe fifteen people besides the girl in the building at this point. A few we can peg as real bruisers, but we can't be sure of the rest. I don't like that we're going in as blind as we are. This is where clusterfucks happen." He must have caught the last of the Donaldson's explanation from the hall. Hill grabbed Donaldson's hand and popped his shoulder with the free hand. "Several people arrived at the local just before seven hundred hours. A lot of activity right around that time."

"Seven to seven." Enrique muttered and then looked sheepish when he realized he'd spoken aloud.

Never one to let an iota of information slip by, Donaldson zoomed in. "What?"

"Seven is a very powerful number in Palo." Studying the ceiling, squinting like he read messages in the tiles, "So we have a few hours, I think. They start at seven with the preliminary ceremonies. Twelve hours later…that's it." Enrique shook himself out of his trance. Explaining for those who hadn't had the benefit of two weeks of being part of the investigation, "Our theory is that they want to take her at the same hour and on the same day she received Lady Death. She, ah, swore to be a follower of *La Santísima Muerte*. According to an invite we found, the ceremony where she became dedicated was at seven. That would be my guess."

"We don't go for guesses in the Bureau," Donaldson growled. "Are you sure?"

"Not a hundred percent, but I'd put my paycheck down on it."

"A month's or a week's?" Wyatt teased.

His response of, "Two months," earned him a whistle from several in the crowd.

"Well, we're waiting for the AG to come through with a warrant." Donaldson studied the map. "So, let's go over who does what and where. We don't have time to do a true scale floor plan. This is going in as blind as I ever want to."

Chase used the wait to memorize the floor plan. The SWAT cycled through various scenarios. Hungwell kept butting in, trying to act like he knew tactical extraction techniques. With the first few words out of his mouth, most of the room knew he was full of shit. Chase mumbled something about idiots and rope, earning a snort from one of the SWAT guys. His nametag said Makum.

Makum marked out distances with his thumb, probably doing mental conversions of the layout. "Where'd you serve?" The way he said it, the guy knew Chase wouldn't blow smoke.

"Panama, parachuted into Kuwait, got out and joined the Bureau before Somalia. You?"

"Persian Gulf." With the barest jerk of his head, Makum indicated Enrique was the focus of his next question. "Him?"

Chase didn't have to even ask what Makum meant. "No service." A soldier sizing up the troops before battle—who you could count on and who you couldn't. There were a lot of ways to make the list. "But when you start seeing alligator heads on sticks and chicken sacrifices, call him."

"Is that what we're heading into?" A seasoned soldier, a police veteran, and still Makum's eyes went wide at that news. The other members of his team crowded round. "I mean, our briefing said drugs, hit man and some of his cronies wanted to do a number on a girl who ratted them. Close quarters, high-powered weapons. Crack house shit with guys who aim better." They all nodded in unison, tracking Enrique's meander towards their huddle like he held snakes in his hand. One square-jawed, buzzed-cut mass of police bravado cut down by whatever visions their minds conjured up. Murders they dealt with day in, day out. Add the word ritual to it and they were lost.

Chase let the pause settle about their shoulders, add its weight. Slowly, "Yes, but…"

Makum swallowed, "I hate buts."

Enrique's glare chastised Chase for trying to weird SWAT out with ghost stories, although only a little. He refused to be contrite. Without missing a beat in the conversation, Enrique slid into instructor mode. "These guys practice something called *Palo Mayumbe*. Black magic. They don't just want to kill Carmen. They're probably going to sacrifice her." His telling was far less dramatic than Chase's, but far scarier because of how clinical the delivery came.

"Holy shit." Makum hissed. He turned to Chase, the look in his eyes pleading with Chase to admit to pulling their legs. "Is what he saying true?"

There was no way to give Makum what he wanted. "That's what we think."

"They'll kill her," Enrique kept talking, briefing them, "and then get the flesh off her bones—burial, boiling—and trap her spirit in a cauldron so they can use it to cast black magic. Her patron saint is the representation of death, a female grim reaper. A very powerful spirit, if they can capture it. And the fact that she pissed Garcia off," he shrugged, "probably lets him really enjoy the whole process." Enrique's bright smile took the edge off the statement. "Okay, now, let's talk about some of what you might see that doesn't go with the standard crack house."

As Enrique began his impromptu briefing on the paraphernalia of *Palo*, Chase decided to take a breather from map reading. The lawyer for the Attorney General's office would hit San Fernando soon and then they'd be rolling. Only traffic between downtown Los Angeles and the outskirts of the city would determine exactly when. The brass had decided on a federal warrant although they could have done a quick and dirty one before one of the LA County criminal judges in at the San Fernando Courthouse. A federal warrant marked it as a federal matter, keeping the chain of command from getting mucked up—no interagency bickering between local law enforcement.

Chase sorted through the various piles of duffels and junk looking for his war-bag. Time to do a once over of his personal body armor and sidearm. Then he'd give the rifle they'd provided him a thorough inspection. He didn't doubt LAPD kept their stuff in top shape; their own lives depended on it. Still, this was his life and some other agency's raid gear.

A cough at his shoulder caught his attention. Chase looked up from the business of hauling his bag from the bottom of the pile and found Wyatt standing next to him. Instead of making Chase come up, Wyatt knelt. "Need a hand?"

With a grunt, Chase pulled the bag free. "Nope, got it." He managed not to spill onto his ass when it gave. "You ready?"

"As ready as I can be." Wyatt smiled. "So," her voice dropped to slightly more than a whisper, "you and Ochoa were having fun in the car. Wish my stakeout position had been that interesting. I just got some kid sneezing sprinkles off my donuts."

Frost spread across Chase's skin. "Yeah, right, some fun." Somehow he managed to not convey any of the terror rampaging through his mind. Not even a tick in his eye or a flush in his ears. Years of self discipline preparing for moments such as this. "Garcia's right there. He knows me. Had to do something to keep him from seeing me full on. If I'd ducked behind the seat, everyone would have thought I was sucking him off."

"Look." Wyatt smiled. "I'm razzing you. I don't care. You really think *I*, who had to fight the nickname 'Barbie Butt' in the department, really gives a shit?" Her smile faded into a tight-lipped smirk. "I may be wrong, still you really did look like you guys were way more into it than just a ruse." Chase didn't say anything, he waited her out. God knew what Wyatt was driving at. Finally, "You're really one stone-ass bastard. Look, just wanted you to know that they'd asked me to take my breaks where I could check on you two. You were the only ones constantly out of the line-of-sight of the rest of us. So, don't worry. No one who matters would have seen and I ain't going to say shit."

"You want me to say thanks?"

"Nope." Like Chase was a moron, Wyatt rolled her eyes. "But you'd be distracted, just that little bit, wondering about if anyone knew or saw or suspected. It'd eat your attention up. And I'd like to keep," she flicked her thigh with her thumb and forefinger, "this 'Barbie Butt' from getting shot off. So there you have it."

Self-preservation Chase could handle. This wasn't *you owe me one*. It was *I'm taking care of my skin*. Chase unzipped his bag and began to sort through. "In that case," his voice smiled even if he kept his expression neutral, "Thanks."

"No problem." Wyatt smacked his shoulder as she stood. "Tell Ochoa stay safe and keep cool."

Chase's response was cut off as the AG strode in with a warrant in hand. Donaldson barked out, "Let's roll!" and the room sputtered and roared to life like a Sherman tank ready to blaze into combat. Shoving his arms into his vest as he stood, Chase caught sight of Enrique. All the SWAT guys pounded his back and pumped his hand. A man with a straight line to Jesus wouldn't have gotten that camaraderie.

As he grabbed both rifles, Chase gave them a final once-over, lingering on Enrique's a bit more than his own. He could strip and rebuild an M-4 in his sleep. Most cops, most agents, never had occasion to get that personal with their weapons. Still the M-4 was a good choice. You never really needed to put it on full auto. Bump fire gave you a good burst of spray without losing control. The standard M-4 operated smooth, accurate and tight. Its jamming record remained low.

All good things to have on your side in close quarter combat.

Chase passed Enrique his weapon. They followed the black vests stamped Police and FBI out the door and to a waiting set of vans. SWAT got the cool vehicles. The stepchild of the War on Terror, law enforcement agencies across the country received equipment normally only found on military reservations in the funding splurge. Of course, LA and the surrounding cities were a war zone like no other. Combat medics treated fewer gunshot wounds in a year than your average County Medical resident saw in a month. In bum-fuck Texas you probably didn't need a tank. In Los Angeles, the gangs used weapons capable of piercing even that armor.

Spilling out of the van, they hurried to the wall of the warehouse and pressed themselves flat. SWAT would go first. The rest of their team would follow to mop up any mess. SWAT argued for a solo go. The Bureau nixed them. Instead of a handheld battering ram, the lead officer wrapped chain through the pull down security gate and the handle of one of the glass front doors. The length ran across the lot to the reinforced rear bumper and tie-down of the van.

He—Chase assumed it was a he by the build, but armor and helmet made it hard to tell—pumped his fist, signaling ready. When all three entrance sites were ready, a staccato bark of "Go!" cracked across the radios. Tires spun on heat-softened asphalt and the chain went taut. For all of a moment the metal fought, groaning out its death grip on the foundation. Then, with a final screech, it gave and flew across the parking area.

No knock and announce on this gig; it was more dangerous to broadcast their presence before entering, both for Carmen and the law enforcement personnel. The Hudson v. Michigan rule combined with exigency insured they wouldn't lose evidence by doing it this way. On the go signal from their squad leader, Chase, Enrique, Wyatt, Hungwell and a shitload of cops Chase didn't know funneled through the gaping wreck of glass double doors. More poured into the building from the rear dock access and a side entrance. The office building stood two floors, the back warehouse rising the height of both stories. All coordinated for a bum-rush on a *Palo* ceremony. None of them knew exactly what to expect.

Cop shows painted a house search as a yelling, headlong purge. This was hushed efficiency in action. As quietly as possible, they moved into the first floor. Not like they didn't think whoever was inside didn't know someone was coming in. Still, the goal was to not be the loud, bumbling idiot with the target pained on your chest. Group entry—loud. Individual progress—very quiet.

It upped the survival odds considerably.

Drums sounded above them. A hard, hollow pounding made by fists against skin stretched over sounding boxes echoed through the warren of rooms. The off-cant rhythm throbbed in Chase's blood. Every procedural manual Chase ever read warned against going into a building if you didn't know exactly where a hostage was located. They had no fucking clue where Garcia stashed Carmen, although the music from the floors above gave them some idea. But if they didn't move, Carmen would die.

Radio static crackled. "We're blocked." The call came from the SWAT team on the roof. "Roof stair is filled with furniture, trash and everything." Shit. "No way down." There went the tactical advantage of hitting the occupants from the front and back simultaneously.

Enrique moved ahead of Chase, his rifle held tight in the pocket of his shoulder, high and ready, but not in a death grip. Chase did a little better, at least he hoped he did, otherwise his stint in the Rangers was going to come off pretty embarrassing. Each team was assigned a set of offices to clear. Chase and Enrique peeled off to the left, following the SWAT lead. A large open space had one opening in the middle, leading into a hall. A little farther down the wall, a smaller door led into an office. Most of the officers hustled into the hall, quickly clearing the path on the left-hand side. At each space, they lost another pair from the team to clearing duty. Chase and Enrique's turn came next. Their office opened onto another, an executive set up.

They knelt in the hall, their backs against the wall. Enrique jerked his head and Chase knew he was moving. A short hop, spin maneuver, rolled him to the opposite side of the door. Chase reached up and twisted the knob. Slowly the door swung open.

With a nod, they both indicated to each other that they were ready. Chase dropped low, a sniper-style position, Enrique went high. Both kept muzzles trained into the room and used the thin wall for what little protection it offered. The set up gave them a decent clearing vantage for the whole space.

Gnarled and twisted, the form of a man hulked in the corner. As one, both trained their weapons, guns aimed at body mass. Two breaths and Chase realized they looked at a statue. He signaled to Enrique that he was going in. Enrique covered him as he moved through an ethereal semi-darkness. A quick site check told Chase the interior door remained shut. He edged around the perimeter of the room until he reached the statue.

At the base, a large plastic bowl held what Chase thought might be a cat's skull. Seated behind it, a baby doll was draped with a rattlesnake's skin. Feathers and bones stuck out at angles around them. All of it was crusted brown. Chase sure as hell hoped it wasn't with what he thought it might be. Since the whole area smelled like rusted tin left in a bowl of sour milk and baked in the sun, it probably was.

Cutting across the floor, stepping over trash and bottles, Chase moved through twilight. Dust motes swirled in dim shafts barely cutting the gloom. He felt like his body was not the same as the skin he'd gown up in. The drums brought something welling up from deep inside. Something primal. Something not quite mortal or human or caring. Rattles and bangs, like people running pipes across an iron fence, bounced through the halls.

The heat sucked the air from the room, coating the atmosphere with the stale scent of sawdust, burnt tar and rat piss. Drifting in and out of those flavors, the hint of copra. And under it all, Chase tasted the musty tang of old death.

Death rotted and choked with dried, rank weeds.

A flip of his fingers signaled Enrique to enter. Again they wound up on either side of the frame. With the same dance as before, Chase reached over and turned the knob. His gentle push set the door swinging slowly open.

Chase peered around the corner. Dim, dark shapes huddled in shadows cast through painted-over glass. Nothing moved. Drawing back, preparing to enter and clear the room, Chase drew in a deep breath. Cinnamon and flowers hit him hard— Juicy Fruit gum. Chase's heart tried to claw its way out of his chest.

It couldn't be Jason. Even when insanely creepy, the real world didn't harbor ghosts. He counted to ten, backing the fear down. When he hit number eight, Chase heard it—a shuffling, a muffled cough. Up went his hand, stopping Enrique before he could move.

Maybe he'd caught a bit of movement, or the reptilian part of his brain processed a shape hidden in the darkness. It didn't much matter. Wherever, whenever the scent memory came from, gave him enough pause to save him.

Chase crouched low. Behind him, Enrique mimicked the move. Chase closed his fist in a signal for Enrique to stay put, then he counted off with his fingers, Chase set them to go. On three, he rolled through the door, came up and scuttled backward to put the wall at his back. Staccato bursts of fire puffed dust around Chase's feet. Muzzle flash, hints of red paint on white skin, sighted him off. Chase pulled the trigger, aiming a little left and down. Another round combined with the thud of running feet came towards him. With nowhere really to go, Chase backed his way around the perimeter of the room, firing as he fled. Five shots out of his weapon—and Chase would give his left nut that all found true—before any response. Then, a groan and the thud of a body hitting the floor told him he'd figured right and scored center mass. The small, closed space swelled with the odor of unwashed pennies. Chase knew the smell well; fresh arterial blood.

Now Chase, eyes adjusted to the level of shadow in the office, covered Enrique's entrance. Enrique sidled up to the form on the floor, his weapon trained and ready. When he reached the body, he kicked its leg. No movement. A couple more prods without response and Enrique slung his weapon. Chase still kept his trained to cover his partner. In a well-deserved abundance of caution, Enrique cuffed the corpse to a pipe sticking from the wall.

Chase flipped on his light and took a quick moment to case the room. Dull reverberations of gunfire rumbled through the building. It didn't stop the drums. The assailant was dead, or faking it really good. White guy with buzzed hair, face up and staring in that fish-eyed look of death, blood seeped out of several holes in his chest. It only took a second for Chase to process his features. Damn if every shot hadn't been good enough to put most guys down. PCP maybe or some exotic new chemical mix kept him going until something really vital had been hit. From his throat to his navel stretched a trident in red paint. Another trident, one with a rolled tail, bisected the first. Above his heart a red X, Chase had put one bullet right through the center. That probably put him down.

Shivers ran up Chase's spine. He swung the beam away from the dead man and about the room. None of what he saw eased his mind. From a blue-green planter, stone faces shoved inside large conch shells considered them with cowry eyes. Garlands of bright beads festooned the horns of a bull's skull. Alligator heads reared out of pots filled with shells, their jaws gaping wide and bamboo poles jammed around them.

On a small table sat another skull, a human skull, the bone streaked and mottled by time to an orange brown. Only the teeth glowed grayish white when the light of the flashlight hit them. Coins glinted in each open socket, like silver mirror eyes. Wedged in the gaping, bare jaws, caught between the teeth, a tarnished FBI badge with blind justice stamped on the face and the spread wings of the eagle perched above the shield disappeared into the maw. Chase didn't have to even get close enough to read the numbers.

He knew.

The badge belonged to Jason.

Chase switched off the light and closed his eyes. His skin crawled with the weight of the darkness, but he had to readjust his night vision. When he opened his eyes, everything seemed soft focus, blurrier yet somehow sharper than before. He reached out and touched Enrique's shoulder. A little electric charge wicked up his arm. They smiled at each other and eons passed in a second. Combat rush; it'd been years since Chase tasted it.

More gunfire. If he focused, Chase figured the sound emanated from near the stairs in the warehouse. It'd be a corridor of death trying to go up the narrow flight, even if it was open to the warehouse. Too many opportunities to pick people off from the side or above. One of those wild thoughts hit him and he figured what the hell? Chase tapped Enrique's arm and pointed to the front of the building. He mouthed the word 'elevator' and smiled as Enrique's face registered shock.

As fast as they could move in the trash-strewn halls, he and Enrique headed back the way they came. Finished with clearing their rooms, Chase picked up three SWAT members, Wyatt and Hungwell and gave them a five-second run-down. A hasty radio transmission gave the code summary for his plan. He prayed to no one in particular that he didn't get them all killed.

Scratches, like rats on acid against a window screen, flowed under the pounding of the drums. Metallic rattles mixed with guns barking overlaid the cutting whirr of helicopters hovering above the building. When he'd tried to whisper to the other officers, they could barely hear. He'd damn near ended up yelling. They rushed to the front and headed right through the reception area and right again. Two more SWAT, Makum and another introduced as LaFlore, covered the old freight elevator. The gate was already back so Chase yanked on the door handles. He tugged down and pulled back, like heavy weight

French doors. It gave, indicating the lift was grounded on the first floor.

As gently as possible, Chase edged the doors apart, but bi-part systems and old hinges were never quiet. Hopefully, with all the drumming, clanging and gunfire, the elevator's mechanics wouldn't be overly noticeable.

When he rolled the doors open, the sound of the drums almost swallowed them in a wave of noise. Crates, broken furniture and other odd bits clogged the lift. No way to get everyone on. God, he was stupid or suicidal to be trying this. Hopefully anyone upstairs would figure it was stupid or suicidal to take the freight elevator and most of the thugs would be at the big action on the stairs.

Truly old style, the elevator operated by rocker arm, making users adjust for level. It wasn't level. The elevator floor sat a good three inches above the lip of the main room. That meant the doors didn't lock if the unit didn't dock. Chase counted his blessings.

They jammed into the small space—six officers from various agencies. Three of the SWAT would have to stay behind. Chase would have preferred Hungwell to remain, but the guy muscled in. Still, he got Makum and his partner LeFlore.

Chase managed to convince Hungwell, Wyatt and Enrique to lie on the floor. If they didn't bring the elevator fully level with the upper floor, it'd give them a decent chance. Well, Wyatt and Enrique didn't need convincing. Chase had to keep LeFlore from punching Hungwell. Chase pulled rank as FBI and cowed the man down. Hopefully, he would live to not regret the decision. All of the negotiation, arguing and resolution were conducted without words.

Flattening themselves against the chicken-wire and metal-framed walls, presenting as narrow a target as possible, Chase and the SWAT pair would take the big risk. Possessed of more sense than pride, Chase put the highly trained officers closest to the doors and told them to determine how and when they would execute. He positioned himself as an over-trained elevator operator.

Chase rocked the switch and hoped that the mechanics worked and had power. Otherwise he was going to look like an idiot. Wire mesh let broken light through the top of the carriage. Swaying far above, near the gear housing, a single dim bulb swayed on a dangling cord near the gears. A gentle shudder accompanied by the creaking of cables indicated they were moving. Maybe Garcia used the lift, kept it maintained.

The counterweight shushed past them on the right wall. Chase braked so that the lip of the second floor was about two-thirds down from the top of the elevator. It'd give them a minimal amount of cover. Makum nodded to LeFlore. The entire elevator took a collective breath of stale, overheated air. LeFlore jumped, grabbed the door release and, using his weight-momentum to spring it, shoved it open. The wood shot back, banging against the wall. Using the edge of the floor as both cover and stabilization, he aimed his rifle into the room and yelled, "Police! Down! Now!"

Chase, standing behind him, saw two sets of red eyes open and focus on them. His ability to breathe at a normal rate took an impromptu vacation. A low, primal growl reverberated under the drums, rattles and gunshots. So human, but not, it plucked every hair on Chase's neck as it throbbed through his senses. Shit, candles, hundreds of them flickered in the room, the sputtering light reflected in the men's eyes. Signs and symbols painted in white covered their bare chests, streaked their faces and wound down their arms.

LeFlore ordered, "Down!" again.

Screaming, one jumped to his feet. LeFlore jumped onto the lip at the same moment. A small compact machine gun appeared in the other man's hand. Makum released the other door, using the momentum to launch him into the room. The ethereal confusion of combat time swam through Chase's head.

One minute he was in the elevator. But then he was out, without knowing he moved. Gunfire, close quarters gunfire, chewed at his nerves and deafened his ears. A flash of bare skin near him and Chase loosed a burst round. Pistol fire echoed in the elevator shaft. He couldn't check because the guy was on him, all corded muscle and rage. Chase's rifle spun from his hands as they went down.

All the air left his lungs as his back hit the floor. Somehow he managed to grab the attacker's wrist, the hand holding the sub-machine gun. The heat from the barrel seared his face while bullets chewed up the wall behind them. Chase looked into a face wearing the mask of insanity. Eyes bigger and brighter than the moon glared at him.

From the corner of his vision, Chase saw the boot coming. It caught his attacker in the ribs, knocking him up and back and off. Chase rolled to his knees, scrambling to gain his feet. He smacked the dropped Uzi, sending it skittering into a pot which toppled over, spilling foul smelling dirt and bones. Then the guy was on him again. Biting his neck, behind his ear where the armor didn't cover. Chase dropped, using his weight to slam the guy onto the floor underneath him. Votive candles and hot wax spilled everywhere.

Barks of gunfire erupted around them. The distinctive three-burst pop of the police assault rifles mixed with the chatter of small machine guns. Echoes rebounded so much in the tiny space that Chase couldn't fix on the locations. For two seconds he allowed himself to hope that Enrique was okay. Then it was back to saving his own ass.

They rolled. Fingers clawed at Chase's face, searching for his eyes. When they came to a halt against the wall, Chase was on the floor, the guy on him. Fuck! Wordless, driven, he kept at Chase. Chase bit one of the hands that strayed too near his mouth. The guy didn't even scream. Then they both jerked back. Chase managed to wrench himself free. He spun to find Makum with his rifle stretched between his elbows and across the attacker's throat. Not technically a legal chokehold maneuver, but who the fuck cared? Still trying to catch his breath, Chase stumbled to Makum's aid.

The guy, maybe half the weight of Makum, tossed the SWAT officer about like a rag doll tied to a dog's back. Chase grabbed his rifle from the floor and swung it like a baton across the guy's shins. The blow connected so hard Chase felt it in his shoulders. The assailant didn't go down. He didn't yell or scream or roar. Instead, a low, syllabant hiss that ran nails down Chase's spine slipped through his lips.

Again and again, Chase went for shins, ankles and knees, the vulnerable spots, until he lost count of the blows. Finally, he managed to sweep the guy's legs out from under him. He went down with a thud, Makum landing on top. Between the two of them they managed to cuff his hands and legs. A third set of cuffs, Chase's sole set, they used to complete a hog tie, linking the bracelets through the chain on the wrists and ankles.

Subject subdued, Chase took a quick inventory of personal damage and surveyed the scene. A lot of bruises, scratches and a bitten neck. He was getting too old for this shit. Everything hurt. Enrique, Wyatt and LeFlore crouched by the exit door, trading fire with unseen suspects. Useful items, like file cabinets and a battered desk, had been piled up as a temporary barricade. It afforded better cover than the paper-thin walls.

Chase danced over candles glowing within glass jars. The flames flickered in time to the clanging of cowbells and chatter of gunshots. Shadows seemed to writhe and jump with the rhythm. Chains rattled. At least the damn drums had stopped. He slid down next to Enrique and took a deep breath. "Where's Hungwell?"

Squeezing off a round, Enrique mumbled, "Elevator." His face was grim. "Not pretty."

First he risked a quick glance over the lip of the overturned desk. Nineteen-seventies metal office décor proved useful for once. Plates piled high with coconuts and green bananas rested before a series of pots. Someone had chalked irregular tic-tac-toe boards over the fruit. Random littering of Bacardi bottles, some empty, some full, added more hazards between the vessels. Huge cast iron kettles dominated. Most kept natural metal although a few had been painted red, white or blue. Others seemed to be glazed pottery pots, the sort you'd find at any mass market garden store. One rust-colored pot hosted various machetes, knives, feathers, two mousetraps and a crucifix. Beaded strings and large toy keys wound about its base.

In the quick look, Chase hadn't seen any of the *Muertos* or Garcia. 'Course there were two offices on the other side to provide cover. "Is he dead?"

"Nope." Wyatt snorted. "Not that lucky. That freak jumped in the elevator all painted with shit. Sprayed off a wild round and his gun jammed." She flipped down and yanked a clip from her vest. A quick set of snaps and Wyatt reloaded. With a shake of her head, she conveyed a bit of the sympathy her words didn't. "Guy's wigged out on something. Starts stabbing Hungwell with the blunt barrel of his gun. We can't get him off. Hungwell's on the floor, lost his rifle. Finally, I guess Hungwell gets his spare piece from his ankle holster. I think he put all five rounds in the guy before he stopped moving." A quick jerk of her head toward the elevator, "We did the tourniquet pressure thing. Hungwell had to take himself down. You guys were over there with the other idiot. Enrique and LeFlore started on the door, keeping everyone else from joining our little party. SWAT'll get him out and send backup."

"You going to join this party?" Enrique snapped.

Back up and sighting down his barrel for anything that moved, Chase teased, "Wouldn't miss it." Shots rang out above their heads and they all ducked back. Popping back up to return fire, Chase got a good view of the room.

Beaded baskets hung from the overhead pipes, feathers spilling from their mouths. Another large pot, like the kind decorative trees came in, hosted fishing poles, nets and various bits of tackle. One guy lay sprawled across his long box drum. Blood pooled underneath the instrument. Empty cigar boxes jammed every corner and lip of shelf. Mounted on the wall, a trophy buck's head stared sadly out into space. Wedged within its impressive rack was a red playground ball.

Bloated and dark, one iron cauldron dominated the middle of the room. Twisted branches jutted from its mouth and a bright steel chain cinched the belly. From within the tangled mess of twigs, feathers, broken glass and odd trinkets, a human skull glared out at them. Everything was crusted over with the same brown-red substance—some stains darkened to almost black, others still fresh enough to recognize as blood. It spattered the walls and floor.

Carmen lay on the floor before the pot. Crosses cut into her arms and legs seeped blood onto the wood. For moment, Chase thought she was dead. His soul melted into his shoes. Then he saw a twitch and a tremble. There might still be hope. The mechanics in the elevator shaft whirred. Hopefully that signaled the arrival of cavalry.

Nine officers in full SWAT gear poured into the room. They'd have had to pack in like sardines for that hop. They crab-walked to the barricade and Makum fell back to brief the new arrivals on the situation. While they didn't have radio silence enforced, no one wanted to go broadcasting plans.

"Okay," Makum edged up between Chase and Enrique. "Y'all need to pull back. We're going for a full assault up the stairs and from here." Barely visible between the dim light and shadow cast by his riot helmet, his smile flashed. "Stand pat. We'll tell you when the movie's over."

Chase wasn't stupid enough to argue. Apparently, Enrique and Wyatt had brains to spare as well. They all traded positions with SWAT members, moving off to crouch by the elevators. Best to let the guys trained to do it do it. When the go signal hit, all hell broke loose. Gunfire and yells and commands of, "Down!" and "Drop it!" The three of them stayed where they were. They'd just be in the way. Still it was hard, listening to the fights and bullets. Finally, someone yelled, "Clear!" Seconds later another voice announced the same. It seemed an eternity until the last, "We're clear!" sounded. By then Chase's legs had damn near gone to sleep on him.

He hustled into the main room, Enrique and Wyatt on his heels and broadcasting their movement so as not to get mowed down by friendly fire. Chase skidded to a halt at the cauldron, almost dropping on his ass as his heel slipped on the blood-drenched floor. The whole damn building was a freaking bio-hazard. Managing to catch himself before he fell, Chase knelt next to Carmen. She looked tiny and frail, somehow older than the young woman in the photos Chase memorized. "Hey, Carmen?" He stroked her arm, sticky with drying blood.

Lacerations, welts covered every visible inch of skin. They'd shaved her head, cut symbols and hash marks into her scalp. Fresh wounds layered older ones. "You okay there?" A low moan answered him. God, he was surprised she was even alive with as much blood as she'd apparently lost. "Don't worry. I'm here. My name's Chase. I'm with the FBI." Enrique squatted beside him, his hand dropping lightly on Chase's shoulder. "We're not going to leave you."

CHAPTER TWENTY

Chase made good his promise. He and Enrique stayed with Carmen until the ambulance arrived. The hustle and bustle of a final clear swirled around them. There were tons of wounded to be processed through on-site triage. Thankfully, most of them weren't law enforcement. Carmen went out in the first wave of injured. Enrique kept whispering to her, in Cuban-flavored Spanish, that she'd be fine as they jogged with the gurney to the ambulance. The bright lights outside, once they burst out the front, hit Chase's eyes hard, made him blink.

EMTs swarmed the scene, as thick as law enforcement had earlier. They worked at stabilizing her and other victims. Right now they seemed intent on keeping Carmen from going into deeper shock than she already was. Helicopters, mostly belonging to news channels, chewed the smoke-flavored air above them. Reporters and plain old rubberneckers clogged the margins of the street, held back by a thin line of police tape and sheer force of officer willpower.

"*Compa*," Enrique stepped up and grabbed his arm. "She wants one of us to stay with her."

"Probably," Chase thought for a moment, "it ought to be you...in case she says something in the ambulance we need." He didn't want to split up from Enrique, but it didn't make sense otherwise. One of them should stay with the star witness. "You okay with that?"

"I'll survive." Enrique smiled. Like he sensed Chase's agitation, he asked, "You going to be alright?"

Blowing off the disquiet in a breath, Chase answered, "Yeah, I'll work on processing the scene with the locals. Catch a ride back." He offered a return smile to Enrique. "Look, I'll get a hold of you in the next couple days. Okay?" Chase meant to hold to the promise, he really did.

"Sounds good." Enrique punched his shoulder and then headed off toward the ambulance. Warm skin, dark hair and eyes; Enrique's flashed a last final, bright smile out the back. It was all Chase had to hold him for a while. A sinking feeling of loss rode up his spine as the ambulance doors shut, cutting off his view of Enrique. Chase shook it off as the ambulance roared away, sirens wailing about the carnage it left behind.

As Chase turned back toward the warehouse, Wyatt ran up to him. "Hey, Nozick," she called out "Makum's looking for you."

He stepped in to meet her as she slowed. "Why?"

"They got a bunch of guys in the loading dock area." Wyatt rubbed the back of her hand across her forehead. Now she looked nothing like a Barbie doll, unless it came in a female SWAT model. Blood, grime and spent powder streaked her skin. Sweat plastered her hair to her scalp. She sneezed, blowing out some of the crap clogging her nose and added, "Makum thinks one may be our guy, Garcia. But no one will talk. The other Feds say you've met him."

Chase coughed himself. The stench of the building warred with gun smoke and made it hard to smell anything else. "Yeah, I have, sort of." He fell into step beside Wyatt as the detective headed back into the building. "He shot me and my partner. Up close and pretty personal."

"Okay, then." He got a grimy smile from her. "This feels good huh?"

Chase shrugged. "Sorta."

"Why sort of?" Wyatt held open the door for him.

Really, Chase didn't want to go back into the scene. Nightmare-making, that was about the best his brain could encompass the various horrors inside. "Would have been better if Jason Olhms was alive to see it go down." He sucked in one last breath of marginally fresh air and walked through the door.

"So it's real personal." Wyatt's tone had volumes of understanding hidden in the simple words.

"Yep." Chase left her at one of the rooms. As a detective on the scene, she'd help process the evidence. He didn't need her to babysit his walk to the back of the building anyway. And it gave him time to prepare. Thinking about all the things he'd say to Garcia when he saw him, about Jason Olhms and the family he left behind. About a thousand cruelties the man had carved into people. A few short steps with those thoughts and Chase realized they didn't matter. Garcia wouldn't ever understand. He couldn't feel other people's pain, not as anything but his own pleasure.

Chase dodged around officers and agents in the hall. He pushed through the loading dock doors and out in the back. A dozen men stood facing a green painted wall, their hands laced above their heads. Various officers worked at searching the suspects. Some wore the telltale marks of a shoot out; bandages and blood. "Hey, Makum," Chase yelled out to the SWAT team leader. "I hear you got a line-up for me." Several of the suspects sat against another wall, looking morose and handcuffed by zip-ties.

The officer mumbled something Chase missed to another officer then waved Chase over. "Didn't really think of it that way, but yeah." Indicating the various men in custody with a waggle of his finger, he asked, "You know Garcia by sight?"

"I do." Chase's gaze crawled over the men. "Couldn't forget his mug if I tried." The real tall guys he ruled out right away. He jabbed his finger at four men, three of them in white shirts and the last in red. None of them stood over five-six. "Turn those guys around."

"You heard the man." Two officers stepped in and manhandled the suspects Chase indicated away from the wall. "There's my lovelies." Makum growled without humor. "Which one's my star player?"

Second white shirt from the left, even after the years, Chase knew Garcia. A jagged scar cut across the bridge of his nose. Close-cropped gray hair faded silver at the temples. "This asshole." Chase moved right up to stand before Garcia. The last time they'd been this close, both wound up shot. "Hey Al, long time no see." As Chase talked, another officer patted Garcia down before handcuffing him. The shoulder of Garcia's shirt was saturated in the rust brown of drying blood. Someone'd cut off one leg of his pants just below the knee. More bandages, seeped in blood, wrapped Garcia's calf.

"Agent Nose-pick," Garcia gritted his teeth, "been a while. How's your partner?"

"See," Chase laughed, refusing to let Garcia's dig about Jason get to him, "now the stunt with the dead chicken? Far more impressive than the elementary school humor." Shaking his head, he shot back, "The whole curse thing really got the heebie-jeebies running." Then Chase smiled. Poisonous, deadly, and promising retribution, all the hate Chase held for Garcia poured out of his expression. It was the only visible flare of emotion Chase would allow himself. He reined it back, forcing his grin to a bitter smirk. "But I guess now that I'm standing here and you're standing there in handcuffs, it doesn't mean much."

Garcia shrugged. "Not so long as I have what's yours."

Taking a wild guess, he drawled out, "You mean Agent Olhms' badge." Chase echoed Garcia's gesture before crossing his arms over his chest. "No, that's going back with me."

"No," Garcia hissed, "I marked *you*. I put my fingers inside you with those bullets in your neck." His grin was twice as evil as the one Chase had attempted. Of course, Chase figured that's because he was still human. Garcia lost that a long time back. "The curse is there, with them. You feel it every time you look at the sky or down at the ground."

"Not so much, actually." Chase wouldn't let himself slide down into anger again. He'd given Garcia that one glimpse. More than that and the man would win without winning. "Saw one of your own doctors. Pulled some mumbo-jumbo and said he took it out with just his hands." Garcia blanched a little. Chase figured Garcia realized there was nothing further to hold over him. That made him powerless. A guy like Garcia always wanted to stay one up even if he was two down. Chase tapped the back of his neck where the skin stretched tight. "Scars haven't bothered me much since then. Figure if you can put a curse under my skin, he can pull it out."

Makum coughed. "Look," he gave Chase a sympathetic twist of his lips, something that said he wouldn't say a word if Chase had taken a swing at Garcia and was impressed as hell that Chase hadn't. "Now that the criticals have gone, we got to get this lot to County for medical."

Not taking his eyes off Garcia, Chase nodded. "The wheels of justice, they just roll on, don't they?" Garcia didn't say anything. Not that Chase really expected him to. "Get him out of here. I'll get my turn with him later."

"Got it." Makum barked out, "Move 'em!" While the officers herded the men into a waiting van, he turned back to Chase. "You are one cold SOB. I'd have been pissed as hell at him. Don't think I would have restrained myself as much."

"Had too many years to get mellow." Chase snorted. "Not worth it. Just isn't."

Clapping his hands together, almost in a parody of prayer, Makum added, "You're just a saint, we all know it." Then he shook off the playful attitude. "Look. I know you'll do your own statement. Do me a favor and just give one of the detectives a rundown of what you saw? It'll help our processing."

It would take weeks for the FBI's reports to be processed and forwarded. Protocol didn't say Chase had to give a report, but it didn't say he shouldn't either. "No problem."

"Great." Makum ushered him towards a man in jeans and riot vest. "This is Detective Lagle. Professional courtesy, Lagle, the Agent's giving us his time." With a slap on the back, Makum ambled off to work the scene. Chase spent the next hour filling the detective in on what he'd seen and heard. It all sounded jumbled to his own ears and he'd lived through it. Hopefully, by the end of it all, the various agencies could piece together everything that went down, clear officer-involved shootings into the justified category and start building the case against Garcia's men.

After a quick thanks for his time, the detective pocketed his notes and walked away. Chase wandered through the scene in the way police wander, being extraordinarily careful not to step on anything, touch anything or disturb anything he hadn't already stepped on, touched or disturbed. As he headed toward the front of the building, down the hall, a sweet scent worked its way past the cloying odors left by blood sacrifices and a shoot out. Chase paused. The doorway at his left, the room he and Enrique cleared. Chase turned and the smell of Juicy Fruit gum hit him head on.

There was no reason for it, but the aroma called him, drew him into the room. Bright flares flashed through the other open doorway. Each step nearer the scent grew stronger until the scent of the gum overwhelmed everything else. The room where he'd killed the guy hadn't changed much, except the lights were on and Chase could see the full nauseating extent.

The paint on the dead guy's chest seemed brighter somehow. Probably lividity, blood seeping towards the lower portions of the body, making his chest a pale canvas. Above the corpse, a crime scene technician positioned his camera and snapped another shot.

Under the light, the haunting images of eyes and beads came off as badly done fun-house props. The bull's skull was painted with wavering symbols drawn by an unsteady hand, the beads broken and garish. All the pots with their symbols and statues looked more like trash piles than altars; shells available at any dime store market mixed with broken window glass and stones. Even the alligator heads were of the sad tourist trap type used to sucker tourists at Everglades' gift shops.

Still, in the middle of the room on a TV tray table covered by a vinyl cloth sat the skull and the bowl and the badge.

"You dusted in here?" Chase managed to croak out the words.

"Yeah, they dusted." The tech looked up from his work. "Not much good it's going to do though."

"Need someone to bag in here?"

"If you want to start." Swinging the camera around the room, he added, "I've photographed everything in here already. Is there a reason," the guy paused and read the letters stenciled on Chase's flack vest, "Agent, you don't want to wait for the crew to come through?"

"That badge." Chase pointed to the skull swallowing metal. "It's FBI. It was my partner's." He was going to throw up if he had to smell that cloying sweet scent any longer. "I want to bag it and lodge it…don't want its significance to get lost in the shuffle."

Fishing in his bag the tech came up with a manila folder and a set of Latex gloves. "Be my guest then." He shook the paper open and held both out to Chase. "Just make sure that my department knows your department has that bit, okay?"

Chase took the gloves and snapped them onto his hands. Then he snagged the bag and set it on the table next to the skull. "I'll turn it in to the right people, don't worry." Gently, he removed the coins, setting them on the table as well. Then he worked the jaw open. Wiggling the badge until it came loose, Chase held it up and breathed deep. He could almost taste the gum, the smell was so strong. "Goodbye, Jason." Chase whispered so that the tech wouldn't hear then dropped the badge in the evidence bag. As he sealed it, wrote his name and badge number on the front, the scent faded, drifted off to be lost among a thousand other odors warring in the room.

For a moment Chase stood there, not knowing what to think. Then he decided it was best just to accept and move on. If he thought too deep on it or too hard on it, he might just run screaming. He owed Jason better than that. "Thanks." Chase said that loud enough for the tech to hear. "I'm going to go turn it in."

"Okay." The guy didn't even look up this time, just kept snapping photos.

Chase made his way out of the room, the barest whiff of Juicy Fruit trailing him. It took a bit to find the right person to turn the evidence over to. Then he got wrapped up in explaining the significance of that piece and the FBI's interest in it. By the time he untangled himself, it was approaching midnight. His phone had vibrated a couple times, the numbers showed as Enrique. Chase figured he'd return the calls in the morning.

Yawning, he looked around for a ride. A cluster of SWAT hung out at one end of the street. Someone there should be able to help him at least get back to the station. From there he could wrangle a drop off at his hotel. He staggered in that bone-weary but still moving way in the general direction of a ride. As he moved, Chase unhooked the *collare*, pulled it off his neck and slid the beads into his breast pocket. No reason to keep wearing it now. He didn't even know why he'd kept it on for so long.

"Agent Nozick!" The call stopped Chase in his tracks. He turned and caught sight of another agent, at least if the stenciled FBI on his vest was an indicator, running toward him.

"Yeah?" Chase waited for the man to catch up. "What can I do for you?"

"I've been looking for you." The man puffed it out as he slowed. "SAC called in. You need to head back to Jacksonville."

Chase looked for a nametag and found one that said Frankle, at least what he could read from the streetlights. "Kinda was planning on it sometime."

"Not sometime…now." Frankle, Chase would call him that until corrected, grabbed his arm and started tugging him in the opposite direction. "I'm to take you back to your hotel. We've got a flight out for you in four hours. If we run, we'll make it."

Protocol dictated he stayed until the paperwork was done. Chase dug in his heels. "I've got local reports I've got to do." You didn't leave others to clean up your mess.

"Don't worry about it." The guy kept going. "SAC says they'll get it when they can. But they want you at your home office tomorrow morning and then Miami to start putting together the case. They're not sitting on this. They want charges filed against Garcia for Agent Olhms' murder before he has a chance to make bail out here. Let's go. You're going to be buried in paperwork for a while…bet it feels good though to close this one."

"Yeah, I guess." Shit. Well, he'd call Enrique later after he got done in Miami maybe and slept some. Marching orders and all. You didn't buck the FBI.

CHAPTER TWENTY-ONE

Bubbles of conversation swirled about Chase. A storm of chatter that broke against his senses like water hitting the shore. Fingering the *collare* around his throat, he reminded himself to breathe. Aware. Awake. Sobriety at nine-thirty p.m. Chase couldn't remember the last time that had happened. Ice rattled in his glass as he set it on the bar.

"So, *Compa*," a warm hand settled between Chase's shoulder blades, "funny meeting you here." Enrique hooked a stool with his foot and settled down next to Chase.

The pseudo-Moroccan décor hadn't improved any since the first time. Mid-week, however, killed most of the crowd. Chase propped his elbows on the rail and snorted, "You're a card, you know that?" The mirror behind the bar reflected Christmas baubles hung on strings from a swag of fake greenery. Off in the corner of the bar, a tiny tree huddled among bottles of expensive vodka and rum.

"I should have been a comedian instead of a cop?" Enrique caught the bartender's attention and signaled for a drink. "Looks like things are all wrapped up now." His tone sounded brighter than Chase earned a right to. A lot of missed calls and unreturned voicemails, yet Enrique'd been all up for meeting tonight. The guy gave him space, didn't try and force a connection when Chase needed to think. It was more than Chase deserved.

"Yeah, well, we have Carmen." A swig went down tasteless and flat. Chase glared at his glass as though it had betrayed him. "I think it's going to take a few years of therapy to get over some of the crap she went through, but she's a strong girl. Reviewed her statement." Keeping to the case, even if it was rehashing old news, was safe. "Looks like Garcia promised her brother that he'd give him back his soul, but he had to return some stuff. Garcia has him do some cleansing rituals and paint himself up. Everyone's buddy-buddy, all is forgiven."

The bartender sidled over and Enrique ordered. When the guy headed off to mix it, Enrique went back to Chase's comment. "Stupid jerk." With a small cough, Enrique seemed to apologize for talking ill of the dead. Twisting slightly, Enrique's knee brushed up against Chase's leg. Then he rested his elbow on the bar and his jaw on his fist. "He believed him."

"Yep," Enrique's touch felt so damn good, insanely so. Chase shifted on his seat so that he could steal a little more contact. Enrique was so much better than he deserved. "Carmen's in the car and tried to talk him out of it. Probably Garcia's thugs were tailing them. But he gets to the meeting point, leaves Carmen in the car. Carmen's cycling through her emails and text messages, trying not to be nervous. Bang, bang goes Garcia's little gun somewhere down in the river. Carmen freaks."

"Let me guess," Enrique leaned in as he fished his wallet from the back of his pants in anticipation of the bartender's arrival, "drops the phone." Bills exchanged for his drink, Enrique settled back on his stool. Somehow he managed to move even closer to Chase in the process.

"As near as she can remember." The Feds pulled Carmen out of Los Angeles as soon as she was stable enough to move. Bruised a few local egos and stepped on some jurisdictional toes in the process, but the FBI did that sometimes. Carmen, in the Fed mindset, *belonged* to them. Chase interviewed her and gave his bosses the notes. They hadn't bothered to pass them on to LAPD yet. "She tried to run but the *Muertes* caught her before she got too far. And then the fun began."

The fun had been too much, too weird and strange for him to handle. There had to be space between Chase and the West Coast for him to process it all—remove it to a safe corner where the dead didn't come floating around unseen but smelling of Juicy Fruit, and cards were just something you played poker with. Unfortunately, Enrique was part of that, the weirdness. Then, after the memories had cooled, the routine of Jacksonville started to eat him until he could barely tolerate it

Stuffed in the pocket of one of his dress shirts, Chase discovered the cast off *collare* and put it back around his neck.

All he could think about was Enrique, and not just the one-hand assist type thinking. He'd find himself dunking a bit of donut in his coffee and wondering what cases Enrique had in his queue. Cycling through the radio and Chase'd catch some Latin pop and stop surfing.

He was stuck, stuck on Enrique for more than a month.

Oblivious to Chase's thoughts, Enrique filled him in on the LAPD events. "The coroner says we'll probably never know where the baby in the jar came from." Chase didn't need it. The Bureau got the reports and passed them down to him. Still, he liked hearing it from Enrique, just because it was his voice. "Been in the formaldehyde long enough to degrade DNA or even to tell how long it'd really been there. And, *shinga*, who knows where the hell Garcia picked it up anyway. The press is still having a field day with the shit."

"I know." Field day wasn't the half of it. "I've stopped watching the news."

Moments of silence drifted between them. Nothing uncomfortable. Neither seemed to feel the need to do more than be together. It was a nice feeling, one that Chase missed.

After a bit, Enrique slid his hand across Chase's shoulder. He tensed for a moment, and then remembered where they were. Any other agent would have as much explaining to do about their presence as Chase would. He could relax.

"The badge belonged to your partner I hear." A comfortable, sympathetic squeeze followed. "The one Garcia shot."

"Yeah." Grateful for the contact, the empathy, all of it, Chase put his hand on Enrique's and squeezed back. "Eventually they'll return it to Jason's wife. They'll need it out here for the trial."

Tentative, hesitant, Enrique asked, "You'll be around for that?"

"Wouldn't miss it." No way would he miss it. Chase dropped his grip and so did Enrique. Again they sat, not talking, sharing space. Chase could be like that forever with Enrique.

Strangest feeling he'd ever had, knowing that about someone. "I, ah." Still, he wasn't certain Enrique was in the same mode he was. Broaching the next subject might not go as well as Chase hoped. "I'm being transferred, you know."

"Transferred huh?" Enrique's face froze for an instant, but Chase caught the hint of fear. Fuck, he was already all the way on the other side of the US of A. Maybe he thought Chase would use it as an excuse to blow him off. "Any place good?"

After a month of thinking, wishing, remembering, no way would he blow off Enrique. "Do you consider Southern California good?" In fact, he'd fight hard and dirty to keep Enrique from blowing him off.

"Really?" A lot of hope and excitement swarmed under one word. Nope, he wasn't likely to have to fight. "Would it be too much to hope for Mid-Wilshire?"

"Yeah." Chase snorted. "Not that lucky, they're putting me in Long Beach at one of the resident agencies. I've been so wrapped up in this shit, I hadn't gone through all my emails. I mean, there's been talk of moving me for a while. But, the Bureau moves like molasses in January most of the time. So I didn't expect it to happen any time this decade."

"Long Beach," Enrique considered his drink, "that's not a bad commute from Silverlake." Then, all smiles, he looked up. "Actually it's a *pendjo* of a commute, but doable." Chase could live on that smile. "This calls for a drink to celebrate. What you having?"

The second bombshell of the past month. "Club soda."

"What?" Enrique damn near choked out the word. "I didn't hear that right."

"Yes, you did."

"I'm trying to wrap my mind around it." Slowly, Enrique set his glass on the bar. Then he turned and stared hard into Chase's eyes. "Explain before my head blows up trying to figure it out."

Shit, after the fight they'd had about Chase's drinking, this was going to go down like a horse pill coated in rubber. "You know when we were at Dr. Jonas' clinic and he, ah, well it seemed like he took some metal out of my neck."

"Yeah."

For a moment he debated on how to tell Enrique. Then Chase remembered it was Enrique. If there was one person in the world he'd never have to explain the why of the what he did to, it was the man sitting on the bar stool in front of him. "I sent the pieces off to the lab for analysis. The results came back. They can't say exact but there's a high degree of similarity between the fragments and the bullets that killed Jason. Tech said close to an eighty-five percent lan-grove match, give or take a few because, and I quote, 'looked like they'd been stuck in a side of meat for a few years.'" It all spilled forth in one tidal wave rush.

Enrique chewed on the inside of his cheek a bit before asking, "So, that freaked you into sobriety?"

"No," Chase admitted, "that freaked me into a fifth of Scotch." Again, Enrique was probably the only one he knew he didn't have to preface the drinking with, minimize it. He'd seen Chase at his worst and still stood by him. "But, shit, something happened with Jonas, it's just too weird. And when I came out of the hangover, as usual, I felt like someone gut punched me. One of the things Jonas told me was that I was verging on some serious damage. Since the bullets were possibly real, I figure he might not be as full of shit as I thought. So, I hauled my butt over to a doc-in-the-box in Jacksonville. Nice physical, lot of blood tests later…"

Enrique jumped in, his voice tight, "Cirrhosis?"

"Actually, Pancreatitis, at least that's the part that's causing my stomachaches." Chase grimaced. "The docs think my liver's inflamed though, probably some fibrosis. To really know that, they'd have to cut."

"*Shinga.*"

Okay, enough about his health, Chase latched onto that topic. "I always thought fuck was pronounced *ch-ing-ga.*"

"Yeah, if you're Mexican." Enrique slapped Chase's bicep with the back of his hand. "Don't change the subject. That's what scared you?"

Chase blew out a deep breath. "Big time." He raised the glass filled with club soda and saluted the air. "So far so good staying off the sauce. I'm the kind of guy who just needs the right kick in the ass, you know."

"Hasn't been too bad then, staying away from *mofuco*."

"No, it's been absolute hell." Another admission he didn't want to make. "But I can do it. I will do it. I may fall off the wagon, but I'll catch up to it again."

"You need help," Enrique's hand dropped to Chase's knee and he leaned in, "*Compa*, you know I'm here."

"Sure about that?" Being with a drunk could be hell. Being with a drunk trying not to be a drunk could be worse than hell. "It's a pretty big commitment to make. You may end up with me sloppy and on your shoulder a few times before I've turned it all the way around."

"I think so. I mean, hell, I'm gay, you're gay." A laugh came up short and ended in a cough. "We're in law enforcement…there's a big plus there. And then, you already know my biggest secret."

"It's not that you're gay?"

"Naw," he teased, "that's only a secret to some people. That I'm an *aborisha*, with Santeria. The department would really not understand it. Expert is one thing, involved is another. And DeVaca called. He thinks I should do the *aseinto*…become initiated as a *santoro*." He shrugged as a wry smile slid across his face. "Animal sacrifice and all."

"You're not going to kill a goat while I'm over for dinner or anything?"

"Maybe a chicken." Chase felt the blood rush from his face and Enrique laughed. "I'm teasing. That's for big ceremonies, not my little house for Chango, but it is a commitment."

"So you think we can make it work?"

Enrique stood and stepped in. Pressing close to Chase, running his hands down Chase's arms, he added, "I think there's enough there I'm willing to give it a shot. You, FBI?"

"I'm going to hear that as a tease for years, aren't I?" Chase looked up into a warm face with a smile all for him.

"Yep."

"Well," he slid one arm around Enrique's middle. A hot body, one he knew and desired, hid under a layer of cotton. "If that's the worst I got to deal with, I think we might have a shot."

"So my place or the back room?" Enrique pressed his cheek to Chase's forehead. How a simple touch felt so damn right seemed beyond Chase's ability to determine.

"I'm getting too old for that crap." He squeezed, pulling Enrique into a bear of a hug. "I'd much rather hang out in bed at your place." Plus bars and a recovering drunk—not a good idea. "I really, really want a drink right now."

Enrique pulled away, dragging Chase off his stool. "Then let's blow. I think I know something that will distract you for a bit." Chase didn't even have to guess at what it was. Frankly it didn't matter. Blow job, fucking, sitting on the couch watching TV, any and all of it would be great so long as it was with Enrique.

ABOUT THE AUTHOR

JAMES BUCHANAN, author of over ten novels and single author anthologies, lives in a 100 year old Craftsman in Pasadena with her SexyGuy, two demon spawn and a herd of adopted pet dogs, cats, rats and fish. Between managing a law practice with SG, raising kids and writing books, James volunteers with the Erotic Author's Association and Liminal Ink as well as coordinates the newsletter for the ManLoveAuthor's co-op. James has spoken and read at conferences such as Saints & Sinners and the Popular Culture Association. In the midst of midlife crises, James bought and learned to ride a Harley – it went with the big, extended-cab pickup. James has been a member of CorpGoth since 1993 and been known to wear leather frock coats to court. If you don't find James at the computer working on her next book, you're liable to find her out on the bike.

Visit James on the web at:

http://www.james-buchanan.com/

http://eroticjames.livejournal.com/

http://groups.yahoo.com/group/eroticjames/

SERVICEMEMBERS LEGAL DEFENSE NETWORK

Servicemembers Legal Defense Network is a nonpartisan, nonprofit, legal services, watchdog and policy organization dedicated to ending discrimination against and harassment of military personnel affected by "Don't Ask, Don't Tell" (DADT).The SLDN provides free, confidential legal services to all those impacted by DADT and related discrimination. Since 1993, its inhouse legal team has responded to more than 9,000 requests for assistance. In Congress, it leads the fight to repeal DADT and replace it with a law that ensures equal treatment for every servicemember, regardless of sexual orientation. In the courts, it works to challenge the constitutionality of DADT.

SLDN   Call: (202) 328-3244
PO Box 65301   or (202) 328-FAIR
Washington DC 20035-5301   e-mail: sldn@sldn.org
On the Web: http://sldn.org/

THE GLBT NATIONAL HELP CENTER

The GLBT National Help Center is a nonprofit, tax-exempt organization that is dedicated to meeting the needs of the gay, lesbian, bisexual and transgender community and those questioning their sexual orientation and gender identity. It is an outgrowth of the Gay & Lesbian National Hotline, which began in 1996 and now is a primary program of The GLBT National Help Center. It offers several different programs including two national hotlines that help members of the GLBT community talk about the important issues that they are facing in their lives. It helps end the isolation that many people feel, by providing a safe environment on the phone or via the internet to discuss issues that people can't talk about anywhere else. The GLBT National Help Center also helps other organizations build the infrastructure they need to provide strong support to our community at the local level.

National Hotline: 1-888-THE-GLNH (1-888-843-4564)
National Youth Talkline 1-800-246-PRIDE (1-800-246-7743)
On the Web: http://www.glnh.org/
e-mail: info@glbtnationalhelpcenter.org

If you're a GLBT and questioning student heading off to university, should know that there are resources on campus for you. Here's just a sample:

US Local GLBT college campus organizations
        http://dv-8.com/resources/us/local/campus.html
GLBT Scholarship Resources
        http://tinyurl.com/6fx9v6
Syracuse University
        http://lgbt.syr.edu/
Texas A&M
        http://glbt.tamu.edu/
Tulane University
        http://www.oma.tulane.edu/LGBT/Default.htm
University of Alaska
        http://www.uaf.edu/agla/
University of California, Davis
        http://lgbtrc.ucdavis.edu/
University of California, San Francisco
        http://lgbt.ucsf.edu/
University of Colorado
        http://www.colorado.edu/glbtrc/
University of Florida
        http://www.dso.ufl.edu/multicultural/lgbt/
University of Hawai'i, Mānoa
        http://manoa.hawaii.edu/lgbt/
University of Utah
        http://www.sa.utah.edu/lgbt/
University of Virginia
        http://www.virginia.edu/deanofstudents/lgbt/
Vanderbilt University
        http://www.vanderbilt.edu/lgbtqi/

Stimulate yourself.
READ.
www.manloveromance.com
THE HOTTEST M/M EROTIC AUTHORS & WEBSITES ON THE NET

Breinigsville, PA USA
19 October 2009
226084BV00001B/9/P